Snowed in at the Wildest Dreams Bookshop

Snowed in AT THE WILDEST DREAMS BOOKSHOP

GRACIE PAGE

First published in the United Kingdom by Harper Fire,
an imprint of HarperCollins *Children's Books*, in 2025
HarperCollins *Children's Books* is a division of HarperCollins*Publishers* Ltd
1 London Bridge Street
London SE1 9GF

www.harpercollins.co.uk

HarperCollins*Publishers*
Macken House, 39/40 Mayor Street Upper
Dublin 1, D01 C9W8, Ireland

1

Text copyright © HarperCollins*Publishers* 2025
Cover illustrations copyright © Katie Foreman 2025
Cover design copyright © HarperCollins*Publishers* Ltd 2025
All rights reserved

ISBN 978–0–00–878842–1
A CIP catalogue record for this title is available from the British Library.

Typeset in Adobe Caslon Pro by Palimpsest Book Production Limited, Falkirk, Stirlingshire
Printed and bound in the UK using 100% renewable electricity at
CPI Group (UK) Ltd

Conditions of Sale
This book is sold subject to the condition that it shall not, by way of trade or otherwise, be lent, re-sold, hired out or otherwise circulated without the publisher's prior consent in any form, binding or cover other than that in which it is published and without a similar condition including this condition being imposed on the subsequent purchaser. No part of this publication may be reproduced, stored in a retrieval system or transmitted in any form or by any means, electronic, mechanical, photocopying, recording or otherwise, without the prior permission of HarperCollins*Publishers* Ltd.

Without limiting the exclusive rights of any author, contributor or the publisher of this publication, any unauthorised use of this publication to train generative artificial intelligence (AI) technologies is expressly prohibited. HarperCollins also exercise their rights under Article 4(3) of the Digital Single Market Directive 2019/790 and expressly reserve this publication from the text and data mining exception.

This book contains FSC™ certified paper and other controlled sources
to ensure responsible forest management.

For more information visit: www.harpercollins.co.uk/green

Chapter One

Ever since she was little, Ivy Pearson had imagined escaping Fox Bay, the tiny coastal town where she had spent her entire life. She had pictured a grand farewell. A tearful, cinematic departure at the train station. Her mum, begging her to stay, to reconsider leaving them for art school. Her little sister Liv, wailing, promising that she'd keep her side of the bedroom tidy if only Ivy would stay. Her best friend Raye, clinging to her, telling Ivy that life without her would be dull and boring. Teachers apologising for misunderstanding her creative genius. The cool kids admitting they had always secretly been jealous of her.

Because this was *it*. This was Ivy's goodbye to Fox Bay with all its quirks and bizarre traditions and anyone who didn't understand her artistic genius. She was going to Cornwall Art College in Truro, where she could finally start her new life as a painter and, she thought hopefully, as muse to an artist as brooding and introspective as herself.

In the event, her send-off committee had consisted only of her mum and Liv, waving cheerfully and asking her to text when she arrived. Raye had already left for her textiles course in Glasgow. No one had cried and no one had begged her to stay. It had all been considerably less dramatic than Ivy had thought.

And Ivy *certainly* hadn't imagined returning to Fox Bay with her tail between her legs less than three months later.

When she had set off for art school, Ivy hadn't exactly considered where she would spend the holidays. Perhaps one of her cool new friends would ask her to stay in their New York apartment or she would have been given an internship at a gallery in Paris. None of that had materialised. The many galleries she wrote to never replied. Three months in, her social life at college was best described as a disaster. And she had nowhere else to go but home.

So here she was, still in her ratty rainbow-striped cardigan, her long, red hair still wavy and unmanageable, still driving her mum's old Fiat 500, still winding her way through the streets of a town she had spent years dreaming of leaving.

Cornwall Art College had not been exactly what Ivy had imagined. Yes, the buildings were beautiful, smart and modern. Yes, there were impossibly cool people with blunt fringes who discussed art theory over their sandwiches. Yes, the teachers wore long scarves and were terrifyingly intelligent. And yes, after years of feeling like a fish out of water, Ivy was finally among people as creative as herself. But for some reason, nothing about art college was clicking the way she had thought it would.

Part of the issue, Ivy thought as she bemoaned the lack of a functioning heater in the car, was that she hadn't been able to afford to live in the college halls. Instead, her mum had found her a room that was miles from the college on the top floor of an elderly couple's house. It meant Ivy never seemed to be invited to the cool parties, where, presumably, intense artistic conversations were happening over red wine. And she'd failed to become anyone's muse.

Correction. She *had* been someone's muse, for a few short weeks. Raff from London, with cheekbones and a leather jacket, had asked her for coffee on the first day and they had instantly bonded over their love of Neo-Expressionism. For a few blissful weeks, it had been all Ivy had imagined – intense, 3 a.m. conversations about the meaning of life and whether it would have been better to be an artist in 1920s Paris or 1960s New York. But then Raff had dumped her at a toga party with the immortal line, 'I just don't think you're my muse, Ivy,' right before disappearing off into the sunset (or rather into the student union bar) with another first-year called Aurélie who – *oui* – was French and had transferred to Truro from the Beaux-Arts. She even wore a *beret*. How could Ivy Pearson, resolutely ordinary, from just up the road in Fox Bay, possibly compete?

To cap it all off, Ivy thought, as she forced the car into gear up the hill between her mum's flat and the centre of town, passing the post office with its traditional hideous winter snowscape, her art was a flop. Unlike her adoring Sixth Form art teacher, Miss Wheeldon, her new tutors didn't seem to think much of it at all. She was beginning to wonder if venturing out of the small pond of Fox Bay might have been a massive mistake.

In Fox Bay, at least Ivy had stood out. In a sea of tanned surfer kids, she and her best friend Raye were the striking, artistic types, with their love of indie music and ripped jeans. At college, it seemed that *everyone* saw themselves as striking, artistic types. Ivy was just one of many. Her heavy fringe and paint-spattered DM boots were practically a uniform at art college. And, far from being blown away by her work, her fellow students seemed almost . . . underwhelmed.

'I just don't really *get* it,' drawled a tall, elegant girl called Imogen, when Ivy had presented her piece to the class, halfway through term. 'It's not speaking to me, you know, authentically?'

'Yeah,' said Raff, his arm slung round Aurélie. 'I feel like your concepts are confused, Ivy. Maybe you need to be less rigid in your approach.'

Less rigid? What did that mean? Ivy understood that being an artist meant dealing with critics. But it seemed that no matter how hard she worked, her work was somehow lacking. As the first term drew to a close, as crit after crit had ended badly and the winter break loomed, she'd felt uneasy; that she wasn't making the most of the opportunity she had wanted since she was little. She *had* to succeed. Art college was everything she had ever dreamed of. Her big chance. She couldn't fail at the first hurdle – could she?

Her final tutorial of the term had taken place in the large first-year studio that smelled of turpentine. The end of term meant the submission of their first long-form project, a major piece of coursework. Everyone else had spread their work across the long tables or hooked up projectors to display audio-visual work.

Ivy had known before she walked in that her project wasn't great. Sheepishly, she had fiddled with the sketches and mumbled behind her curtain of red hair about *permanence* and *ephemerality*. The unimpressed silence that greeted her explanation said it all really.

'Stay behind, will you, Ivy?' her tutor Jess had said casually as the other students packed up to go. Jess had glossy black curls and wore jumpsuits with bold prints. She used phrases like 'let's try digging deeper into your practice'. She also didn't suffer fools or floundering students. Ivy was starting to suspect she was one.

Ivy sat while the last students had left the room. Then she watched and cringed while Jess had slowly flicked through the half-empty pages of her sketchbook, frowning.

'So,' Jess said gently at last, closing the book, and turning her piercing green eyes on Ivy. 'This final project. It's worth thirty per cent of your overall grade you know.'

'Yeah,' said Ivy uncomfortably.

'Remind me of the thesis here, will you?' Jess tapped Ivy's sketchbook with one black-painted nail.

Ivy scrambled for the words she had used earlier. 'I was thinking about ... exploring the relationship between impermanence and the – the ephemerality of self.' Even as she said it, she wanted to cry. What did that even *mean*?

Jess nodded thoughtfully. 'Right. Impermanence. Ephemerality. Aren't they kind of the same thing?'

Ivy swallowed. 'Um. Yes?'

There was another silence and then Jess had leaned forward. 'Listen, Ivy. I know the first term at college can feel overwhelming. Especially with commuting and living off-campus. I'm very sympathetic to that, believe me. But this project is important. You know that, right? It's your summative work for the first term. You can see how hard everyone else has worked. It *has* to be signed off when you get back after break. It is crucial to your overall mark for the year.'

Ivy nodded mutely.

'And to be blunt,' Jess continued, 'right now, I don't see a *project*. I don't see *anything*.'

Harsh, Ivy thought. But, she had to admit, possibly fair.

'You've got the technical skill, of course,' Jess went on. 'There's no doubt about that. You wouldn't be here if you didn't. Your line work is excellent, really extraordinary – some of the best I've seen. But this course isn't about being good at drawing. It's about putting yourself out there, allowing yourself to be vulnerable.' She tapped the sketchbook again. 'At the moment, something isn't working.'

Ivy bit her lip. The worst thing was that Jess wasn't being unkind; she was being honest.

'If you're stuck,' Jess added, 'find what you care about. Draw that. And remember to . . .'

'To dig into my practice, I know,' finished Ivy.

Jess smiled. 'You can do this, Ivy. I should be accepting the final projects now, but technically I can give you till the first week back. Take the winter break to figure this one out. What *matters* to you artistically? What speaks to you? What do you enjoy drawing, what feels important? Find that and the rest will come.' She pushed her chair back. 'Let's come back in January with some fresh ideas and a fresh attitude, okay? Because you have it in you. I know you do.'

'Thanks,' said Ivy. She had gathered up her work and left the studio that afternoon feeling nothing less than crushed. She had ducked past the student union, knowing that everyone would be in there celebrating the end of term and their successful projects, and driven back to her lodgings, miserable thoughts churning round her head.

Were ephemerality and impermanence the same thing? Yet again, Ivy had a growing suspicion she'd made the biggest mistake of her life. The last thing she'd painted with any conviction had been a half-finished seascape in September that she'd immediately flipped face-down on her desk. It had reminded her of home, and the last thing she wanted to paint was anything inspired by Fox Bay.

And now it was the end of term. The crowds of exciting, Bohemian new friends Ivy had thought she would make had obviously not materialised, nor had the longed-for internship in Paris. Ivy had no hot artist boyfriend to bring home and show off either. With no money and no offers pending, Ivy had realised she had no choice but to go back. Back to Fox Bay, back to the room she shared with Liv, to figure out her end-of-year art project in a place she knew better than the back of her hand, where literally nothing exciting or inspirational ever happened.

'Of course you must come back!' her mum had said delightedly down the phone when Ivy finally summoned the courage to call and admit defeat. Her mum was permanently enthusiastic about life and love, despite a succession of failed relationships. 'I'm sorry the internship didn't work out, but I can't wait to see you and Liv will be *thrilled*. Not to mention everyone else here. Everything is exactly the same in the flat, love. We haven't changed a *thing*.'

Ivy blinked back tears. It was comforting hearing her mum's warm, lilting voice. But . . . *everything is exactly the same. We haven't changed a thing.* She could just imagine it – the same mismatched furniture, the same cramped little kitchen, the same bedroom, one half papered in Velvet Underground posters and prints of expressionist art, the other covered in Lilo & Stitch and Minions.

'Great,' she said in a small voice.

'Fox Bay will probably roll out the red carpet. Or at least, Fin will bake his special cheese scones for you.'

Fox Bay would be the same too, Ivy had thought gloomily. The bakery, with Fin setting out the bread at exactly the same time every morning (Ivy had to admit to missing those cheese scones). Wildest Dreams Bookshop, with its eccentric owner Josie doing sun salutations in the doorway. The Mariner's Arms, with its resident golden retriever and Simi and Lou behind the bar. Old Bill, smoking his pipe in his sea captain's hat;

Tamsin, selling her crystals; Skye, making coffee at the Driftwood Café; Kate at the surf shop teaching the new generation of surfers . . .

Nothing ever changed in Fox Bay and Ivy couldn't believe that anything ever would.

'And all your school friends will be so pleased,' her mum had gone on happily. 'Erin, Mei, Callum.'

'They're not my friends, Mum,' Ivy muttered. 'They think I'm a loser. They only used to invite me to things because they felt sorry for me. I bet they were relieved I never went.'

Mei, Erin and Callum were nothing like her and Raye. They did regular Fox Bay things like surfing and partying on the beach, while Raye and Ivy had preferred to listen to music in their rooms and plot their escape. And Raye had been non-committal about the break, wanting to hang with Cleo, her new girlfriend. Ivy wasn't sure when she'd be back.

And there was another thing to consider. While Ivy's mum was just about scraping together tuition fees for Cornwall Art College, Ivy would still need to work during the holidays. She needed a job.

'I'll ask around,' her mum had said, clearly running through her mental roster of Fox Bay job vacancies. 'Lou's started doing delivery pizza, so maybe you could do some shifts with the car, but I'm not sure it's quite taken off yet and the Fiat is pretty unreliable, as you know. Or Simi might need help behind the bar at the Mariner's Arms now that Jacob's away with Anna . . . I saw Skye the other day back for the holidays, so I'm not sure there will be anything going at the Driftwood . . .'

'Thanks, Mum,' Ivy said. 'I was sort of hoping for something during the day so I can do my project in the evenings. But if you hear of anything . . .'

'I'll do my best,' her mum had promised.

But all her mum's leads – handing out fliers for Old Bill's new boat tours, wiping tables at the beach café – came up short. In the end, Ivy had rung Raye.

'I've got the perfect solution,' Raye told her. 'Wildest Dreams. It's the most low-maintenance job *ever*.' She had worked at the haphazard bookshop part-time for years.

'It's incredibly chill,' Raye assured her. 'You remember – I was mostly reading or catching up on gossip. Okay it got pretty busy towards the end of last summer but that was exceptional circs. It'll be perfect for your needs.'

Stacking shelves during the day sounded more appealing than pulling pints at night, Ivy thought.

'Do you think Josie needs anyone?' she asked.

'I bet she does,' Raye had said. 'I just had to tell her I couldn't help out this winter as usual. Josie is the best. If anyone is going to support your artistic endeavours, it's her. She is *all* about living for your art. Besides, she's too loved up with Fin these days to make anyone work *that* hard. You could do a lot worse than Wildest Dreams. I'll text her now and ask.'

'Thanks,' Ivy had told Raye. 'I guess I'm coming home. Are

you not coming back yet then?' She'd tried not to sound too hopeful (or desperate).

Raye laughed down the phone. 'And miss the end-of-term parties? No way! Besides,' her voice turned coy, 'Cleo's parents are coming to Glasgow in a couple of weeks and she thought maybe we could all have dinner together. Pretty big, huh?'

'Pretty big,' said Ivy, trying not to sound like she cared too much whether Raye made it or not. Like she wasn't at all jealous of Raye's cool new life. 'I guess I'll see you when I see you.'

'I'll try and make it back for New Year,' Raye said breezily. 'And,' she went on mysteriously, 'wait till you see Fox Bay. I went back for Reading Week and let me tell you, you're in for a surprise. Things have changed since you were last there.'

'Really?' Ivy said, hardly listening. 'Change, in Fox Bay? I find that hard to imagine. Have they repainted the station sign? Or put in new speed bumps by the Co-op?'

Raye had cackled. 'Just wait and see, Ivy. Wait and see.'

When Ivy reached the centre of Fox Bay, on her way to meet her mum and Liv at Cod Almighty for a homecoming meal, she realised that Raye had been right. Something had definitely changed.

Take, for instance, the train station. Forcing the wheezing car into a space, Ivy stared in amazement. Usually, only one or two passengers would alight at Fox Bay, if that. It wasn't uncommon to be the last passenger on the train by the time it made it all the way down the coast to the town. Today, though, crowds of people poured off the train, chatting excitedly.

Ivy climbed out of the car and caught snatches of their conversations.

'This place is so cosy!'

'Shall we hit the bookshop first?'

'Or the Unmissable Gems of Fox Bay boat tour maybe?'

'A cream tea at the Mariner's?'

'We *need* to get one of Fin's cinnamon buns.'

Bewildered, Ivy headed along the pavement to Cod Almighty. Her mum and Liv were in the window, holding up a sign that read WELCOME HOME IVY! She went inside and allowed herself to be enveloped in her mum's warm, slightly bony hug. Her mum was a whirlwind of energy, all sharp angles and elbows, with freckles and thick red waves of hair like Ivy's. She was also the kindest person Ivy knew and an eternal joiner, signing up for everything from the PTA to the Litter Collection Team; all in spite of the long hours she worked as a receptionist at the doctor's surgery.

'Darling,' she whispered into Ivy's hair, 'look at you! All grown up! My clever art student.'

'We missed you,' whispered her little sister, Liv, burying her own curly head into Ivy's waist.

'You've got so tall,' Ivy said, extricating herself from her mum's hug and rumpling her sister's hair. 'You're going to be taller than me soon.'

Liv, who was nine years old, very practical and wanted to be the next Sheryl Sandberg 'so that someone in this family makes some money' wrinkled her nose. 'I doubt it,' she said matter-of-factly. 'Your dad was six foot five and my dad was, and I'm quoting Mum, a short arse.'

'I don't think I said that about him, love,' her mum said, going pink. 'Come on. Let's get Ivy some tea.'

'What,' Ivy said, gesturing to the people bustling along the pavement, 'is going on here and what has happened to the sleepy little seaside town I left behind? Is there some new festival I don't know about?' It was the only explanation she could think of. Fox Bay had a penchant for eccentric traditions and festivals, going big on things like Pancake Day, egg rolling, midsummer rites and Samhain. But it was usually confined to the locals. Ivy couldn't remember anything bringing in the tourists like *this*.

'Of course, you haven't been here since it all kicked off.' Her mum had tucked her arm through Ivy's. 'Remember when that writer, Kathleen Lee, came here last summer? You were away on that residency, but I told you about it.'

Ivy remembered, of course. A celebrity romance author called Kathleen Lee had launched her book in a hidden bay in their town. The launch had gone viral, with an exclusive signing from Kathleen Lee at Wildest Dreams, stoking the book's already mammoth pre-sales and turning it into a phenomenon.

'But it wasn't like this,' Ivy said, bewildered.

'Well everything just snowballed after that,' her mum said. 'Some big travel writer from the US wrote a feature calling Fox Bay *England's Secret Seaside Paradise*. They said we were "the

UK's answer to Stars Hollow". And since then, it's just been hordes of tourists.' Her mum sighed. 'Which I suppose makes this secret seaside paradise rather . . . *unsecret*. Good for the local businesses though. The bookshop is especially popular, of course.'

'Wow,' Ivy said. 'I didn't realise it had got so big. Is Kathleen Lee really that famous?'

'She's huge. There's even talk of a movie of *Ocean Deep*. Although that might just be a rumour. I haven't seen an announcement yet. You know what this place is like for gossip.'

As they navigated their way back to the car after finishing their chips, Ivy found that the town was indeed crawling with tourists, thronging the cobbled streets, taking selfies in front of Old Bill's boat, posing with glass bottles fitted with tiny paper scrolls on the shoreline, buying crystals at Tamsin's shop and having coffee outside the picturesque Mariner's Arms.

'Gosh,' Ivy looked around in amazement. 'It's quite a change. I'm not used to seeing this many people at once in this town.'

Her mum laughed. 'And you always said nothing happened here! Well, now look.'

It was true. Ivy had left to discover the outside world at the precise moment the outside world had come to Fox Bay.

Chapter Two

On her first day at Wildest Dreams, Josie had brought Ivy up to speed.

'The tourists mostly don't buy much, and they like taking photos reading by the fireplace – but don't let them light it, darling, I suspect it's a death trap. It's for something called TikTok. And then they usually head off for sightseeing.'

'What else is there to *see*?' Ivy had asked, confused.

'Oh, Old Bill has his tours – Unmissable Gems of Fox Bay, that's what he's calling it. He takes tourists out in his boat, they go to Seal Island and back, then they have tea at the Mariner's and go home again. It's all fairly harmless and it's been great for the town.' Josie added coyly, 'I've decided to capitalise on all this attention myself – it's called a side-hustle, apparently. I've moved in with Fin – my beau, darling, I refuse to use the word boyfriend – and I'm renting out the top two rooms to tourists. They think staying in a bookshop is unbelievably charming. So if you could take on the *tiniest* bit of the housekeeping I'd add that to your wages.'

'What have the guests been like so far?' Ivy asked suspiciously.

'They've been very interesting,' said Josie evasively. 'We've had a meditation teacher who was here to run a sound bath, only she insisted it had to be at 3 a.m. because that's when the vibrations are strongest. And then there was the meteorologist who put a telescope on the roof to observe the lunar eclipse, but he broke his ankle getting down, poor man. Had to be airlifted off, can you believe it? And then there was this couple on a romantic getaway – but then the man's wife came to confront them, right in the middle of the children's story time.'

At Ivy's appalled face, Josie had rushed on. 'But our new guest won't be anything like that. A very nice American woman. No trouble at all from the sounds of it,' Josie had told her. 'Quiet, bookish. No telescopes or tuning forks or other people's husbands, darling, I promise. Her name's Brooke Wakefield and she's arriving in a few days from California for some *peace and quiet* – her exact words. Sightseeing, sea air, that sort of thing. She said she's a huge Kathleen Lee fan and they're always delightful. And she's booked the flat for weeks.' She beamed at Ivy. 'You'll take it on, won't you, darling?'

Ivy had nodded, praying Brooke was indeed as low maintenance as she sounded. But as she arrived at the bookshop on Thursday morning, the day of Brooke's arrival, she was feeling mildly terrified remembering the horror stories about the previous guests. However, she did need the extra cash.

The grey, drizzly weather just about suited Ivy's mood. The key stuck slightly in the old lock and Ivy had to give the bookshop door a purposeful shove with her hip before it gave way, the familiar jangle of the bell overhead echoing through the empty shop.

Wildest Dreams was still half-asleep, cloaked in a hushed wintery grey, although shafts of weak sunlight were breaking through. The fairy lights strung across the shelves blinked sleepily to life as Ivy flicked the switch, revealing the bookshop in all its cheerfully chaotic glory. An old windchime with a sun, moon and stars swayed gently in the draught from the door. There was the window seat, piled with mismatched cushions and paperbacks; the cloth toadstools leading to the kids' corner round the back. There was a home-made wreath Josie had fashioned, enthusiastically stuffed with holly, pinecones and bits of foliage so that it now looked like a festive hedgehog. Glass bottles, remnants from the legendary Kathleen Lee book launch last summer, still glinted on the shelf, some filled with fairy lights, others with beach pebbles and paper scrolls containing peoples' love stories from all over the world, in all different languages.

Ivy let out a deep breath. Minus the customers and demanding guests, Wildest Dreams felt like a sanctuary of sorts. When it was quiet, with its crooked shelves and tea rings and Pushkin the cat, who tolerated Ivy's presence with regal disdain, she caught a whiff of the cosy old shop she remembered from childhood, before it had become so busy and popular and had a bit of a glow-up. A place to sit and read. A place of dreams. She wondered if Josie missed that peacefulness too, in spite of all the success and attention.

As she headed further into the shop, Pushkin launched himself on to the counter with a dramatic yowl.

'Oh, hello,' Ivy said, stroking his soft black ears. 'Are you having a rough morning too?' Josie had told Ivy that she'd tried to relocate Pushkin to Fin's flat with her but the cat had stubbornly refused, marching back to Wildest Dreams every morning with his tail held high and dragging his claws along the wooden floors when they had tried to move him. In the end, Josie had let him stay, adding 'loveable bookshop cat' to the rooms' online listing.

Pushkin pulled away from Ivy's ear-stroking and glanced meaningfully towards his bowl. Ivy sighed and went to fill it. She tugged off her scarf and oversized coat, pulling her bright auburn hair out from the neck of her cardigan. She glanced at the display of cosy romances, resenting their glittery optimism and cheerful titles. *Fireside Flirtation*, *Snowflakes and Swooning*. Ugh. She knew exactly how they would all end. That the big-city lawyer would settle for a life in the sticks or the family farm would be saved from ruin with some ridiculous and impractical solution that would suit no one in real life but somehow, in a romance, worked.

'Whatever,' muttered Ivy crossly, trying not to think of Raff and Aurélie and sparkling lights in Paris.

The shelving system at Wildest Dreams was proudly *non-linear*, as Josie had told Ivy on her first day. She wanted the customer's experience to involve 'intuitive browsing' and once compared the shop's labyrinthine layout to 'a literary treasure map'. After her introductory tour, Ivy had privately called it a nightmare.

The previous assistant – Josie's niece Anna, who Ivy had never met but whose colour-coded notes gave serious Virgo vibes – had apparently tried to wrangle the sections into order, and had left copious instructions as to how her system could be followed. But Wildest Dreams was not a shop that was easy to tame. Josie had eschewed most of the categorisation in favour of her own system, and her system was chaos.

'Anna is a darling girl,' Josie had told Ivy, 'but she needs to relax a little. I thought Bali would bring that out in her, but even her backpacking plans were organised on colour-coded spreadsheets.' She smiled. 'Still, I hear she and Jacob are having a wonderful time in Australia right now without any plans at all. It just shows you, darling, when you follow your heart, incredible things happen.'

Anna had spent last summer in Fox Bay and, after a romance with the town's hottest bad boy, surfer Jacob, had promptly ditched uni in favour of what seemed to be an extended gap year. Ivy wasn't sure she wanted to throw her own life up in the air in quite the same way.

The winter sun was making an attempt to shine through a break in the rain as Ivy made her way behind the counter, brushing aside a scattering of dust. She pulled off her gloves, shoved them into the pocket of her coat, now hanging on the peg, and turned to the tea station that had been wedged on to a makeshift side table by the till so the holidaymakers could use the kitchen.

Ivy craved a decent espresso most mornings – the true artist's drink of choice, she had decided – but she couldn't afford to visit the Driftwood Café on a daily basis. Besides, she thought irritably, the café was always full of the popular surf kids. Despite growing up by the sea, Ivy couldn't swim and definitely couldn't surf. The old gang – Jacob, Seb, Isla and Skye – might have moved on, to travel, work and college, but new cool kids always sprang up to take their place. Kids who threw parties on the beach and danced at night to the flickering light of the bonfire.

Ivy filled the kettle and put as much ground coffee as she dared into the cafetière. *These inane rom coms aren't going to shelve themselves*, she thought. She had better get started, with or without decent caffeine. She headed into the back room of the shop and—

Ivy shrieked and was instantly mortified. She never shrieked.

A boy about her age, maybe a little older, was doing a downward dog on the rag rug. A boy with chestnut-brown hair falling into his warm brown eyes. Lean, tanned and balanced effortlessly, his long limbs silhouetted by the grey morning light filtering through the window.

The boy didn't even flinch. He moved fluidly into a different stretch, glancing up at her with a bright, unbothered smile.

'Oh hey! Sorry, didn't mean to scare you. I didn't realise anyone would be here so early. I'm Trip.'

Chapter Three

Ivy stared at him, her heart thumping wildly, wondering if she was interrupting the politest robbery of all time.

'I was expecting you at some point of course,' he went on, still smiling at her. His accent was American, Ivy thought dazedly, broad and cheerful, like he came from someplace sunny and relaxed. 'Josie said you'd be in this morning. You must be Ivy.'

'I . . . what?' Ivy managed, finding herself frustratingly unable to string a sentence together. Her gaze caught on his muscles in his loose vest, effortlessly holding his yoga position.

'My sister's Brooke Wakefield. Josie's guest? She's upstairs, sleeping off the jet lag. We got here last night. I'm staying here too. Originally it was just going to be Brooke, but she showed me the photos of this town and this bookshop and I had to see it. It's spectacular! But yeah, Josie didn't mind. In fact, she said I brought great *psychic energy* to this place. Which is already as amazing as I expected, by the way. I feel like I'm in a picture postcard. And I haven't even seen it in daylight yet!' Talking all the while, he flowed unselfconsciously into some kind of warrior pose, muscles shifting yet again.

Ivy's brain finally kicked into gear. The pieces clunked into place. Clearly, Josie's new lodger, Brooke, came with a brother attached. Another person to accommodate, an unnervingly cheerful and unnervingly handsome person with long limbs, unruly chestnut hair and caramel-brown eyes, doing yoga on the shop rug and chatting away without a care. *Thanks for letting me know, Josie*, Ivy thought, smoothing her unbrushed hair and rubbing sleep out of her eyes.

'Um, okay. Well, welcome to Wildest Dreams,' she said. 'Tea?' She was meant to look after the guests, after all. 'Coffee? Chai?'

'No, thanks,' Trip said, without breaking his pose. 'I thought I might get a green juice later. Get some vitamins in after the flight. Maybe an echinacea smoothie or something.'

'Sure,' Ivy said. She didn't want to break it to Trip that the closest thing Fox Bay had to a smoothie was probably mushy peas from the chippy. 'Good luck with that.'

'I'll just finish up here and then I'll come and introduce myself properly,' Trip said. He gave her an unexpectedly sweet smile. 'See you in a minute, Ivy.'

Ivy had just managed to make a coffee that was strong enough to wake her up – even if it did taste of mud – shelved the rom coms and was immersed in a new edition of the *Paris Review* when Trip appeared.

'Hey!' he said. 'Oh man, this place is so charming. I can't get over it. Even that refrigerator. Look at it. Super neat.'

Ivy turned the page without looking up. 'It's a fridge. A fridge that looks like it's from the 1970s. In fact, I think this whole place is one big health and safety violation.'

'And these coffee cups!' he went on, picking one up. 'Brew and Prejudice. That's funny, isn't it? Because—'

'Yes,' Ivy said, groaning internally. Trip was clearly someone who enjoyed puns. That wouldn't get old *at all*. 'I get it. Like *Pride and Prejudice*, but it's . . . a brew.'

'That's right.' He beamed at her. 'So cool.'

'Josie designed the mugs and had them made at the print shop. They're full of typos. Look closely and you'll see she's spelled "prejudice" with two js.'

Trip was seemingly undeterred. 'I love how much personality this place has. And it's so peaceful. The sea, lulling you to sleep . . . it reminds me of home.'

'Which is where?' asked Ivy, turning the page, although she couldn't concentrate on her article over the sound of Trip's enthusiasm.

'California.' He leaned on the counter, eyes bright and expectant. 'Mostly in Santa Cruz. So what's your story? Josie says you live in Fox Bay?'

'I grew up here,' Ivy said shortly. His wide brown eyes were still fixed eagerly on hers so she found herself carrying on. 'I should have been born in London but Mum moved here when she was pregnant because she'd met a Cornish guy. They had my little sister Liv and then the Cornish guy moved to Spain. We think, no one seems too sure.'

'Awesome,' said Trip. 'Growing up here must have been amazing. I bet you're out every day in the summer, catching waves.'

'Nope,' Ivy told him, turning back to the *Paris Review*. 'I'm a freak of nature. The only non-surfer in Fox Bay. When I walk through the streets the townsfolk point and stare.'

'Oh,' he said, sounding a little uncertain.

Ivy sighed. As usual, her sense of humour, such as it was, had fallen flat; not that she cared. She was used to blank stares.

Then, to her surprise, Trip said, 'Do they ring a bell as you walk past and pelt you with rotten eggs?'

She glanced up at him, startled, and saw a smile tugging at his mouth. 'Not quite,' she said. 'But I have to warn you, the stocks are still in the town square.'

He grinned. 'Noted. So are you back for winter break?'

'Yeah, I'm at art college in Truro right now.'

'Wow. That's *so* cool. An artist. You must be full of ideas.'

Ivy froze for a fraction of a second, a page half-turned, the smile stiffening on her lips. The words hovered awkwardly. *Artist. You must be full of ideas.*

'I guess,' she said. 'Whatever. Look, Trip,' (was that really his name?) 'I should get on. Lots to do. Josie might plan her day according to the lunar cycles, but she also works me pretty hard.'

To her relief, Trip took the hint. He stood and tied his hoodie round his waist.

'I'm gonna head out for a quick run, anyway. I read that running at sunrise helps your circadian rhythms and resets your body clock after a long flight. Jet lag hack, I guess. See you later, Ivy.'

'See you,' muttered Ivy, watching as he bounced out into the rain.

The moment the door clicked shut behind him, Ivy let out a breath and put down her magazine. It was *way* too early for that much conversation and enthusiasm. Too early for anyone that cheerful. She relished the sudden return to silence, moving to the kids' corner and straightening scattered cushions, aligning the tiny chairs round the table.

She refilled Kathleen Lee's display, knowing that fans would make a beeline for it the second the door was unlocked. Somehow, Wildest Dreams had become the official Kathleen Lee stockist. Feeling obscurely sorry for the local authors, such as Serena Woods, she pushed some of their books to the front of the display, hoping they would get picked up too.

A few minutes later, Josie arrived, humming and windblown, her grey curls wild, with a fresh box of paperbacks and a baguette from Fin's bakery in her arms. 'Goodness, the rain is coming down now!' she exclaimed. 'You're here early, darling. You're always so punctual. It worries me, Ivy.'

'Isn't punctuality a *good* thing in an employee?' said Ivy, wrapping her rainbow-cardigan round herself against the sharp breeze from the open door.

'Well, I suppose, although frankly I think good time-keeping is overrated.' Josie set the box on her hip and kicked the door shut behind her. 'Being on time *is* useful, I suppose, when you have trains to catch and shops to open – but in the grand scheme of things it's a bit dull. I wouldn't have had half the adventures I've had if I hadn't missed the odd flight or two. You're young.' She waved a hand. 'You should be staying out late, partying, sharing ideas, thoughts with like-minded souls. You should be texting me to say you're not coming in at all because you've – you've run off to Marrakesh with a poet!'

'I'll bear that in mind,' said Ivy. Like there was anyone she would want to run off to Marrakesh with, she thought.

'Good.' Josie set the box down with an exhale. 'Have you met Brooke yet?'

Ivy shook her head. 'She's asleep. Or so her terrifyingly perky brother told me.'

'Oh, so you met Trip, did you?' Josie said. 'An unexpected addition but I said he was very welcome. *Such* a nice boy. So enthusiastic. Most young people seem depressingly jaded these days.' A sly look came into her sparkling sea-green eyes. 'And my goodness, he's a handsome boy. Those dimples.' She added casually, 'He's about your age, darling, isn't he?'

Ivy stifled a groan. 'Whatever you're doing, please don't.' Josie was about as subtle as a plank. The last thing she needed was Josie deciding that she and Trip were like-minded souls and should run off to Marrakesh together, because Ivy would never hear the end of it.

'What?' Josie laughed. 'I was only thinking that you could show him around. Explore Fox Bay together.' She winked. 'By moonlight, perhaps.'

'I'd rather eat a Kathleen Lee hardback,' Ivy said. 'Or reorganise the Russian poetry shelves.'

Josie tapped the box. 'Fine. *Someone's* got to put these on display.'

'Perfect,' said Ivy, taking it and heading to the romance shelves. 'This should take a nice long time.'

Josie called after her, 'Suit yourself! But don't pretend you didn't notice those dimples!'

Ivy set to work, muttering under her breath. *Trip.* Seriously, what kind of name was that? She shelved another book with a little more force than necessary.

'You're an artist? That's so cool. You must be full of ideas.'

Sadly not, Trip, Ivy thought bitterly. She was an idea-free zone. She shuddered anew at the thought of her final tutorial.

Find out what you care about and start from there.

The shop door chimed open, and Ivy instinctively braced herself for the influx of customers. She peered round the shelves into the front of the shop. But it wasn't a Kathleen Lee fan or an eager shopper. It was Trip again, this time with wet hair and a soaked T-shirt.

'Good morning, darling,' Josie said. 'Nice run? Did you do the route I suggested, along the cliffs?'

'Yeah. It was perfect. Wet, but perfect. Fox Bay,' Trip declared, still catching his breath, 'is *even better* in golden hour.'

Golden hour. Ivy snorted. She considered telling him it wasn't called *golden hour* here. It was just 'morning' and besides it was pouring with rain. But she decided against it.

'Do you want me to help out at all, Josie?' Trip was asking.

'No, no, darling,' Josie said. 'Don't be ridiculous. This is your holiday. What is it with you serious young people? Always looking for jobs.'

'It's called a cost-of-living crisis,' Ivy told her from the romance shelves. 'That plus student loans.'

'Ignore Ivy,' Josie said. 'Go and find a book and read. I can recommend some excellent avant-garde Russian authors.'

'I *do* have some reading to do for college,' Trip said. 'Oh hey, Ivy,' he said, turning to her like they were already best friends.

'What are you studying?' Ivy asked, to be polite.

'I haven't made my mind up on what I want to major in. Or which college I want to go to, to be honest. But I'm leaning towards Philosophy. I want to study the mechanics of joy.'

Ivy groaned. 'Of course.'

Just then, the door opened again and this time a group of five people came in, clearly from out of town, all clutching *Ocean Deep* totes stamped with a glass-stoppered bottle and a cluster of seashells.

'Have you heard the rumours about the film?' said one. 'I hope they can get Jacob Elordi to play the captain.'

'I heard they might go for an unknown for Lily,' said another.

'And the sequel is meant to be in the works too,' a guy said excitedly. '*Ocean Far*. You find out all about the captain's younger brother. I wonder if we can pre-order it here? The owner is friends with Kathleen . . .'

'I think I'm needed,' said Josie. She took a bite of her baguette and sighed. 'Of course, all this business is wonderful, but does anyone miss when Fox Bay was just a *little* quieter?'

Chapter Four

By the time Ivy flipped the sign from *Open* to *Closed* that evening, her brain felt like sludge. Like any spark of creativity she might have once nourished had been snuffed out by the endless, incessant questions.

Do you have the book? The one with the green cover? Or maybe blue? I saw it on TikTok.

Do you have anything about war but not sad?

Which Kathleen Lee should I get if I don't like misunderstandings? Or romance? Or dogs?

Ivy's feet hurt from standing; her cheeks hurt from polite smiling; her throat hurt from forced small talk. Josie had left early for a yoga session and never returned, probably struck with a sudden desire to hike or paint. Trip had vanished that afternoon and his sister still hadn't emerged from her room. Ivy didn't mind. Alone was good.

She drove home breathing deeply, without even the crackly old car radio for company, imploring inspiration to strike. She could squeeze in half an hour of sketching and brainstorming after dinner – if she could only think of something to draw. At the moment her mind was a whirl of receipts and queries and orders.

She parked outside their block and climbed the flight of stairs to their flat, fantasising about an evening to herself. Maybe Mum might have taken Liv to something after school – neither of them could resist an activity. But when she unlocked her front door and stepped into the kitchen, the noise hit her: the familiar hum and clutter of chairs scraping, something bubbling on the stove, and her little sister holding forth at full volume.

'Ivy!' Liv squealed, launching herself across the kitchen. 'You're late! We waited *for ever*! We have NEWS!'

'Hi,' Ivy said, caught in a tight, pasta-sauce-smeared hug. She picked a piece of onion out of Liv's hair. 'Smells amazing. Also, ow.' She prised Liv off gently. 'Sit down, okay?'

Her mum, sliding garlic bread on to a plate, gave her a worried look. 'You seem exhausted, love. I can't believe Josie is working you this hard.'

'It's not Josie,' said Ivy wearily, slumping into her usual chair. 'It's life.'

'Yeah, she's always like that now,' Liv said cheerfully. 'It's all part of her art school persona. Grumpy with everyone.'

'It is not!' cried Ivy indignantly. 'And I'm not!'

Ivy's mum bit her lip, clearly trying not to laugh. 'Oh, I don't think that's true, Livvie,' she said. 'Poor Ivy is just a bit tired.'

'But this will cheer her up,' Liv said, doing a drumroll on the Formica table. 'Wait till she hears what we're planning! Wait till you hear, Ivy!'

'Brace yourself,' her mum said, piling spaghetti into a bowl for her. 'And eat up, love. You need some energy.'

'Go on then,' said Ivy, picking up her fork. 'Tell me all about it.'

'Fox Bay Primary is putting on a *winter spectacular*!' Liv jiggled in her seat. 'Like a real show, with tickets and lights and everything! We're raising money for the library!'

'Ah,' said Ivy. 'Is this one of Mr H's wild plans, by any chance?' The primary school headmaster was notorious for impenetrable, confusing and frankly disastrous events to aid the community in some form or another. They were almost always a shambles, but the people of Fox Bay always showed up dutifully anyway.

Her mum laughed. 'You guessed it. Only, I have a good feeling about this one.'

'Mr Hargreaves says it's not going to be a normal nativity. And it won't be weird like last year where Baby Jesus turned into a Christmas pudding. It's going to be all about Cornwall! Like, history, folklore, pasties, smugglers – everything!'

Ivy smiled at her little sister. Liv had inherited their mum's enthusiasm for a project, although thankfully she was far more practical. 'You're fundraising for the library with smugglers? In December?'

'Yes!' Liv looked absolutely thrilled. 'Mr H let us brainstorm and then everyone's ideas are going in. He promised. It's genius – he says so.'

'But the end of term is in, like, three weeks,' Ivy pointed out gently.

'He says that's *ample* time,' Liv told her. 'What does ample mean?'

'It means enough, and he's wrong. I always thought Mr Hargreaves was delusional,' said Ivy, digging into her pasta with her fork. 'And now I know it.'

'*I* think it sounds inspired. The library is desperate for funds. And *so many* tourists will be here,' her mum said, filling Ivy's water glass as she sat at the table. 'It's the perfect time to draw a crowd. Mr H is cannier than he looks.'

'If you say so,' Ivy said. 'It sounds chaotic.' She added absently, twirling spaghetti, 'They'll need all the help they can get.'

'Exactly! Which is why,' her mum said, 'I volunteered *you* to help, love.'

Ivy paused, fork halfway to her mouth. 'You what now?'

'You're head of props and set design!' her mum said brightly, like she thought Ivy would be delighted. 'We told the show committee how talented you are, didn't we, Liv? They signed you up right away.'

Liv nodded, her mouth full of spaghetti. 'Mum told them you're an *artistic genius*.'

'Mum,' Ivy said, slowly, putting down her fork, 'you do know I'm working full-time through the holidays, right? And working on my art project. My incredibly important, thirty-per-cent-of-my-mark project.'

'Well, yes, but you've got your evenings. And it's not like you're *doing* anything with your art right now.'

Ivy winced. 'Thanks.'

'You know what I mean. It's a good cause. And I think you might enjoy it. You were always amazing at making sets and things when you were little. You used to put on plays all the time.' Her mum rested her chin in her hands and looked at her daughter. 'I'm worried about you, love.'

'Oh not you too,' said Ivy. 'I've already had the lecture from Josie about how I'm young and I should be out having adventures or running away to Marrakesh or something.'

'Well, she's not wrong,' her mum said. 'Maybe not the running-away part, thanks very much, Josie – but all the same . . . You're up at the crack of dawn for work and then you come home and stare at your sketchbook for hours but never seem to draw anything and then you go to bed early. And then you get up and do it all again. Not much of a holiday for you, is it? I think you seem . . .' She hesitated.

'What?' said Ivy defensively. 'Go on, what do I seem?'

'You seem lonely.' Her mum sighed. 'I think doing the props for this show would be fun, if you let it be.' She nudged her daughter. 'Fun, remember that? Before you got so serious?'

Ivy stared at her spaghetti. 'You really signed me up already?'

'Head of props,' Liv echoed proudly. Her face was practically fluorescent-orange with tomato sauce now. 'You're going to make a giant castle out of papier-mâché. And probably a fishing boat. And some fish.' She waved her hand. 'Mr Hargreaves says it's a work in progress. He's got Mr Patterson to do the script. He's the new top primary English teacher and he's studied avant-garde theatre.'

'Great,' Ivy said flatly. 'So this winter if I'm not making papier-mâché while kids perform avant-garde theatre I'll be surrounded by tourists at the shop with Josie badgering me to learn Russian poetry and flee the country. Plus, a guy who thinks yoga is a personality.'

'Who is the guy?' her mum asked, bewildered by Ivy's litany.

'Oh, never mind,' Ivy said. 'Some new paying guest of Josie's. His sister's here for a holiday and for some reason she brought along her irritating brother – they're posh Americans who want a quaint British winter. Little do they know they've moved into the world's most chaotic Airbnb. What a holiday.'

'That's the spirit, love. The first meeting is next week.'

Liv beamed. 'It's going to be *amazing*.'

Ivy sighed, stirring sauce through her spaghetti. She was meant to be having an artistic breakthrough, not painting sets for a school show, doing endless shifts in the shop and housekeeping for a cheerful American boy called Trip.

Who, for some reason, she kept picturing in his yoga gear.

Chapter Five

Over the next few days, Ivy began to wonder if Trip had cloned himself. It was the only logical explanation. Because he was *everywhere.*

No matter how early and how quietly Ivy had crept into the shop, there he was. At the counter before she'd even switched the kettle on, raving about the 'best croissant I've had since I was in Paris' (Fin's almond ones, obviously). Then again at the Co-op, comparing oat milks and chatting away to Sarah, the bemused but charmed shelf-stacker about whether pea protein was actually more sustainable. Later that week, Ivy noticed him outside the Mariner's Arms, helping Simi unload casks of beer.

'Thanks,' Simi had said, wiping her hands on her jeans. 'Whoever you are, you're a lifesaver. I wasn't sure I'd manage that on my own.'

'No problem,' Trip had said. And with a cheerful boy scout's salute, he'd headed off. *Probably to adjust his circadian rhythms or something*, Ivy had thought bitterly, watching him go.

On Monday, a cold, misty morning, she sought refuge in the Driftwood Café, where she found Skye, Fox Bay's coolest inhabitant, freshly back from London for the holidays, chattering away to Trip like an old friend as she frothed milk.

'I can't believe you were at Coachella this year,' she was saying, as Ivy waited to order her double espresso. 'I was there too. It was so cool.'

'It *was* cool,' Trip said happily. 'There should be more festivals like that, only smaller and at more accessible price points. You know, I can totally imagine a festival *here*, on the beach.'

Skye's eyes widened. 'Now that would be awesome . . .'

Ivy exited swiftly, without ordering. She really didn't need the coffee and any more of Trip's seemingly boundless good spirits and big plans. On the way to the shop, she ran into Old Bill, Fox Bay's unofficial mayor and teller of tall tales.

'You have that Trip chap staying at the shop, don't you?' he asked Ivy, pushing back his sailor's cap. 'He's a good lad.'

Ivy groaned. 'Not you too, Bill.' Surely *someone* in Fox Bay was immune to Trip's relentless charm offensive.

'Lad says he's going to show me some of those yoga moves he's always doing,' Bill told Ivy, shifting the pipe that was permanently welded to his mouth. 'Says it'll keep me limber which is important for bone density as you age. And he wants me to give up smoking. Got to watch my chest, he says.'

'How's that working out for you?' said Ivy, looking meaningfully at the pipe, which Bill lowered sheepishly.

Ivy unlocked the shop to find a woman sitting at the counter, wearing expensive-looking gym gear, reading *Variety* and drinking from a KeepCup.

'Oh hi,' said Ivy, wrestling the door shut. 'You must be Brooke, Josie's mysterious lodger, sister to the most cheerful man in the world.'

The woman considered her. She had Trip's chestnut hair and brown eyes, although her hair was cut in a sleek bob and her eyes had a sharper, more knowing expression. 'And you must be Ivy, the mysterious housekeeper. Thanks for the towels – I assume that's you.'

'Yeah, that's me,' Ivy said. 'Josie's paying me a bit extra for housekeeping but I'm really studying art and . . . anyway. How are you finding it here in Fox Bay?'

'It's only the most picturesque Airbnb ever.' Brooke's tone was dry. She cricked her neck. 'Even though that bed is a killer. And that shower isn't exactly warm.'

'I tried to tell Josie Wildest Dreams needed some more improvements before she could rent it out. I think she's hoping the view makes up for everything else.'

'It is a great view,' said Brooke, turning back to her magazine, clearly shutting down the conversation. While her brother could talk for the USA, she was clearly a woman of few words.

'So you're a Kathleen Lee fan, then?' Ivy asked.

'Not really,' said Brooke. 'I just came here for the vibes.'

Ivy frowned – hadn't Josie said that Brooke was a fan? Just then, the door opened. 'Hey!' Trip beamed, appearing in the doorway with coffee. 'Brooke, you're up! And you've met Ivy!' He handed Ivy one of the takeaway cups. 'I got you one too,' he said. 'Hope that's okay. Skye said this was your order. Double espresso?'

'Thanks,' Ivy said, taking the cup, feeling a surge of gratitude. 'I really fancied a coffee that doesn't taste of dirt this morning.'

'Isn't this place awesome, Brooke?' Trip said, his gaze lingering on the carved ceiling beams and little stained-glass panels above the door.

'It's great,' said Brooke, still immersed in an article.

Trip was drinking his coffee and scanning the *Fox Bay Sentinel*. 'There's so much cosy stuff to do here,' he said. 'Look at this, Brooke. A winter pageant, put on by the local primary school. How cute is that?'

Did he ever stop talking, Ivy wondered. As though reading her mind, Brooke glanced up and rolled her eyes affectionately. 'He's like this *all the time*, you know,' she said to Ivy. 'Doesn't pause for breath.'

'Yeah,' said Ivy, fighting back a smile. She hadn't expected Trip's sister to be so different to him. 'I've noticed.'

Trip waved the paper, unfazed. 'It's part of a fundraising drive to save the library. We should see if we can help. Brooke, you'd be good at—'

'I'm on holiday, remember?' said Brooke sharply. Ivy was sure she shot her brother a warning look and he fell silent.

'Why did you pick Fox Bay? It's so out of the way,' said Ivy, watching Brooke closely. There was something odd here, she thought. She just couldn't put her finger on what.

'Why not?' Brooke said with a shrug. 'I liked the idea of a nice old-fashioned English winter.'

'In a town with no good hotels, one restaurant and a pizza

van? In an Airbnb with a terrible mattress, a cold shower and no functioning coffee machine?'

'Brooke works all the time,' Trip chimed in. 'I think she's just looking to switch off for a bit. If Brooke's not organising or booking or scheduling something, she's lost.'

Brooke smiled thinly. 'That's because *someone* has to think five steps ahead.'

'What do you do?' asked Ivy.

'Consulting. Boring.'

'Ivy's an artist,' Trip said.

'Good for you.' Brooke stood and stretched. 'Well, have fun kids. I'm going for a walk – alone.' She pointed a finger at her brother. 'Got that, Trip? Alone. I want peace and quiet, not having you point out every landmark you've decided is totally adorable.'

Trip grinned. 'She's kidding,' he told Ivy. 'She loves me really.'

Brooke rolled her eyes again, then headed out into the morning mist that still shrouded the cobbled streets, leaving behind the faintest scent of expensive perfume. Ivy watched her go, frowning. Had Brooke seemed oddly evasive about her reasons for being here? Or was Ivy so bored of Fox Bay life already that she was imagining drama where there wasn't any?

Trip sipped his coffee happily. 'She liked you.'

'Really?' said Ivy. She hadn't got warm and fuzzy vibes from Brooke.

'Yeah! I could tell. She doesn't open up like that to just anyone.'

If that was Brooke opening up, Ivy wasn't sure she wanted

to get on her bad side. She took a sip of her own coffee. Hot, bitter, delicious. 'This is really nice coffee,' she managed. 'And it was . . . very thoughtful of you to get it for me.' She headed into the stock room with a backwards wave. 'Now if you don't mind, I have to work.'

After their brief meeting, Brooke remained as reclusive as Aunt Josie had promised, preferring to hole up in her room typing furiously on her laptop, holding long, muttered calls, or going for solitary walks along the coast. In contrast, Trip remained ever present; always cheerful, always smiling, with his perfect hair flopping on to his forehead.

'That young man,' Josie remarked the next day while restocking the history section, 'has a very distracting energy.'

'Distracting?' asked Ivy.

Josie laughed. 'Not to *me*, of course, I could be his grandmother, but you know what I mean, don't you? I'm surprised you can do any work at all with him around. Those eyes. Have you noticed the dimples yet?'

Ivy had no intention of agreeing out loud, but she was keenly aware of Trip's dimples. And also his eyes, and the way they changed according to the time of day. Caramel brown in the morning sunlight, wide, warm brown as he burst in with some other new and apparently utterly charming Fox Bay discovery, crinkled with laughter in the twilight of closing time when he told them some hilarious anecdote from around the harbour. Never had Ivy met someone so enthusiastic about everything and anything. Which was very annoying. In fact, Trip was entirely lacking in the sort of intellectual depth that Ivy needed right now.

'I do wish you'd show him around a bit, darling,' Josie said now. 'It feels churlish not to. Fox Bay is full of glorious secrets that only the locals know. The poor boy must be getting a bit bored, with his sister up in her room most of the time.' Josie lowered her voice. 'It's quite odd behaviour. But I was thinking – maybe she has *burnout*. I hear lots of young people have it these days. I do wish she'd let me cleanse her aura.' Josie shook her head worriedly. 'I hope she's having a nice holiday here. Anyway, it must be dull for Trip. Why don't you take him on a tour?'

'I'm too busy to babysit Trip,' Ivy said firmly. 'If Trip wants a tour he can pay for one, along with the rest of the tourists.'

It was true – she *was* busy. Each time Trip had stopped to talk in the last forty-eight hours, Ivy had had her hands full. Literally. Once with a stack of paperbacks, once with a hair-raising inventory that Josie had blithely asked her to 'glance through' and once with her phone buzzing from the winter pageant WhatsApp group that Ivy had been added to against her will.

As if on cue, it buzzed now in her pocket. She pulled it out. *178 unread messages.*

Ivy groaned and started to read, scrolling through a fast-raging argument. She had suspected the show planning would be a nightmare and so it was proving. Mr Hargreaves, sweetly eccentric but ineffectual, had no more control over the Holiday

Show Planning Committee than he did over his students. The committee were growing anxious. The teacher heading up the direction, Mr Patterson, had ideas that were *so* bold and *so* experimental that Ivy thought privately they hovered on the edge of lunacy.

Things were escalating by the second. Mr Patterson had floated the idea of the entire show being performed in Cornish and there was now a vigorous debate raging over whether they could light an actual bonfire *on stage* to represent Midwinter traditions. Mr Patterson suggested the smugglers could also fight the tax collectors in a 'politically loaded act of defiance'.

Technically, Ivy didn't need to do anything until rehearsals started the following week, so she could – again, technically – ignore these messages. But Ivy found that if she didn't nip the ideas in the bud, the group got more and more carried away. Every time she reached for her sketchbook to do some actual art, her phone buzzed. Or someone came in to ask for the latest Kathleen Lee. Or Trip appeared, trying to talk to her about running or yoga.

It was all too much. With a sudden burst of decision, she muted the show WhatsApp and flung her phone in the drawer along with a heap of rubber bands and some crystals.

There. She wanted as little part in the show and the attendant madness as possible. Once a loner, always a loner.

It was much safer that way.

Chapter Six

On Wednesday, Ivy decided the week was flying by with unnerving speed and that she had to at least try and do *some* college work. She motored through her morning tasks at the shop, finally clawing back a free hour before the rush started, sitting down with a muddy coffee, determined to get something, anything, on the page.

She decided to try a mindfulness technique they had studied in college in the first week to 'loosen them up and get the creative juices flowing'. She picked up her pencil, set it on the page and closed her eyes. Quick pencil lines, letting her mind go where it chose and allowing her fingers to follow. It was surprisingly soothing. An image came unbidden to mind: a shop, drowsy with early morning sunshine, bottles glinting in the pale light, the clutter of books and cushions and a windchime above the door . . . she drew on, smiling slightly, lost in the moment, letting the lines flow from her pencil . . .

At last, she opened her eyes and frowned at the page. There was a tall figure, doing some sort of yoga pose, hair falling into their eyes in a way that seemed unnervingly familiar.

Ugh, thought Ivy, and slammed the sketchbook shut.

Enough of this, she thought. If Trip was invading even her private thoughts, not to mention her sketchbook, it was time for baked goods. Fin had told her yesterday that he was planning on making his mythical cheese and chive scones this week and if anything would aid artistic thought – or at least make Ivy feel better about being an artistic failure – it was one of those, warm from the oven and smothered in lashings of butter.

She hopped off her stool and stuck her sketchbook into her coat pocket. Maybe there *were* a few things worth returning to Fox Bay for.

Ivy ducked into the bakery, planning to grab the goods and go. But Fin was out back and she found herself wedged between a tray of cinnamon buns and a tall girl ahead of her in a tan coat, with perfectly tousled hair, listening to Taylor Swift so loudly that Ivy could hear the strains of *All Too Well* even through the earphones.

It was nice being back here, she thought, in this cosy space. She'd been buying cakes off Fin ever since she was small when he had decided to turn his hobby into a business. To pass the time, she took out her sketchbook and began to draw, trying to tune in to the smells and warmth of the little bakery, the rows of croissants and baguettes, the old-fashioned till, the railway clock on the whitewashed wall—

'Ivy?'

Startled, Ivy looked up from her drawing to see the girl in front had taken her earphones out and turned round. Of course. Erin-from-school. She should have recognised her from that perfectly tousled honey-blonde hair.

Erin looked exactly the same as she had at school, only somehow even prettier and shinier. Along with her friends Mei and Callum, Erin had slipped effortlessly into the vacuum created when the previous cool kids Skye, Jacob, Seb, Isla and their gang had left Fox Bay. But while Jacob and co had been known for trouble-making – late-night parties and drinking on the beach – Erin had been an earnest force for good. She was always hosting a beach barbecue for charity or organising litter-picking or getting the choir to sing at the retirement home or running for leadership positions at school. Erin was popular *and* effortlessly good at everything. She was also, infuriatingly, nice.

Which somehow, Ivy thought, made her more annoying.

She and Ivy had technically been friends, in that they both did art, and Erin was so determinedly sociable even Ivy's icy stare and curt answers hadn't put her off. But Ivy had assumed that she was just acting out of obligation and this would fizzle as soon they left school. Now, Ivy quickly shoved her sketchbook with its uninspired croissant drawings into her pocket. It was too early and too hot in the little bakery to be confronted with the most popular girl at school.

'Hi, Erin. You must be back for the break,' she said.

'Yes! Ivy! No way. I *thought* that was you, given you were buried in a sketchbook as usual.' Erin gave one of her trade-mark wide smiles, revealing gleaming white teeth. 'I picked up on the general scornful vibe, along with the red hair.'

Ivy gave a weak laugh. 'It's kind of my signature look.'

'That and your cute old cardigan,' said Erin affectionately. 'Look, you're still wearing it! We all used to tease you about it, didn't we?'

'I remember,' said Ivy, through gritted teeth.

'I can't believe you're back!' Erin said. 'Still doing art? Of course you are. You were always so *committed*. Oh my god, Ivy. Remember your GCSE project? The three-foot mermaid with the broken heart? And Ms Leach cried.'

'Ha.' Ivy managed a shrug. 'Yep. Still doing my art.' *Sort of*, she thought. 'I'm at Cornwall Art College.'

'We should hang out while you're home,' said Erin, her smile firmly in place, eyes fixed on Ivy. 'Cal and Mei are back too and they'd love to see you. Everyone's got so much exciting news to catch up on!'

'I'm super busy right now – I'm working every day at the bookshop,' said Ivy hastily. The last thing she wanted was to hear everyone's exciting news. She cast a desperate look around for Fin, but he must have still been getting the bread out of the oven. 'And I'm going to be helping with the school show.'

'Wait, that's *you* working on the show?' Erin said, her eyes widening. 'My sister Lucy, you remember her? She's in Year Four. She said someone's moody older sister was going to make a life-size lobster costume for the maritime number. I should have known!'

Ivy sighed. 'Yeah. That's me.' She had no choice but to make conversation. 'And you're at Bristol, right?'

'That's right. Psychology. Loving. It.' Erin beamed. 'Isn't uni *amazing*?'

'Amazing,' said Ivy woodenly, willing Fin to come out with the scones. 'Just . . . amazing.'

'Well now that I've run into you, you've *got* to come out tomorrow night,' Erin said. 'I won't take no for an answer. Everyone's heading to the Mariner's.'

'Who is everyone?' asked Ivy, stalling for time.

'The gang, Ivy!' Erin shrieked, like they hung out all the time. 'Callum and Mei. Like the old days. Only we can drink legally now, of course.' She winked. 'Not that it stopped us before, did it? Although Simi was always so strict about letting us in the pub. Now we can have a civilised G+T and share all our news. What do you say?'

Ivy hesitated before her eager gaze, casting around for an excuse. 'I don't know . . .'

'Come on,' Erin coaxed. 'It'll be a fun night. Apparently there's some new guy in town who is always doing yoga on the beach, which is bold given the weather. Mei says he's *ridiculously hot*. She wants him to come along. Funny name . . .'

Of course. 'Trip,' said Ivy resignedly. 'He's Josie's new Airbnb guest at the shop.'

'Perfect! Well you can bring him along with you,' said Erin, clapping her hands. 'That works out nicely.'

Ivy opened her mouth to say no. But that suddenly felt like admitting defeat.

'Okay,' she heard herself say. 'Just for one drink.'

Erin grinned. 'Yes! Nice one! I've got your number of course. I'll add you to the WhatsApp and message you the deets.'

To her relief, Fin came out just then with a tray of golden scones that smelled delicious. 'Ivy, I saw you waiting and knew you'd want one of these,' he said, tucking it into a napkin for her. 'And take this for Josie, will you?' He handed her a fresh loaf.

'Thanks,' Ivy mumbled, backing away.

'See you tomorrow!' trilled Erin, waving vigorously as Ivy hurried out. 'Can't wait!'

Chapter Seven

The following evening, the shop was quiet in the last half hour before closing. Dusk had fallen outside and the streetlights were coming on slowly. Ivy was restocking the window display with winter-themed books. She was positioning *The Wolves of Willoughby Chase* just so, when Josie appeared in the doorway, clutching a calculator, a pencil stuck into her grey curls, clucking disapprovingly.

'What on earth are you still doing here, darling?' she said. 'It's gone half six. Well after closing time. I thought you'd left *hours* ago.'

'I don't mind working a bit late,' said Ivy, glancing furtively at the clock. She'd been thinking that if she worked *really* late, she could legitimately miss the pub.

'What are you doing tonight?' Josie asked innocently. 'Didn't you have some plans? With your old school friends who invited you to the pub?'

'Um, yeah, sort of,' mumbled Ivy.

'I see.' Josie's eyes narrowed. 'For a moment I thought you might be using work as an excuse not to go. But that's silly of me. Why *wouldn't* you want to get out there and have some fun with people your own age?' The words *for a change* hung unspoken in the air.

Ivy sighed. Josie acted vague ninety per cent of the time but she occasionally had moments of terrifying perception. 'Fine, you've got me,' Ivy admitted. 'The thing is, I don't want to go. They'll all have had an amazing first term, whereas I'm in a rut.' She flung a piece of crepe paper seaweed crossly over *The Lion, the Witch and the Wardrobe*.

'Darling, being in a rut is just the universe telling you it's time to expand. Think of it as an invitation.' Josie snapped her fingers. 'I know what you should do. You should take Trip.'

'Erin did want me to ask him,' said Ivy. 'But I'm sure he's busy—'

'It's perfect. The poor boy must be bored rigid. One can only do so much yoga. And the pub is a British rite of passage,' Josie said, already reaching for her phone. 'I'll text him now. Besides,' she winked at Ivy, 'he'll create quite a stir at the Mariner's Arms.'

'I don't think he'll want to go and hang out with a load of strangers,' Ivy said, as the bell above the door jingled and Trip strolled in as if on cue, cheeks pink from the cold, hands stuffed into the pockets of his navy pea coat.

'Hey,' he said. 'Is Brooke back?'

'She's upstairs. But Ivy's going to the pub tonight,' Josie said hastily. 'And we were just saying that you should go too. Experience some British culture. A pub night – it's an institution.'

Trip's face lit up. 'A pub night?'

'I don't think the Mariner's counts as culture,' Ivy said, but Josie was already shoving her coat at her.

'Go. Be young. Be fun. Be free. Don't let Lou give you her new Cornish pasty pizza, it was really quite strange. Maybe chopped carrots don't work with melted cheese . . .'

Trip gave Ivy a hopeful grin, eyes wide and earnest. 'Would you mind if I tagged along?'

Ivy hesitated. It wasn't that she minded, exactly. After all, she was only planning on paying a flying visit to forestall any future invitations. But Trip was so . . . *happy*. Golden and sunny, with his great hair and his constant good mood. Whereas she already felt like a flat, grey smudge next to most people, let alone him.

Still, she didn't have much choice, not now Josie had forced her hand. And Erin and Mei had seemed ultra-keen that Trip should come along. Ivy would be doing a good deed by bringing him. And at least she would be walking in with the hot boy who everyone was curious about . . .

'Fine,' she said at last, grabbing her scarf. 'Let's go.'

'Have fun, darlings!' trilled Josie as the door shut behind them. 'Don't do anything I wouldn't do – and that rules out *nothing*.'

The walk to the Mariner's Arms was long enough to be awkward with someone you barely knew. *Not* that Trip seemed to feel a trace of it.

'The light's different here,' he said. 'And the sea smells different too.' He breathed in. 'Sharper somehow than California.' He nudged Ivy gently. 'Can you smell that?'

Ivy found herself breathing deeply. The wind picked up as they turned on to the narrow street that led down to the harbour, the scent of salt and woodsmoke hanging in the air. A smell she knew in her very bones. For good or bad, it was the smell of home, she thought.

'What part of California are you from again?' she asked, curious in spite of herself. She had always wanted to visit California, where so many great artists had come from. 'Was it Santa Cruz?'

'My parents live outside of San Francisco in this fancy suburb.' Trip had a smattering of freckles on his cheekbones that she hadn't noticed until now. 'My grandma's house is right on the coast though. She grew up in England actually, near London, but then she became the queen of the Santa Cruz hippies.'

'What's Santa Cruz like? What are the vibes?'

'Constant sunshine, surf, tacos, yoga studios.'

Ivy sighed, thinking of how far away it sounded from her own upbringing – windswept days shivering on the beach, school trips to the local farm and fish fingers for tea. 'I'm beginning to understand you.'

He looked at her. 'What do you mean?'

'The constant good cheer. The yoga even when it's freezing out. The optimism. The green juice . . .'

Trip laughed. 'Hey, I'm getting used to all the caffeine and lack of vitamins. But maybe Fox Bay needs a little spirulina. Old Bill could certainly use it I reckon, from his description of his bowel movements.' He winced.

'I don't want to know about Old Bill's bowel movements, thanks very much. That's another thing,' Ivy said accusingly. 'Giving Fin recipe tips. Helping out Simi. You've only known these people for about five minutes but you talk about them like you're best friends.'

Trip shrugged. 'They're nice,' he said simply. 'I like talking to them.'

'They're *weird*, like everyone here.' Ivy kicked a pebble and it scudded across the cobbles. She could feel Trip looking at her. 'What?' she said accusingly.

'Oh, nothing.' He gave her a sidelong smile. 'It's just . . . weird is good. Isn't it? I think so anyway. The best artists must have been pretty weird, right?'

'Hm,' Ivy grunted, thinking that the inhabitants of Fox Bay were weird because they'd never experienced life outside Fox Bay, rather than because they were secretly artistic. They turned the corner by the old post office, their steps falling into an easy rhythm. The glow from a streetlamp caught in the tousled waves of Trip's chestnut hair.

'So are you still deciding on colleges?' she asked.

'Yeah. I have a place at Stanford,' he said. 'And another at NYU and another at BU in Boston. And some others outside of the States.'

'Whoa,' said Ivy, startled. 'That's . . . a lot of universities in a lot of different places.' And she'd thought Fox Bay to Truro was a big move.

'Right. It's weird because usually I know exactly what I want to do but with this, I just can't decide. It feels too big, you know? So I took this year off. Deferred my place.'

'Seriously?' asked Ivy bluntly. The idea of deferring college, the place she had dreamed about for so long, seemed incomprehensible.

Trip hesitated for a second too long, a contrast to his usual ready answers.

'I just needed a break,' he said eventually. 'My sister and I had a busy year. So we decided we'd do something new. Travel a bit.'

Ivy glanced up at him. Trip was usually an open book, but now it felt like there was something he didn't want to tell her. She remembered the air of mystery she'd felt around Brooke. 'Remind me what your sister does again?' she asked.

'Um. Sales. Logistics.'

Ivy frowned. 'Sales *and* logistics?' She was sure that Brooke had said she did consulting.

'Something like that. Look, we're here.'

They had indeed reached the pub and its warm light spilled across the street. Ivy stopped, eyeing the front door warily. Laughter was filtering out, along with the smell of spiced cider and fried food.

'You sure you're ready for this?' she asked.

Trip looked up at the creaking old sign swinging above them, then back at Ivy. His expression was unusually serious as he said, 'Are *you* ready for this?'

Ivy gave a short laugh. 'Don't worry about me.'

Still, she didn't move. On the other side of the door, amidst the comforting chaos of the Mariner's Arms, her past was waiting. She had imagined returning to Fox Bay one day a completely different person, preferably a hugely successful artist. And now here she was, back again within a matter of months, even more insignificant than before.

This is ridiculous, she told herself. She would know half of the people in the pub. One drink and then she'd leave. She just had to be brave and—

Get it over with, she thought. She took a deep breath and put her hand on the door handle. Waited.

'Should we . . . go inside?' Trip asked gently, after a minute.

'Oh. Yeah, sure,' Ivy said, flushing, and pushed the door open.

Standing on the threshold, she was met with the warm and cosy pub she remembered. But she'd never seen it this busy in winter. More tourists than usual, presumably chasing the cosy season vibes they had read about on Instagram. The fire was roaring and there was a low hum of chatter.

Looking more closely, Ivy could see that the Mariner's Arms had also had something of a glow-up while she had been away. New cushions on the mismatched benches. The drinks menu scrawled on chalkboard included a handful of cocktails – Fox on the Beach, the Cornwallpolitan – when before it had been pints or soft drinks only, or occasionally some mulled cider. But the bones of the place were the same. Twinkly fairy lights looped along the low ceiling beams, the scent of rosemary in the air.

And she could see the familiar figures of Simi behind the bar and Lou gathering up glasses.

'Look at this place,' Trip said beside her. 'This is like . . . everything I thought a British pub would be but better. It's like we stepped into a movie.'

'That's Fox Bay for you,' Ivy said wryly, as Old Bill belched loudly on the bar stool beside her. 'Movie material. The quaintest small town that ever was.'

Trip was looking around delightedly. 'It sure is,' he said. 'There's even a *dog*. A golden retriever.'

'You'll get along well,' Ivy muttered.

'Ivy! You're back!' Ivy could see Simi waving them over from behind the bar. She beamed at Ivy as they approached. 'I thought I noticed a certain pre-Raphaelite beauty walking around Fox Bay.'

'I wish,' Ivy said, smiling in spite of herself. She always appreciated a compliment from elegant, intelligent Simi. 'Simi, this is Trip. He and his sister are staying at Josie's for the holidays. He's come all the way from California.'

Simi leaned across the bar and held out her hand. 'Of course. My saviour from the other day. One of Josie's latest guests. I didn't catch your name?'

'I'm Trip,' he said, offering his hand with one of his wide, sweet smiles. 'Ivy let me come along tonight. She's been stuck with me at the shop.'

'Poor girl,' Lou chimed in, appearing with a wooden board of pizza and looking Trip up and down. 'I'm sure it's been a terrible hardship for you, Ivy.' She smiled innocently at her and Ivy shot her a look. 'The usual, Ivy? Lemonade?'

Ivy nodded. 'Yeah, I still hate beer.'

'I'm trying to persuade Simi to make the place a bit more upmarket, given all the tourists. More mocktails and bar snacks and things.' Lou held out the tray. 'Cornish pasty pizza? It's a new one for me but I thought some of these tourists might go for it.' She frowned at it. 'I'm trying to persuade them it's a Cornish delicacy.'

'Er, no, thanks,' said Ivy, recalling Josie's warning about carrots and cheese.

'I'll have some,' said Trip, taking a piece. He took a bite, blinked and started to chew fast. 'Are those . . . peas?' he asked, through the mouthful. 'And potatoes? And ground meat? On a pizza?'

'Yup,' said Lou. 'Do you like it?' she asked hopefully.

He gave her a thumbs up as he chewed, seemingly unable to swallow. 'It's like nothing I've ever had before,' he said sincerely. As Lou turned away, he widened his eyes desperately at Ivy. She bit back a laugh.

'It's disgusting, isn't it?' she said, handing him a napkin.

Then she swiftly took the remaining pizza from him and dumped it in a flower pot.

'Thanks,' he whispered, looking a little pale. 'I think Josie's right. I don't know that carrots work on a pizza.'

'Lou's an amazing cook,' Ivy said. She thought Lou looked a little tired. 'I think the pressure of catering to all these tourists might be getting to her. She should stick with what she does best, which is pizza *without* carrots.'

Ivy took in the scene as Lou poured their drinks. It *looked* like the same old pub night – the benches full of people crammed elbow to elbow, the regulars huddled by the dartboard, Old Bill holding forth to a large table of tourists with some real or imagined sea exploits. But the closer Ivy looked, the more she was certain that there was a subtle shift. More unfamiliar faces. She could see a couple of women taking a selfie with their pie and mash.

'Isn't this cute? *Just* like the pub in *Ocean Deep*,' sighed one.

'I know. We should go down to the beach tomorrow and find that adorable old sea captain . . .'

Ivy felt a flicker of panic. This didn't feel real, somehow – not like the Fox Bay she knew. Once, these oddities and quirks had felt normal, all Ivy had ever known. Now they seemed a bit pretend, like a collection of picturesque sights filtered through Instagram rather than the real place she had grown up in. Ivy had a sudden urge to sketch the scene before her, before it was swept away altogether. *The one night I leave my sketchbook behind*, she thought ruefully.

'Ivy, Trip, hi!' Erin arrived in a camel coat and ankle boots, her hair glossy and freshly waved. 'Lou! Simi!' She rushed round the bar to hug Simi. The others came in behind her, ordered their G+Ts and pints and located a snug in the corner. Ivy found herself wedged between Callum and Mei, while Trip and Erin sat opposite.

'How's things?' Ivy asked awkwardly, deciding to be the one

to break the silence. 'Callum, are you at Exeter now?' Callum had been the star of school football and had even been scouted for Manchester United's Youth Team. He'd decided he wanted to stay closer to home, which had always seemed pretty inconceivable to Ivy.

'Yeah, I'm studying product design and running the student radio station there too,' he said. He seemed even taller and broader than he had been at school. 'It's great. We have to play all the regular stuff of course but we're allowed to play one song every hour that is unsigned so that's really fun. And I'm first-year head of the student union.'

'Wow,' said Ivy. 'I didn't realise you were such a *joiner*.'

He laughed. 'I found my thing, you know? Music. And I'm dating someone too.' He blushed. 'He's called Lucien. He writes poetry.'

Poetry? Ivy didn't remember Callum so much as opening a book outside lessons, what with all the football and beach parties. 'Congratulations. What about you, Mei?' asked Ivy, turning to the pretty girl at Callum's side, praying that just one of them was having a terrible time or even an average one.

'Well, you know I'm doing law at Bristol,' said Mei, swishing her elegant bob. 'Which is going really well. And I'm working part-time at the Clockwork Rose. Have you heard of it? It just won a mixology award.'

'I've heard of that,' said Trip. 'This travel blogger I follow was recommending it. Apparently it's one of the UK's coolest bars.'

Mei smiled up into his face. 'You should try it if you ever come to Bristol,' she said sweetly, fluttering her lashes.

'Isn't uni a blast?' sighed Erin, taking a large swallow of her drink. 'I really feel like I found myself there, you know? Like I became the person I was always meant to be.'

'Absolutely,' said Mei.

'Totally,' agreed Callum.

Ivy sat back, feeling more crushed than ever before, as they chattered away about the trips they were taking, the clubs they were joining and the adventures they were having. She and Raye had always rolled their eyes at the gang behind their backs, but now they seemed . . . happy. Fulfilled. Living rich and interesting lives. Whereas Ivy, in her paint-spattered DM boots and oversized cardigan, was the one who seemed lame.

'And how's the art going, Ivy?' Callum asked at last, when there was a lull in the conversation. Ivy had just taken a gulp of lemonade and she choked on her drink as everyone turned to look at her.

'Oh, um, it's great, thanks,' she managed. 'It's great to be around so many other creative types. To be challenged artistically, you know?'

Callum nodded politely. 'You're at the Cornwall Art College, right? My friend is there,' he said. 'Imogen, do you know her?'

'Oh yeah,' said Ivy, flushing. 'Imogen. She's . . . nice.' Imogen was friends with Raff. What if she had told Callum about the loser at art college?

'She was pulling her hair out over her final coursework. Apparently you don't pass the first year without it?' He shook his head. 'That's *seriously* harsh.'

'Yeah, wow,' said Trip. His wide brown eyes turned to her. 'How did yours go, Ivy?'

'Well, it's a very competitive course,' Ivy said, fiddling with her paper straw. She thought of her empty sketchbook and Jess's worried expression at her last tutorial, the blank faces of her classmates as she had mumbled about impermanence. 'I'm still adding some . . . finishing touches. But I'm very nearly there.'

'The details are important,' said Trip. 'So what's the story with Lou and Simi? I haven't spoken to them much.' Ivy glanced at him. Had he realised she was floundering and changed the subject?

'One of the top love stories of Fox Bay,' said Erin. 'Simi was some high-flying management consultant till she gave it all up for this.'

'My parents say she and Lou are being really mysterious . . .?' whispered Mei. 'They keep driving to Truro and giving vague excuses.'

'Yeah and Mum said they've been sneaking off a lot lately and getting people to cover shifts,' Erin said. 'Do you think they got married? Eloped?'

'Or maybe they're house-hunting,' added Callum. 'And they're planning to move.'

The attention moved on to Fox Bay gossip and Ivy sank into herself. She felt like a ghost. A sad, shadowy, drab ghost.

Trip, on the other hand, seemed like the brightest person in the pub. Ivy kept sneaking glances at him, wondering how anyone could look so impossibly perfect. His sweatshirt clung to him in all the right places, his hair was tousled like he'd just come from the sunlit beach (despite it being pitch-black, damp and freezing when they had walked over) and he seemed to draw people to him. The gang clearly *loved* him. Other customers stopped to chat, asking about his accent. Even the pub dog loved him, resting his head on Trip's knee under the table and looking at him adoringly, while Trip stroked his ears.

'And what about you, Trip?' Mei said at last, leaning forward. Ivy had forgotten how pretty Mei was, with her glossy black hair and long lashes. 'What brings you to Fox Bay? Shouldn't you be surfing in California?'

Trip laughed. 'At this time of year? I don't want to be a Californian stereotype.'

'Oh?' Mei leaned in still closer, clearly enjoying herself. 'So you're a rebel?'

'I've been taking a year off,' Trip said, and again Ivy caught that hint of discomfort she had sensed earlier, the slight flush on his cheeks. He was normally so easy that the reserve jarred.

'Like a gap year?' Erin asked.

Trip nodded. 'Something like that. I wanted to see a bit of the world.' He added quietly, almost to himself, 'You can have a lifetime of adventures just by saying yes.'

'A lifetime of adventures?' said Erin, looking confused.

His flush deepened. 'It's a family saying,' he said. 'I'm trying to live by it.'

'Where have you been?' Ivy asked longingly. She had never left England.

'Um. Everywhere,' Trip said with a sheepish smile. 'Mexico for a surf camp and to see some distant relatives. Iceland for a glacier hike. Rome for the history. Sardinia for the pasta. Paris for the art and the food. And now . . . here.' He gestured around at the pub, like Fox Bay was just as special.

Ivy felt a surge of envy. She thought of her mum fretting over her fees, the tiny, cramped room where she stayed in Truro, stuffed with her art materials, the hours commuting on buses in the dark. The way she'd come home for the holidays not because she *wanted* to, but because it was the only place she could live rent-free. And here was Trip, flitting across countries, no looming deadlines, no extra jobs to pay for petrol, no guilt. Offers from high-end colleges whenever he decided to make a decision. *Lucky him*, she thought. Must be nice to go wherever the wind took you. No wonder he was always so thrilled with life.

'Honestly,' Trip said hastily, as though reading her mind, 'it's been great, but it's also kind of terrifying. Everyone else has a plan, you know?' He gestured to Erin, Mei and Callum. *Not me*, Ivy thought.

'You guys seem so certain about what you want to do,' Trip continued, 'whereas I keep thinking . . . what if I pick wrong?'

There was a beat of silence. Ivy caught his eye, and for once, he didn't look like his usual cheerful, confident self. He looked, briefly, as uncertain as she felt.

'Welcome to the club,' she muttered, before she could stop herself. 'Nagging uncertainty. Existential dread. It sucks.'

Trip gave her a brief, tentative smile. 'Thanks.' He gathered himself. 'So you guys have all known each other since school?'

'Yeah,' said Mei. 'Only Ivy was always a bit of a loner.' She shook her head, smiling. 'She and Raye were too busy being arty and mysterious to hang out much.'

'Yeah,' said Callum, laughing. 'Ivy, remember when you called me a philistine for putting your picture the wrong way up?'

'Or when you wore that placard for a week as performance art,' said Erin. 'Teachers kept begging you to take it off because you couldn't fit through doors.'

'Yeah, I remember.' Ivy felt herself tensing. For some reason she didn't want Trip to think she had been an outsider at school. A weirdo. Even though she had admittedly been both of those things.

But Trip just shrugged. 'Ivy sounds like she was pretty cool at school,' he said, looking right at her with his warm, caramel eyes.

Ivy rolled her eyes. 'Oh, please,' she said. 'Whatever.' But she couldn't help it. She was smiling. Someone – even if it was a bizarrely cheerful and aimless globe-trotting American tourist – thought *she*, Ivy Pearson, was *pretty cool*.

'Ivy's all right,' said Erin, grinning at her. 'Or she would be if she cracked a smile more often.'

Callum nudged Ivy affectionately. Mei giggled. The dog

wagged his tail vigorously and licked Trip's hand. Just for a moment, Ivy saw the pub through Trip's warm, delighted gaze. Saw her old school friends as funny and welcoming. Saw the fairy lights and worn tables and even the disgusting Cornish pasty pizza as charming.

She *had* missed Fox Bay, she realised, with a faint pang in her chest. She just hadn't known it till now.

After three drinks instead of the promised one, Ivy decided it was time to leave. It had been okay, she thought cautiously – better than she had expected, anyway – but she didn't want to push it. The others gathered their things as well and headed out into the night.

The air was bitterly cold. Eyes watering, Ivy zipped up her coat and rubbed at her arms as the group stood outside, chatting and making vague plans for the weekend.

'Hot chocolates at the Driftwood on Saturday, Ivy?' Mei said. 'Are you in?'

'I'll probably be working,' Ivy said evasively. 'And doing stuff for the school show. Mum's roped me into helping with the props.'

'Wait, *we* could help with the show too,' said Erin suddenly. 'Remember Mr H's shows in primary school? I miss doing them together. And Lucy is dead excited about it. Do you think they need an extra pair of hands, Ivy?'

'Yeah,' said Callum. 'I could help with the sound maybe.'

'And I can do stage-manager stuff,' said Mei. 'I'm used to

bossing people around behind the bar. I even have a headpiece from when I was Leavers' Prom co-ordinator.' She beamed at Ivy. 'We could hang out properly. I want to hear more about your art project.'

'And you didn't tell us whether you met any hot guys at college,' said Erin.

'Um,' said Ivy, the warmth she'd felt in the pub rapidly fading, 'I'll ask Mr H if he needs anyone.' If she didn't *accidentally* forget, she thought. She could keep up the pretence that everything was fine for a few hours, but any more than that would be hard.

'Yeah, text us and let us know. Night, guys!' Erin called, looping arms with Mei and Callum. 'So good to see you!'

'You too,' Ivy said, waving.

'I'll walk you back,' Trip said.

'You don't have to,' she said. 'My car's parked a bit away from the bookshop. I'll be fine on my own.'

'It's okay, I'd like the walk. If you want the company.' He hesitated. 'Or maybe you're ready for a bit of peace and quiet?'

Ivy groaned internally. She *was* ready for peace and quiet and she wasn't sure Trip had it in him to be quiet for more than a minute at a time. 'How about we walk and . . . don't talk?' she said, trying to be as tactful as possible. 'Can you manage that, do you think?'

'I can try,' Trip said seriously.

'Fine. We can walk back along the beach in that case.'

They set off along the sand, the warmth of the pub quickly

fading behind them. For a few blissful minutes, neither of them spoke.

Then Trip broke.

'Your friends are great,' he said. 'Super welcoming.'

'They're not actually my friends,' Ivy said quickly, and then felt bad. She tried to explain. 'I mean, we didn't hang out all that much at school. It was mostly just me and Raye and then those guys were more like . . . acquaintances I saw every day. Because we all did art together. Otherwise, we don't have much in common. They're too popular for me.'

Trip walked quietly for a minute. '*They* seem to think they're your friends,' he said at last. 'They seem to really like you.'

Ivy let out a sharp laugh. 'Of course you'd think that. Because everyone *does* like you.'

He frowned. 'That's not . . . do they?'

'Yes! Everyone loves you, ergo you think everyone is great. It's *infuriating*,' Ivy snapped, surprising them both. *Where had that come from?*

Trip slowed to a stop, looking at her, clearly also confused. 'Hey. What's wrong?'

She stopped too and stood looking at him. *What's wrong?* She didn't know exactly. Trip was looking at her, entirely serious for once. Like he really wanted to know. And all of a sudden, words were bubbling to the surface.

'I feel like I'm failing at everything,' she found herself saying. 'You heard the others. They're loving uni. Having this transformative experience. Finding themselves. Whereas me? I spend most nights alone in a bedsit. Everyone's out there doing all these amazing things and I can't even *draw* anything lately. I'm an artist and I can't draw!' Her voice rose to a wail.

Trip opened his mouth but before he could speak, she carried on. 'I hate commuting for college every day. I hate leaving the house when it's dark and getting back when it's dark and missing out on all the fun stuff. It's *lonely*. I let a stupid pretentious art boy break my heart. I'm behind on my project and my tutor Jess thinks I'm rubbish. And the worst thing is, she's right.' She let out a hard sob, unable to keep it in any more. 'I thought art school would make me feel like I was finally becoming the person I always knew I *could* be, once I left this place. Growing up, I always had this – this *spark* when it came to art. Like it was meant to be. But it's not what I expected,' she finished forlornly. 'At all.'

There was a long silence. Ivy realised she was properly crying now and she groped blindly in her pockets for a tissue. 'I know it's stupid, I know people have it worse . . .'

'It's not stupid,' Trip said quietly. He pushed a handkerchief into her hand and she took it gratefully, scrubbing at her cheeks. 'It sounds like you've had a really tough time. I get it.'

'You don't get it,' she muttered, but all her anger was gone now and she just felt sad and tired. 'You, Trip Wakefield, are clearly not accustomed to failure.'

'I mean, I get looking forward to something and then it falling flat.' He gave her a crooked smile. 'I meant what I said back there, Ivy. I've known you for a week and I can already tell you're pretty cool. Don't let a bad start at art school put you off what you're meant to do with your life. That spark you had growing up? You'll get it back.'

Ivy looked out at the vast dark sea, speckled with lights, and let out another wail. 'God, you're annoyingly good at this.'

He waited while she wiped her eyes. She looked down at the handkerchief.

'Is this *monogrammed*?' she asked, seeing the initials *E.W.* embroidered on the corner. 'Seriously?'

He laughed. 'It's my dad's. But yeah.' She held out the damp piece of cloth. 'Why don't you, um, keep it?'

'Okay,' she said, stuffing it into her pocket. 'Sorry about that. I'm over it. No more self-pity. I think the lemonade went to my head.' She squared her shoulders. 'Let's go.' Trip opened his mouth and she held up a hand. 'Seriously. I do not want to talk about it.'

They walked on in silence. 'What *shall* we talk about then?' whispered Trip, clearly unable to take it, and Ivy burst out laughing.

'You're ridiculous. Okay, I have a question for you. Is Trip your actual name? Or is it short for something?'

He shook his head, mock-hurt. 'You don't think it's an *actual name*? Wow. Aren't you named after a plant?'

'I'm named after my great-great-aunt. It could have been worse – the other one was called Dorcus. Come on. Is Trip at least short for something?'

He grinned at her. 'Wouldn't you like to know?'

'Triple chocolate cake,' she guessed.

'Delicious, but no.'

'Triplet?'

'Sorry. Just me and my sister.'

'Tripe?'

'I tried it in Paris and no. Not for me.'

Ivy laughed again, startling herself.

They reached her car. 'Well,' she said, brushing her thick hair off her face and rocking back on her heels. 'Sorry again for the dramatics. Thanks for the walk. And the impromptu therapy.'

'Any time,' he said, turning to go. 'See you tomorrow, Ivy.'

She watched him walk off, hands deep in his pockets. *How is even his walk cheerful?*, she thought.

As she was turning the engine over for the third time, trying to persuade the car to start, a text came through.

'Don't make me tell you again. You're pretty cool, Ivy.'

She was smiling as the engine flared into life.

She was still smiling when she pulled up at home. She headed up the stairs, opened the door and stepped inside the flat, shrugging off her coat. Her mum was on the sofa where she was highlighting Liv's script for the show and watching a black-and-white Halloween movie. Ivy tried to sneak past but her mum looked up.

'Hang on,' she said. She reached for the remote and pressed

pause, the frame showing the masked killer with knife raised. 'Something's up. Something is different about you.'

'You know, usually in winter people watch cosy movies,' said Ivy. 'Not slashers.'

Her mum ignored her. 'I've got it. That's what's different. You look almost . . . *happy*.'

'I'm not,' Ivy replied automatically.

Her mum smiled. 'Right. Of course not.' She shrugged and reached for the remote again. 'Well, whatever you are, it makes a nice change.'

Chapter Eight

The next day at the bookshop was a blur of gift-wrapping (Raye had warned Ivy about paper cuts: 'a real hazard of the job') and customers outdoing each other with increasingly impossible questions ('I want that novel about the couple who befriend a fox? It was on the radio?'). Not to mention the growing mountain of WhatsApp messages from the show committee, of which Mr Hargreaves rapidly – and predictably – seemed to be losing control. Ivy muted it on a regular basis for self-care reasons, dreading the imminent beginning of rehearsals when she would have to actually start contributing.

That morning was Story-time Adventure, a regular reading hour that Josie insisted on with the local children – the children being Ivy's least favourite part of the job, with their sticky hands and outlandish questions.

'I'll do it,' Trip told her as she complained over her coffee. He had started to bring Ivy a double espresso on the way back from his run. 'Seriously. I like that sort of thing.'

'You can't like it,' Ivy told him. She eyed him as he checked the weather app on his phone. 'Why do you keep checking? It's cold and grey, basically, for the foreseeable. This isn't California, Trip. You signed up to an English winter, this is what you're going to get.'

Trip flushed and put his phone back in his pocket. 'It says it's going to be unusually cold,' he said. 'I wondered if it might snow.'

'Don't be fooled by Dickens – we don't get white Christmases here,' Ivy said brutally. 'Now are you really sure about doing Story-time Adventure or were you just teasing me? Because the kids will be here any second.'

Of course Trip took to it with ease, happily reading *Where the Wild Things Are*, baring his terrible claws and gnashing his terrible teeth to whoops and shrieks of delight.

'He's a natural,' sighed Josie happily, watching on from the doorway. 'Such positive energy.'

'Unlike his sister,' Ivy said, nodding to Brooke, who was marching across the shop floor on her way out for the day, sunglasses jammed on despite the grey skies, typing furiously on her phone. 'Isn't this meant to be her holiday? Where does she rush off to every day?'

Josie looked after Brooke as she hurried out of the shop, letting the door bang shut behind her. 'I can't make her out either, darling,' she admitted. 'If she's Trip's sister, she *must* have positive energy as well. She probably just . . . hides hers better.' Josie frowned thoughtfully. 'But you're right – I do wonder where she goes every day. Now darling, we must start decorating in earnest this weekend. I refuse to miss an opportunity for extra fairy lights.'

On Saturday morning, Ivy got into the shop early to sketch, away from Liv's endless chatter about the show. She found Brooke already awake and lacing up running shoes.

'So you're an early-riser, beach-runner type like your brother?' said Ivy, still trying to probe their mystery guest.

Brooke shrugged, hoisting one toned leg up on to the stool to stretch. 'In California, getting up at sunrise to do some form of physical activity is kind of part of the deal,' she said.

'Do you also like yoga? And random acts of kindness?' Ivy asked, wondering if Josie was right and the siblings were more similar than she'd thought. 'And dogs?'

Brooke snorted. 'If you're asking if me and Trip are alike, in case you haven't guessed, the answer is no,' she said. 'We're about as different as you could be to a blood relation. He's like the yang to my yin. Case in point? I hate yoga. I spend the whole class thinking about the things I have to do after it's over and wishing I was doing them instead. I hate dogs – the slobber. And as for random acts of kindness . . .' Her voice softened. 'My brother is too nice for his own good.'

Just then Trip himself arrived with damp hair and a paper bag of pastries. 'Did you guys know there's an old lighthouse along the cliff path and over the bay?' he said. 'And also, it's *really* raining out.'

'Nope,' said Brooke, pulling out her phone and scrolling

through her notes app. She absently held out a hand and her brother put a coffee cup into it. 'A lighthouse is *not* on my list of local Cornish attractions.' She looked up at Ivy accusingly. 'Do you know about this lighthouse?'

'Of course I know about it,' Ivy said, biting into her own croissant and wondering why Brooke cared so much. 'It's not in any of the travel stuff though – it's a secret. Fox Bay has a few of those. Secret sights that only the locals know.'

'Interesting,' said Brooke thoughtfully. 'Secret sights.'

'It sounds amazing,' Trip said. 'We should check it out, Brooke. It's all boarded up. Old Bill says it's haunted.'

'Of course he does,' said Ivy, grinning. 'Bill never lets the truth get in the way of a good story. And a trusting American is an easy target . . .'

'Apparently,' Trip went on, 'the ghost of the old lighthouse keeper appears at the window when the moon goes behind a cloud and a beam shines out to sea. Even when *no light should be on*.'

'Sounds dangerous to me,' said Ivy, chewing. 'Someone should warn the Coastguard.'

Brooke took a swig of coffee and made a noise of irritation. 'The lighthouse isn't on *any* of those stupid "Hidden Cornwall" websites I've been using.'

Ivy finished her breakfast, wiped her fingers and picked up the box marked 'Winter Wonderland Window Display'. Josie had asked her to tackle it that weekend – although, once she picked off the lashings of yellowing Sellotape, she realised it mostly seemed to consist of a tangle of fairy lights.

She was wrestling with them – and fending off Trip's offers of help, while Brooke told them to pipe down – when the shop bell chimed and Mr Hargreaves appeared in his usual scuffed shoes and slightly-too-short trousers, rain clinging to his jacket sleeves. His hair puffed out in little white wisps and he looked exhausted-yet-wildly hopeful – his default expression, as Ivy remembered well from countless assemblies in which he had urged them to take up a new cause.

His face lit up when he saw Ivy and she let out a mental groan. Wasn't it enough that she was on the WhatsApp group? Did he have to come to her place of work too?

'Ah, Ivy! There you are!' he said, as his glasses fogged up. 'You haven't been responding on WhatsApp.'

'Where else would I be?' she couldn't resist saying. 'I work here. And, um, I think my phone is broken.'

'I wanted to make sure you're coming to the meeting tomorrow night – Mr Patterson has some questions for you. I've got a wonderful feeling about this show,' he said. 'Cornish culture across the ages. Where the mythical meets the modern.'

'Sounds ambitious,' drawled Brooke. 'This is a kids' show, right?'

Mr Hargreaves beamed. 'It *is* ambitious. As all the best creative endeavours should be.'

'So why does Mr Patterson need to talk to *me*?' Ivy asked suspiciously. 'I'm props only.'

'It's something to do with a new pagan ritual set piece.'

Ivy stared. 'A pagan ritual? In a children's show?'

Brooke cackled. 'Oh, I'm *definitely* coming to this.'

'It's very bold,' Mr Hargreaves said, nodding earnestly. 'But between us, I'm not entirely sure everyone will be on board. Mr Trenwith – do you know him? Always wearing the cargo trousers? He's already threatening to pull his twins out unless we stick to something more traditional and he's very influential on the PTA. Anyway, I'm sure we can come to a compromise. Can I leave the stone circle to you?' He beamed at her. 'I've always valued your vision, Ivy.'

Ivy glared at him. 'You gave me an F in History. When I was *nine*.'

'Well. Yes.' He smiled again, sheepishly. 'I should have realised that you're a creative spirit Ivy and you couldn't be pinned down by facts and dates. I'll see you tomorrow. I'm relying on you!'

Mr Hargreaves bustled out again, taking with him the smell of wet wool. Trip, who had been leafing through a cookbook so quietly that Ivy had forgotten him, said, 'Pagan rites? Sounds interesting.'

'It sounds wild,' said Brooke. Her phone pinged and she glanced at it. 'For god's sake,' she muttered. 'I sent the projections last *week*.'

'I thought you were here for a holiday?' said Ivy suspiciously.

'I just have to pick up the occasional email,' Brooke said. 'Who was that guy?'

'That's Mr Hargreaves, head of the primary school.' Ivy sighed. 'He's notorious for starting big ambitious projects and then never following through, and his latest show is no exception. I've been drafted in to do props.' She chewed her nail. 'Unfortunately, the library really needs the funds so I was hoping this one *wouldn't* be a complete disaster. Plus Liv – my little sister – she's super excited about it.' She shrugged and stood, picking up the fairy lights again. 'But it sounds like it's descending into the usual in-fighting and ridiculousness. The show committee need a firm hand and Mr Hargreaves isn't it.' She shuddered. 'Wrangling children and their parents. Trying to help them remember their lines. Ugh. Who would want to do stuff like that?'

'I mean, I would,' Trip said. 'I love . . . stuff like that. Community theatre.'

Brooke smiled. 'He really does. Freak.'

Trip leaned an elbow on the table. 'Actually, as my darling sister knows, I spent many summers at theatre camp.'

Ivy glanced up. 'Theatre camp? That's not a real thing. Is it? I thought it was a staple of High School movies.'

'Oh, it's real,' Trip said. 'I started when I was nine. I started out as a sapling.' He cleared his throat. 'If you chop *me* down, you chop down *all our dreams*,' he intoned solemnly.

Ivy couldn't help laughing. 'Stop. Oh no. That's so sad.'

'It was a spoken word piece about deforestation. I got a glowing review in the local paper. I preferred being behind the scenes though, so I got into the directing and stuff. Maybe I should offer to help.'

'Or you could stop helping everyone constantly. Why would you give up your holiday to help with the school play, when you could get out of Fox Bay and explore the rest of Cornwall?' Ivy asked.

Trip thought for a moment. 'Because it's . . . nice? In fact, why *don't* you like it, Ivy?' he asked. There was a glint of challenge in his eyes.

Ivy paused, tangled in fairy lights. 'Hang on. I never said I didn't like it.'

'You don't seem that thrilled to be here,' said Trip.

'You really don't,' Brooke agreed.

'Oh.' Ivy found both the siblings staring at her with their matching wide brown eyes. 'Well, I grew up here, you know? No one loves the place where they grew up, do they?'

'Um,' said Trip. 'I mean, I love where *we* grew up. Actually not so much where my parents live, but my grandmother's house in Santa Cruz. It's right on the water.' His voice was dreamy as he went on. 'This old place painted pink and turquoise, with a yard that looks like a wild herb jungle and wind chimes that make music even when there's no wind. A bit like Wildest Dreams, come to think of it. Who wouldn't love growing up someplace like that?'

There was a pause. Brooke shifted uncomfortably. There was that odd undercurrent between the siblings again, which Ivy couldn't quite put her finger on. They didn't mention their parents much, she thought.

'Well, I know you think Fox Bay is a picture postcard but you try *living* in a postcard,' said Ivy at last. 'Stay here for long enough and you realise everybody knows your business. It can get suffocating.'

'In that case,' said Trip, 'why did you come back?'

'Er, I have not *come back*. In case you haven't noticed I'm at *art school*,' Ivy said indignantly. 'This is the *holidays*. I have literally no choice. Not all of us can swan around the world on some luxurious gap year, you know. Sardinia, Rome, Paris and then . . . Fox Bay? Seriously? I blame that article.'

Trip shrugged, looking at the floor. 'It sounded nice,' he said.

'Tell Ivy why you really wanted to come here,' Brooke said. Her voice was teasing, but underneath she sounded unexpectedly gentle.

'Well, I . . .' Ivy was sure Trip was flushed. 'I . . . wanted snow.'

She stared. 'Snow?'

'Yeah.' He nodded. 'Snow on a beach, specifically. I thought Fox Bay might have it.'

Ivy frowned. 'Wait, that's why you keep checking the weather app? Because you came here for snow? That's the weirdest reason to travel halfway across the world I ever heard. And I'm afraid you're out of luck. It's like I said – it *never* snows in Fox Bay.'

'But maybe it will this year,' said Trip hopefully. 'The news says it's unusually cold.'

Ivy opened her mouth to tell him it definitely, absolutely wasn't going to snow because it never had in her whole life, and then caught Brooke's eye. Something in her expression made her shut her mouth.

'Besides,' Trip said, smiling again, 'there's nothing wrong with being weird – you said that yourself.' He nudged her. 'We can be weirdos together.'

Something caught in Ivy's throat. *Weirdos together.*

'You're both very strange,' Brooke said, looking at them with something like affection. 'Now would one of you weirdos fancy doing another coffee run? The stuff in the shop tastes like mud.'

Chapter Nine

True to her word, Ivy attended the meeting the next night. She walked in just as Mr Hargreaves had proudly declared a compromise; Mr Patterson would trim his vision of a full-blown pagan ritual into a modest interpretive dance with scarves and lanterns. In exchange, he had reassured the committee that there would be plenty of sea shanties and Cornish history to satisfy the traditionalists. Everyone was happy.

Sort of, at least. Ivy had a feeling it would only be a matter of time before another argument erupted. The rehearsal seemed ... haphazard.

Ivy sat near the back, sketching rough scenery ideas in a notebook balanced on her knee, but also watching the chaos unfold. At the front of the hall, a gaggle of kids were arguing over who should be King Arthur. One was crying. One was attempting to abseil up the stage using the curtains. Two were picking their noses. Mr Patterson seemed oblivious, directing a group of ten-year-olds through a silent storm dance sequence, which involved a lot of uncoordinated spinning in capes.

'Hi!' came a piercing voice.

Ivy turned to see Erin's sister, Lucy.

'They said you're doing props,' she said cheerfully. She thrust a piece of paper at her. 'So here's the list!'

Ivy took it. 'The list?'

Lucy beamed. 'Of everything Mr Patterson said we need by next week.'

Ivy took the sheet. It *was* as long as her arm and written in frantic black biro with doodles and scribbled notes. Ivy made out the words 'stone circle', 'Stargazy Pie', 'giant mackerel', 'trident?' and 'shoal of fish'.

'*Shoal of fish?*' Ivy asked.

'Oh yes,' said Mr Hargreaves, rushing past. 'Mr Patterson needs those for the set piece with Tom Bawcock. He's envisioning hundreds, cascading down on to the stage in different colours.'

Ivy looked at the stage, where a child had just tripped over a lobster trap. 'This is a lot of work,' she said, 'for one person and some papier-mâché.'

Lucy nodded solemnly. 'That's what Mr Hargreaves said. But he also says you're a genius.'

As the meeting dissolved into disarray, Ivy began to curse her mum for signing her up to this nightmare.

From what she could overhear, the show was a classic Mr Hargreaves shambles in the making, with a confusing script, hordes of unfocused children and competing ideas. It was only a matter of time before another argument kicked off.

* * *

The next afternoon, Josie decided that the shop still didn't look nearly sparkly enough. She staggered in with a huge bag full of holly and silvery winter branches and insisted they strew it around the shop, before covering every available surface in fairy lights. She also found an old record and set it to play in the corner, cranking out crackling, warbling tunes.

By the time they had smothered the shop in foliage to Josie's satisfaction, it was time for another Story-time Adventure. The Sunday session was always packed and Trip was out hiking with Brooke so she couldn't even delegate to him. Ivy read stories until her throat was hoarse. The theme was fairies and sparkle, and she couldn't have felt less sparkly as she worked her way through a big book of fairy tales. When she was done, Ivy staggered into the kitchen for a break and to call Raye.

'Why didn't I get a job back in Truro?' she croaked to Raye down the phone as she splashed tepid coffee into another stupid pun cup. This one showed a cat wearing a flapper headdress and smoking a cigarette, with *The Great Catsby* spelled out in theatre lights. 'I blame you.'

'Me?' said Raye, sounding remarkably unbothered. She was clearly walking outside, somewhere windy. 'How is this *my* fault?'

'You told me the shop would be a breeze – well it's not. There are hundreds of Kathleen Lee fans here on a daily basis, taking selfies of themselves with glass bottles. And this Fox Bay show! It's sucking the lifeblood from me.' She sighed, looking around the little kitchen, at the inspirational quotes stuck to the walls,

Josie's signed photo of some random 70s Russian poet. 'Do you ever question, like, all your life choices?'

'Well, aren't you a ray of sunshine these days?' Raye said. Ivy could hear voices in the background and snatches of laughter. 'Cheer up. The tourists and Kathleen fans will get bored of Wildest Dreams soon and the shop will calm down. What are Josie's guests like?'

'Weird,' said Ivy, lowering her voice. 'Like, very weird.'

'How? They can't be weirder than that tantric couple.'

'It's this guy and his sister. She's some sort of driven exec type with a shadowy job who barely says two words and he's . . .' Ivy trailed off, trying to think how best to describe Trip. 'He's like, insanely cheerful.'

'Okay.'

'You don't understand. It's exhausting,' whispered Ivy. 'He's *relentlessly* positive. He does yoga every morning. His entire wardrobe is expensive knitwear, like he's starring in a Cornish drama. He's constantly bringing people coffee and – and being nice,' she finished. 'And his name is Trip. Trip! Really?'

'Sounds terrible,' drawled Raye. 'Listen, I've got something to tell you that will cheer even you up.'

'Go on.'

'Mum and Dad are determined I'm coming home for this show – it's all they can talk about, you know how intense everyone gets about Mr Hargreaves's productions – so I'll see you in a few weeks. Then you can meet Cleo.'

'She's coming here?' said Ivy, faltering. Raye, partner-in-crime

Raye, fellow loner Raye, had a girlfriend serious enough to bring home for the holidays?

'Yeah!' Raye's voice was happy. 'She's dying to see where I grew up. I've told her loads about you and Fox Bay and all the bizarro traditions. I can't wait for you to meet. I know you're going to love her.'

'I'm sure,' said Ivy. So she could feel like a loser around her best friend too. Fabulous. 'You sound very cheerful.'

'I am,' said Raye. 'The sun is out, which is pretty special in Glasgow. I've just eaten a vegan sausage roll the size of my head. The vintage shops are all open. And Cleo and I are going to a gig tonight. It's that band we were meant to see last month, only we ended up going to this club . . .'

Ivy wedged the phone under her ear and poured yet more coffee as her friend chattered on about her uni exploits. When had Raye, her moody, quirky, fellow weirdo become so . . . chill? Another person having an amazing time at uni?

Just then, she heard a chorus of shrieks from next door, louder than usual, interrupting Raye's story of yet another fun night.

'Sorry, Raye, I've got to go, the children are either killing each other or something worse. Speak soon.'

She hung up and burst into the kids' area to discover that Story-time had, somehow, turned into Sales-time, thanks to Liv and her best friend Bethie's entrepreneurial zeal. They had taken up positions by the door and were corralling unsuspecting customers with festive tickets and hand-drawn posters for the show. Notes exchanged hands and Josie looked on benevolently.

'Please come to our show?' said Liv, smiling winningly at a customer. 'It represents Cornish culture. With stories and song and dance. And maybe some smugglers.'

'It's to save the library,' Bethie was telling a smart woman in a Barbour, rattling a Quality Street tin. 'You like books, right? The library has books.'

Trip, appearing in the doorway in another expensive-looking jumper, dropped a tenner into their tin. His sister, elegant in her yoga gear, stood next to him. 'Look at you two,' he said fondly. 'You're like tiny entrepreneurs.'

'Mr Hargreaves told us to seize any opportunity to sell,' Liv said determinedly. 'And Story-time seemed like an *opportunity*. "A captive audience", that's what he said.'

At the front counter, Ivy wiped the sticky marks off the glass. Why *were* children so sticky? she wondered.

'It's very sparkly in here,' said Brooke, glancing around at the foliage and lights. 'Very Hallmark. I like it.' Her gaze narrowed and her tone became businesslike. 'Ivy. I've been wanting to talk to you.'

'I've been right here,' said Ivy. 'Literally nowhere else to go.' *I wish*, she thought.

'You're a proper Fox Bay local, right?'

'Right,' said Ivy. 'Because my mum has terrible taste in men and unfortunately most of them seemed to live in Cornwall.'

'That,' said Brooke, 'is more information than I wanted. But if you want to make a bit of extra cash, I've got a proposition for you.'

'Okay,' said Ivy cautiously. She'd already been burned by getting signed up to the show without her knowledge and she didn't really have any free time now. Still, the thought of extra cash was tempting. 'What is it?'

'I'd like you to be my tour guide,' Brooke said briskly. She pulled out her iPhone and flipped it round to show Ivy her notes app. 'I wanted to see some Cornish sights but I've done all the standard stuff and you mentioned that Fox Bay has secret things. I'm wondering whether Fox Bay is an untapped resource – more hidden things like that lighthouse, for instance.'

Ivy thought for a moment, casting her mind over all that Fox Bay had to offer. 'The lighthouse up on the cliffs *is* worth seeing. The Mariner's Arms is meant to be an old smugglers' pub – you can see the hidden cellar where they stashed their whisky. Seal Island is pretty special – you can only get there by boat. There's a little cove round the bay, where locals swim as it's quiet. It's where the Kathleen Lee book launch was held.'

Brooke shook her head. 'See? I knew I needed a local's knowledge. This is exactly what I'm looking for. I'll pay you to show me around. Like a real tour guide. The more picturesque, the better.'

'Fox Bay does do picturesque well,' said Ivy. 'I'll check when I'm next—'

'I was thinking tomorrow at seven,' said Brooke. 'We could hike up to the lighthouse as soon as it gets light.'

'7 *a.m.*?' asked Ivy, bewildered. 'Why do we—'

Just then, the bell over the door jingled and Mr Hargreaves burst in, silk scarf askew, looking windblown and utterly frantic.

'Ivy! Thank goodness. Why aren't you replying on the WhatsApp?'

'I muted it,' Ivy told him frankly. 'Why?'

'Have you seen your mother? I've looked everywhere. *No one is answering their phones.*'

'Well, it is a Sunday,' Ivy said. 'People have lives, lie-ins. At least that's what I hear. What's happened? A theatrical emergency?'

She was joking, but Mr Hargreaves only flapped his hands anxiously. 'Yes! It's Mr Patterson. He's in hospital! Appendicitis, poor thing! He can't direct the show and the committee's in absolute bits. No one has that level of experience, no one can make sense of his script. Half of it is written in Kernewek. And his show is so ambitious! We might have to cancel—'

Ivy heard a loud gasp and turned to see Liv, looking as though someone had died. Her eyes filled instantly with tears.

'Cancel?' Liv whispered. 'But we sold *seventy-seven pounds and fifty pence* worth of tickets today!'

Bethie also looked horrified. 'What about the giant Cornish pasty Fin was going to make? He's been practising for weeks. He said we might get into the *Guinness Book of Records*!'

Ivy looked at their stricken little faces and turned back to Mr Hargreaves. 'Hang on, you're going to *cancel the show*? Because one teacher has appendicitis? That seems a bit dramatic.'

'No one else has the experience,' Mr Hargreaves wailed. 'We

need someone who knows theatre and staging and lighting and—'

'I've been to theatre camp!' Trip piped up.

Everyone turned to look at him.

'Oh no,' Ivy breathed. 'Trip, save yourself. Don't do it.'

'Theatre camp?' said Mr Hargreaves, taking an eager step forward, trembling. 'Tell me more, young man.'

'Every summer.' Trip began to tick off his credentials on his fingers. 'Full musicals, blocking, props, ensemble management. I can work a fog machine. And I've been CRB and DBS checked because I toured with an international youth world music group two summers ago.'

Fragile hope dawned on Mr Hargreaves's face. 'You – you could *direct*? At such short notice?'

'I'd love to,' Trip said, without a flicker of hesitation. 'Be my honour.'

Liv screamed, launched herself at Trip like a small hurricane in fairy wings, and hugged him. Bethie applauded. Mr Hargreaves mopped his brow. Brooke let out a small, weary sigh as though this was entirely to be expected.

Ivy gripped Trip's arm and pulled him aside. 'You don't know what you're getting yourself into,' she hissed. 'The people of Fox Bay are fairly deranged at the best of times, but this play has sent them over the edge. You've seen how stressful it all is. No one can agree on anything. This show is like one walking red flag.'

He grinned down at her. 'Hey, someone's got to save the

show.' He looked past her at where Bethie and Liv were jumping up and down, the coins in their tins rattling. 'Look at them. They're so happy.'

Ivy dragged a hand down her face. 'You're meant to be on *holiday*.'

'Seriously, Ivy, this will be fun for me. I like a project. I get bored doing nothing.'

Ivy turned pleadingly to Brooke, who was watching them with wry amusement. 'Tell him not to,' she implored. 'They'll eat him alive. These people need a firm hand, not Mr Nice-and-Enthusiastic.'

Brooke shrugged. 'Don't underestimate Trip,' she said. 'He once stage-managed *Les Misérables* in the Santa Cruz mountains with a cast of ten-year-olds, two cats and a budget of fifty dollars. The play is in good hands, Ivy.'

Ivy groaned. 'Don't do it, Trip,' she repeated.

But Mr Hargreaves was already outlining the rehearsal schedule while messaging the WhatsApp chat the good news, Trip was rapidly taking notes on the back of a receipt and Liv and Bethie were loudly and tunelessly practising their big Arthurian number. It seemed like the show would go on after all, Ivy thought.

She only hoped that Trip wouldn't be broken in the process.

Chapter Ten

On Monday morning, the sky was still ink-dark as Ivy pulled on her thickest jumper and grabbed her Thermos, which had seen her through countless school trips and residentials, shutting the door to the flat quietly. Brooke had texted her last night, her message as businesslike as she was in person.

Still on for showing me and Trip this famous lighthouse? 7 a.m. start? I meant it about paying you. I've checked the local tour guide rates and think this should cover it.

Brooke had then mentioned an hourly rate that was nearly double what Ivy was getting paid in the bookshop. That had decided it for her. If a couple of American tourists wanted to pay her to trek around Fox Bay, she wasn't going to say no.

The drive to the harbour front was peaceful, the town silent. Ivy rolled down the windows, letting in the sound of the wind whistling over rooftops and the occasional squawk of a gull. She could smell the sea. The cold stung her cheeks, but it was the good kind of cold, clean and bracing, and she drove slowly, relishing it.

Trip and Brooke were waiting when she reached the shop a few minutes after seven, steam rising from the travel mugs in their hands. A dog barked somewhere in the distance.

Trip waved like they hadn't seen each other in years. 'Morning, Ivy!' He patted his pockets. 'I brought snacks. Fruit, nuts, chocolate, flapjacks . . .'

'Great.' Ivy hefted the Thermos. 'I brought caffeine.'

Brooke was dressed in a matching navy hiking set, somehow looking both elegant and functional, hair smooth beneath a hairband. She looked far too pristine for Fox Bay, which was mostly all ancient fleece and lumpy cardigans. 'You're late,' she said severely.

Ivy huffed. 'It's *four minutes* past seven.' She glanced at Trip. 'And you're going to freeze to death up there on the cliffs.'

Trip was wearing a navy Aran jumper but no coat. 'Then I'll die doing what I love,' he declared. 'Seeing local landmarks. Finally.'

'Ivy's right,' said Brooke, digging in her rucksack and pulling out an expensive-looking black fleece. 'You'll be cold. Put this on.' She turned to Ivy. 'Right, shall we get this over with?'

'It's a scenic walk, not the dentist,' muttered Ivy, pulling her backpack on. 'Okay. To the haunted lighthouse.'

They headed out of town, walking along the quay where Old Bill, busying himself by his boat as usual, wearing his sailor's cap and with his pipe clenched between his teeth, gave them a wave.

'Off to see the lighthouse, are you?' he called. 'Brave of you. You've heard the stories, I'll bet?'

'Yeah,' said Brooke, pausing. 'Something about a lighthouse keeper?'

'Ah, well since you asked,' said Old Bill with relish, setting down the rope he'd been winding and leaning against the boat. 'It's a sorry tale. Poor Jim Potterill. Lighthouse keeper in 1912. Fell asleep one night when he should have been manning the lighthouse.' Old Bill lowered his voice impressively. 'And that same night, the moon was hidden by clouds and a boat was wrecked. The crew perished. Unable to bear the guilt, Jim threw himself from the lighthouse down on to the rocks below to join them in their fate.'

'Yikes,' murmured Brooke. 'I did not find anything online about *this*.'

'And then ever since, when the moon slips behind the clouds,' intoned Old Bill, 'you can see it. A light lit where no light should be, and a ghostly figure walking back and forth, atoning for his carelessness all those years ago.' There was a pause. 'Aye. Well, take care. Don't want to scare yerselves silly up there on the cliffs and join poor Jim.' Ivy caught the faint wink he gave her.

'We'll be careful,' said Trip. 'Ivy's going to show us the way.' He frowned. 'Bill, you said you were going to cut out the pipe.'

'I've cut right back,' said Old Bill defensively. 'And aye, no one knows the way to the lighthouse better than Ivy – she's been walking these paths since she was a nipper. Plenty of other stories I could tell you about this place. Why there's even a hidden island . . .'

'See you later,' said Ivy, dragging them on towards the Mariner's Arms. She knew that once Old Bill got started on Fox Bay lore, they would never manage to stop him. 'Take anything he says with a seriously large pinch of salt,' she murmured. 'All those stories and tall tales are just that. Who knows if this Jim chap ever existed? Old Bill doesn't even go out on his boat much any more. He just likes playing the part of a wise sea dog.'

'Why not?' said Trip easily. 'If it makes him happy.'

Ivy thought about that one. She couldn't think of a single reason, suddenly, why Old Bill *shouldn't* potter in his boat at dawn, winding rope, pipe clamped in his teeth, terrifying local tourists with his tales of regretful ghosts and souls lost at sea. Not if it made him happy.

'Morning,' called Simi, yawning on the front step of the pub. 'You're up early.'

'Is this your pub?' Brooke asked, raking her gaze over the Mariner's Arms. 'Didn't you say it was a smuggler's hideout, Ivy?'

'That's right,' said Simi. 'A famous smuggling ring used to hole up here. There's a basement full of old rum casks. The owner planned to get rich by turning the ringleader over to the magistrate but the smugglers got to him first.' She drew her finger across her throat. 'Nasty stuff.'

'Hmm.' Brooke squinted up at the topmost windows. 'Do you have rooms up there too? How many?'

'Just the two,' said Simi. 'But I'm thinking of expanding and using the outbuildings now there's so many tourists. I just have to hook up the Wi-Fi and re-do the bathroom. Why, do you need a break from Wildest Dreams? Josie's plumbing getting to you?' She winked. 'I'll do you a deal.'

'Not just now, thanks,' said Brooke crisply. 'So, you'd be able to sleep, what – ten here?'

'I guess,' said Simi. 'Why?'

'No reason,' said Brooke, turning to go. 'Well, see you later.'

She hurried on, and Trip followed. Ivy caught Simi's eye and shrugged. 'Weird,' Simi mouthed.

Brooke *was* weird, Ivy thought. She was approaching their sightseeing as though she were organising a business plan, ticking things off a list. And what was with all the questions? She was the polar opposite of her open, easy-going brother.

At last they reached the start of the cliff path and began the slow climb up, the dark giving way to grey-blue, with streaks of rose and gold that bled across the sky. The sea was a dull mirror at first, then shimmered as the first threads of sunlight touched it.

Old Bill was right. Ivy realised she knew these paths like the back of her hand, her feet unerringly finding the right turnings that were off the main path. She had been coming here all her life. Her mum used to pack her and baby Liv in the car with flasks of tea and sandwiches, drive to the foot of the cliffs and force them on a walk.

Over the years, Ivy had been less and less willing to come.

She'd wanted only to be curled up with her pad and pencils, drawing everything she could see in her mind's eye, making the images in her head come to life. The last time her mum had dragged her up here, the spring before she left for art school, Ivy had grumbled every step of the wet, drizzly way. *This is so boring*, she had moaned. *Can't we ever do something different?*

Now, though, the walk *did* feel different. The salt air, the familiar crunch of the path beneath her boots, the springy grass, the sudden stillness that wrapped around them like a blanket the higher up they got – Ivy knew it from childhood but it also felt like she was experiencing it for the first time. Maybe because she'd had some distance, she thought. Or maybe because she was showing it to strangers.

Their breath clouded in the cold. The sky lightened still more, the crimson sun rising. And then they rounded a corner and, suddenly, they saw it: the lighthouse, standing ahead like a pale ghost from one of Old Bill's stories against the brightening sky. And beneath it, the vast expanse of sea. They stopped, looking up, craning their necks.

'Well, there it is,' Ivy said, breaking the silence. 'The famous Fox Bay lighthouse. You can see why it gets missed by all the tourist websites. From further round the headland you wouldn't know it was here.'

Trip let out a low whistle. 'Wow.'

Brooke whipped out her phone and took a series of pictures. 'Perfect,' she breathed, then tucked her phone away again. 'Very cool. This is just the sort of thing I was looking for, Ivy.'

'It really *is* cool,' Ivy murmured. 'I forget sometimes.'

Trip looked sideways at her, the sunrise casting gold across his face, lighting his rumpled curls like a halo. 'Sometimes a break from a place isn't a bad thing,' he said. 'You come back, you see it differently.'

Ivy didn't reply, hugging her Thermos against her chest to keep out the chill. She wasn't sure she'd go *that* far – Fox Bay was still Fox Bay, with all of its frustrations and quirks – but all the same, she was glad they had come up here today. They stood in silence, letting the wind buffet their cheeks.

Brooke stood slightly apart, looking out at the sea and rocks below. As Ivy watched, Trip walked over to his sister and threw an arm round her shoulders.

'She would've loved this,' she heard Trip murmur. 'Wouldn't she? A dawn trip to a haunted lighthouse?'

Brooke let out a small laugh and Ivy caught her words, muffled by the wind. 'She would have made us wake up *way* earlier than this. 7 a.m. is for layabouts.'

'She would've brought that ratty old tartan blanket and at least three Thermoses,' Trip added. 'And cake. You can't have an adventure without snacks.'

'It would have been *character-building*.'

The siblings laughed softly. Ivy watched them from the corner of her eye, wondering who they were talking about, but not wanting to interrupt. She knew it was time to head back, get some decent coffee and open up the shop. But she was in no hurry to leave, not when the brother and sister were having a moment.

Ivy closed her eyes to the sunrise and breathed in deeply. It felt like real life could be suspended here, with all her worries and cares left somewhere far below. And for just now, she didn't want to go back.

At last, they headed down the path and then Brooke and Trip went out to see one of the nearby fortresses, continuing Brooke's itinerary. Back at the shop, Ivy was soon swept up in work, and the hours sped past.

When it was time for her break, she checked her WhatsApp with caution and saw that debate was raging furiously over Trip's appointment as director.

Wait. You're putting a tourist in charge?

He's not even Cornish. He won't understand half of the references.

Give him a chance. Maybe fresh eyes will be good?

No. We need someone with experience. The show is too important.

Too important? It's a kids' show for god's sake. I vote we cancel it.

Yeah. We've only got two weeks and I can't even figure out what the script says. Half of it seems to be in another language . . .

Ivy bit her lip. There was a rehearsal tonight and she was worried that Trip would innocently be walking into the lion's den. He was too sweet-natured and would be no match for the Fox Bay show committee. At least she would be there, she thought, to offer him some protection.

The rehearsal was at six. Josie vanished at four to teach a breathwork seminar in her friend's barn. After the last customer had drifted out, Ivy flipped the sign to *Closed* and slung her MOMA tote over one shoulder.

Trip was waiting outside in the dusk, checking his phone, beanie pushed back over his hair.

'Ready for your directorial debut?' Ivy asked, as she locked up.

'Absolutely,' he said cheerfully.

'Because you can still back out, you know. Tell Mr Hargreaves you're allergic to face paint and dust. And children. And hiking shorts, of which there will be many in the PTA. Seriously, it's going to be hairy. It already sounds pretty tense on the WhatsApp. My advice? Quit now, before they know who you are.'

Trip only laughed. 'No way, I'm not a quitter. Besides, I don't know what you're so worried about. It'll be fun.'

'I look forward to seeing your impenetrable optimism crushed,' said Ivy, as they headed along the high street.

He ignored her and nodded at her bag. 'That's a cool quote.'

She glanced down at her tote. 'Yeah. It's Jack Whitten. *The purpose of art is to expand consciousness.* He's an American painter and sculptor from the—'

'I know who Jack Whitten is,' Trip said.

'Oh, right,' said Ivy. Unconsciously, she had formed the opinion that Trip's idea of culture involved surfing and green juice.

'I used to go to MOMA a lot. One of my gran's family friends is an artist in the West Village and she was always taking us on what she called *artistic expeditions*. She knew half of the modern artists that exhibited there.'

'Lucky you,' said Ivy enviously. Yet more evidence of Trip's charmed life that she could only dream of.

'*Expand consciousness*. It's a big aim,' he said.

'Yeah.' Ivy sighed. 'And someone like Jack Whitten had stuff to *say*, you know? All the greats did. What have *I* got to say? Not much.'

'You're worried about that big piece of coursework?' He caught her surprised look. 'What? You mentioned it the other night. I was just paying attention.'

'Yeah, I notice you do that,' Ivy said. 'If you must know, yes, I *am* worried. I haven't got much to hand in so far.'

'How much is not much?' he asked.

'Oh,' she said evasively, 'a few sketches.' She met his clear gaze and groaned. 'Well, *half* a sketch, to be exact. The thing is, I don't know what I want to *say*. I've tried making art that reflects social change. I've tried considering political themes. I feel like my brain is going to explode. Everything I try just feels . . . rubbish.'

'I'm sure it's not rubbish,' Trip said. 'It sounds like you're thinking *too* hard. Thought is the enemy of flow.'

'Okay,' said Ivy. 'That sounds very zen.'

'Vinnie Colaiuta said that. A famous drummer. He should know, right? Drumming is all about flow.'

'Another old family friend?' she teased.

'Actually, we did go see him once,' he admitted. 'At a jazz club.'

They passed Fin's bakery, now dark except for the soft lamplight in the flat above, where Ivy knew that Josie would now be making dinner – a concoction of strange ingredients that shouldn't go together and yet, somehow, would prove to be utterly delicious. The window in the bakery was slightly fogged, a silhouette moving inside. Fin prepping for the next day's bread, like he did every night.

The streetlights came on, as they also did at the same time every night. Old Bill was there as always on the harbour, tapping out his pipe, ready to head home. Simi was lighting the candles in the windows of the Mariner's Arms, preparing for the evening shift. Lou was stoking her pizza oven. Kate was locking up the surf shed . . . Everything here in Fox Bay was the same as always, Ivy thought, night after night – routine and cosy and small.

And what's wrong with that? a little voice asked. It wasn't like the outside world had been so great. She had only made it as far as Truro before she'd come scurrying back.

'Can I ask you something?' Trip said, bringing her out of her thoughts.

'Sure.'

'Do you ever draw Fox Bay?'

She glanced at him. 'What?'

'Your art,' he said. 'You said you were exploring all those big themes and ideas, but you've never mentioned anything to do with *this* place. Your home. It's a lot of material right under your nose.'

Ivy considered his question as they walked on, passing the old stone buildings, the fairy lights strung along the windows of Tamsin's crystal shop, the familiar red door of the post office. She thought of the pieces she had done in Sixth Form that her teacher had loved. Large-scale, moody charcoal pieces of the Great Pyramid at Giza, Machu Picchu at dawn, the Great Wall being lashed by a storm. The Taj Mahal, the Statue of Zeus. Places she had never been to except in her imagination; wonders she had never seen except online or in books.

'I don't know,' Ivy said eventually. 'I guess when I think of art, I think of something big and amazing. Why would I focus on something small and unimportant like this?'

Trip was quiet for a moment, then he said, 'If you had something you really wanted to say, right now, something urgent and important – would it be this hard to put your finger on what that is?'

Ivy opened her mouth to argue and he hurried on.

'And don't you think the things you see every day *are* important? Worth noticing? I mean, look at this place.' He waved his arms around at the darkened cobbled streets. 'It's magical. Weird, sure. But full of stories. Half the people in town seem like they've stepped out of a novel. And I bet not all those stories are simple or easy.' He shrugged. 'Look, I'm not suggesting you draw Fox Bay for the rest of your life. But if you're stuck for the next step, maybe this could be your way in. Draw what you see in front of you. It's like Monet said, *Nature is the source of my inspiration.*'

'How many inspirational quotes do you have up your sleeve?' Ivy muttered.

'Just because something is small, doesn't make it unimportant,' Trip said firmly. 'Look at Cassatt, Morisot, Emin. Kids in the bath, an unmade bed. That's life too, isn't it?'

This time, Ivy stayed quiet. *Just because something is small, doesn't make it unimportant.* She could feel something – a prickle of interest that said this was worth investigating.

'I'll think about it,' she said at last. They walked on. She imagined sketching these cobbled streets, shining under the streetlights. Old Bill folding up the rope that would never be used. Fin's silhouette as he moved around his silent bakery . . .

Her phone beeped and she fumbled for it. 'It's your sister,' she said, reading the curt text. 'She's hell bent on us seeing Seal Island tomorrow morning and she's persuaded Kate to take us out before work on Old Bill's boat.' She sighed. 'Why the sudden interest in the meagre sights of Fox Bay and why is it always so *early*? Is Brooke's approach to every holiday so organised?'

'I think she's just enthusiastic about Cornwall,' said Trip, but she noticed he didn't meet her eye. 'Hey, is that the hall?'

The glow of the town hall lights appeared ahead, and the unmistakable sound of small children shrieking drifted towards them.

'Brace yourself,' Ivy said. 'If you think Fox Bay is magical and idyllic, you're in for a rude awakening. Things are going to get real, fast. And by real I mean feral and maybe a bit scary.' She thought for a moment. 'We should have a signal.'

'A signal?' said Trip, the corners of his mouth lifting in a smile.

'Yeah, like if you can't take it any more and you need me to get you out of there, stat. I can fake an emergency with the best of them. Or trigger the fire alarm.' She thought. 'How about *lighthouse*. You say that and I know it's time to scram.'

Trip beamed. 'Excellent. Lighthouse it is. Not that I'll need it. Come on Ivy, have some faith.' He nudged her. 'Let's make theatre.'

Chapter Eleven

The old town hall smelled as it always did; of varnished wood, instant coffee, biscuits and a hint of damp. Ivy knew that smell from childhood. The playgroups she had attended as a toddler and then the countless bake sales and school shows that had taken place here over the years. She knew the battered plastic chairs, the thick, faded red velvet curtains and the temperamental trapdoor in the floor of the stage that had once catapulted Ivy into darkness during a primary school nativity. The space where the audience would sit in only a couple of short weeks had been cleared; a tuneless upright piano sat off to one side. Other than that, it was hard to imagine a show taking place here at all.

Ivy slunk in behind Trip, taking in the scene. There was Mr Trenwith (cargo trousers and all) talking loudly and gesturing angrily at the script. Kids scurried about, one shaking a tambourine, another tangled in a fishing net. A group of parents sat on the stage, drinking coffee from Styrofoam cups and idly chatting, clearly tuning out the whole mess. Mr Hargreaves pleaded with everyone for silence and was roundly ignored. Pages of the script were scattered like leaves in the wind. Liv,

Bethie and their friends were sitting on a ladder, watching with wide eyes.

'Look at this,' said Trip, sounding genuinely thrilled. 'This is great.'

'Is it?' whispered Ivy. 'It looks like this is one step away from *Lord of the Flies*.'

Trip shook his head firmly. 'They just need direction. Don't worry, Ivy. I thrive on chaos.'

Ivy took in a child hitting one of the parents around the ankles with a wooden spade and another eating what she thought was papier-mâché from a bucket. 'Then it looks like you're in for a treat.'

Mr Hargreaves saw them and scuttled over, hands outstretched. 'I'm so glad you're here,' he said, casting a hunted look over his shoulder. 'Mr Trenwith says the twins need *more* lines, but they already have the bulk of the dialogue. And two of the seagulls are off sick. The folk band are refusing to work under these conditions. And—'

A shrill whistle rang out and the crowd, startled, fell silent. Trip clapped his hands loudly. 'Quiet, everyone,' he called, a note of authority in his voice that Ivy had not yet heard. 'Now, my name is Trip –' he ignored the chorus of sniggers from the older kids – 'and I'm going to be taking the reins while Mr Patterson is in hospital. I have a lot of experience with community theatre –' Ivy saw the dull-eyed parents look up with interest – 'and I've familiarised myself with the concept. Interesting stuff. I know that we can pull this into a great show.'

'In less than two weeks?' called one of the parents.

'Absolutely,' said Trip firmly. He dug a huge ring-bound folder out of his backpack, stuffed with paper. 'Mr Hargreaves has given me a copy of the working script and, in my opinion, we have the makings of a hit on our hands. We just need to work together and, er, make some adjustments.' There was a flurry of murmurs and he held up a hand, again with such authority that everyone fell silent. 'But before we do *anything*, we need to go back to basics. Get to know each other.' He pointed to Mr Trenwith. 'Can you help Mr H carry this table into the centre of the room? And you guys,' he pointed at Bethie and Liv, 'bring some chairs.' He smiled around at them all. 'We're going to start with a table-read.'

It turned out that Ivy shouldn't have worried. Trip had, naturally, been a hit.

Less than three minutes into the table-read, he had gently interrupted the painfully shy second lobster's inaudible monologue with his first tactful, encouraging suggestion. He had slashed seven pages of exposition about the rock formation of Cornwall. Then he had suggested shifting the mermaid chorus to the start, thrilling the Year 4s and, when he added that the smugglers should enter accompanied by claps of lightning, there was a round of applause. He was authoritative, decisive, tactful. It was a whole new Trip that Ivy hadn't seen before.

Ivy, listening in while painting a stormy backdrop, could practically feel the hall draw a collective sigh of relief at being in safe hands at last. Mr Hargreaves nodded enthusiastically every time Trip spoke. Even Mr Trenwith seemed to decompress, especially when the twins were allotted the key roles of narrator. The PTA parents, previously bristling with competing agendas and what appeared to be decades of barely hidden grudges, softened. The Year 5 boys, who had sat through everything so far with crossed arms and expressions of utter disdain, were soon animatedly explaining the rules of Cornish wrestling to him, basking in his genuine interest.

About half an hour in, Ivy noticed the door opening and Mei sticking her head round it, followed by Erin and Callum. 'Hiya!' Mei said tentatively. 'Is it still okay to come in?'

'Sure!' said Trip, bounding over and ushering them inside. 'Come in! Everyone, this is Callum, Mei and Erin. They're going to be joining us on the backstage team.' He produced a sheet of paper. 'I've got your spec here. Callum, all the sound tech is over there in the corner and the Year Fives are up for helping. Mei, here's the script and the lighting cues. And Erin, I thought you could vet this for historical accuracy?' He squinted at the script. 'I'm not sure this bit about King Arthur *surfing* to victory can be right?'

As they went off to their respective corners of the hall, Ivy, who had been staring open-mouthed, turned to glare at Trip.

'What are they doing here?' she asked.

'What?' he said, shrugging. 'I asked them to come. They seemed keen the other night. I thought it would be nice for us all to hang out.'

It felt like all of Fox Bay was getting involved. Even Simi turned up halfway through with a tray of sausage rolls 'for the creative team,' she said. 'I told Lou to hold off on the carrots this time. I don't know what's got into her. Her tastebuds are all over the shop these days.'

Ivy, painting on the sidelines but unable to resist watching, began to feel a tingle of optimism as the rehearsal unfolded. Somewhere, underneath the confusion, she could sense Trip pulling it all together. Yes, it was chaotic. Yes, the show was still completely unhinged in concept. But somehow, in spite (or perhaps because of) Trip's bizarre and boundless optimism, for the first time it was . . . working. Taking shape.

'Okay, folks, nice work today. I think we've narrowed down what everyone is doing,' Trip called as the rehearsal drew to a close. He hopped up on one of the wobbly plastic chairs. 'The final scene list. Ready?'

He cleared his throat. 'Here we have the official running order of Fox Bay Primary's Celebration of Cornwall. Reception – Food and the Fishing industry. Year One – Music, including a Fleetwood Mac medley in honour of Mick Fleetwood's roots. Year Two – Dance, with traditional Cornish folk dancing. Year Three – Literature, a chilling scene from Daphne Du Maurier's *Jamaica Inn*. Year Four – Language, including a lesson in Kernewek. Year Five – Sport, a demonstration of Cornish wrestling. Year Six – Mythology and story, the Legend of Tom Bawcock. The Finale will be a dramatic reenactment of Arthurian legend adapted by Year 4.'

'Basically Game of Thrones but with eight-year-olds,' Erin whispered to Ivy and she found herself giggling.

Trip drew a deep breath. 'How does that sound?'

There was a hearty round of applause. The parents came to collect their children and everyone else began to tidy up.

'I'm going to get Liv home,' her mum called. 'She's shattered. See you later, Ivy.'

'Bye, Ivy!' called Mei, scooping up her coat and bag and following Erin and Callum out into the night. 'See you soon! Looking forward to hanging out!'

'Yeah, me too,' called Ivy. *It actually hadn't been too bad*, she thought to herself.

The hall had all but emptied, and Trip and Ivy found each other alone, stacking chairs. There was a small silence.

'I mean,' Ivy said eventually, 'it's going to be a complete train wreck.'

Trip grinned. 'And I, for one, cannot wait. Don't tell me that wasn't kind of fun.'

'It was surreal,' said Ivy, dragging a stool over. She caught Trip's eye and smiled. 'Okay, I admit it. Yes. It was kind of fun. I'm impressed. You got the committee under control in the space of one evening.'

'I have just one question,' said Trip. 'Before I commit.'

'Go on,' said Ivy cautiously.

'What on earth is a Stargazy pie?'

Ivy was still explaining the pie, fish heads and all, to a fascinated-looking Trip when Mr Hargreaves came bustling in from the back room.

'Enough! Let me finish this. Go home, my dears,' he cried. 'You've worked wonders, dear boy,' he added happily. 'Wonders.

There's hope for the show yet.' He shook Ivy's hand enthusiastically. 'I can't thank you enough for introducing us.'

'Great,' said Ivy, extricating her hand. 'Glad it worked out.'

'I'll walk you to your car, Ivy,' Trip said.

They headed out into the night, which had fallen in earnest while they were inside. 'Whoa. When did it get *so* dark?' he said. 'I can't see a thing.'

'The streetlights are out in this bit,' said Ivy, groping her way to the pavement. 'This whole town is an accident waiting to happen. I parked along the harbour. This way. Let's just hope we don't bump into anything or any—'

'Hang on,' said Trip. 'Stop a minute.' He caught Ivy's hand and she felt an odd shiver run up her arm. 'Shut your eyes.'

'Why?' said Ivy suspiciously.

There was a smile in his voice. 'My gran always used to tell us this trick when we were scared of the dark. *Close your eyes for ten seconds and when you open them, everything will be brighter.*'

Ivy hesitated.

'Go on.'

She shut her eyes obediently and Trip counted slowly under his breath.

'*Ten, nine, eight, seven, six, five . . .*'

She opened one eye a crack. His hand was warm and firm in hers.

'No peeking,' he said sternly. She wondered how he knew and shut her eyes again. 'You have to wait the whole ten or else it doesn't work. *Four, three, two, one.* There. Open.'

Ivy opened her eyes and gasped. The harbour was bathed in silver moonlight and Trip was looking right at her, his eyes alight. And he was still holding her hand. He seemed to notice at the same time and let it go.

'Did you just produce a *moon*?' she asked.

He laughed, looking around at the silvered street. 'Um, no. That part was a coincidence. It must have been hidden behind a cloud and came out while we had our eyes shut.' He grinned. 'But you have to admit, it's brighter.'

He was right about that, Ivy thought. Together they began to walk along the harbour, the moon painting the water in silver, and the noise from the town hall fading behind them until the only sounds were an occasional distant splash and the masts tapping as the boats bobbed in their moorings.

'Tonight was great,' Trip said happily, almost to himself.

'You tamed the show committee,' said Ivy, shaking her head. 'No one lit any fires. And no one lost any limbs.'

'Trust me, with some of those stunts Mr Patterson had in the script, it was close. It all could have gone very *Midsommar*.'

Trip walked beside her in companionable silence for a while, hands in his pockets, until Ivy spoke.

'What made you ask Erin and Mei and Callum to help with the show? I mean, you barely know them.'

Trip glanced over at her, his expression thoughtful. 'People mostly want to join in if you ask them.'

'So says a life-long joiner. I can tell.'

He nodded. 'Absolutely. That's one of the biggest things I

learned from my gran. She always had this way of just *assuming* people would want to be part of whatever wild project she was doing. A solstice parade or a spontaneous poetry night or a protest march. She'd ask everyone, the most unlikely people, and they'd usually say yes.'

'She sounds nice,' said Ivy. She thought of Brooke and Trip at the lighthouse that morning and wondered if they'd been talking about their grandmother then. 'Like you. I'd be the one saying no or sitting in the corner.'

'Well, there's nothing wrong with that.' Trip nudged her gently. 'You're nice too, Ivy.'

Ivy flushed. 'I don't think anyone's ever called me nice before.' *Difficult, stubborn, intense, single-minded*, yes. She had been called all those things. But *nice*, no.

'Well, I think you are,' Trip said easily.

Ivy could see her car up ahead and was almost sorry the walk was coming to an end. They reached it and stood there, facing each other. Out of nowhere, there it was again, Ivy thought. That odd, unexpected shiver.

Trip rubbed the back of his neck. 'Night, then. I'll see you in the morning, bright and early for this island excursion.'

'Yeah. Night. Bring a coat this time? It gets cold on the boat.'

'Okay.'

Neither moved.

Ivy said, 'And you'll bring snacks, right?'

Trip smiled a warm, slightly crooked smile. 'Of course,' he said. 'You have to have snacks.'

Chapter Twelve

Liv was asleep when Ivy tumbled into bed. She dreamed a strange confused dream – of tapdancing lobsters performing outside the ghostly lighthouse and Mr Hargreaves conducting, all set to a jazz soundtrack. Trip was there too, hands in pockets, smiling his sunny smile and looking on. *You're nice too, Ivy.* In the dream, Ivy felt like everything was going to be okay.

For the first time in weeks she had slept deeply and was sound asleep when her alarm went off. She sat bolt upright, disorientated, quickly turning it off so as not to wake Liv – why had she set an alarm so early? Then it came back to her. Of course. Her appointment with Brooke, Trip and Seal Island.

Forty-five minutes later, outside the shop, swaddled in all the winter clothes she could pile on, she found Brooke alone, looking as usual effortlessly put together in leggings and a thick padded coat.

'Trip's just getting the snacks,' she said, pulling on thermal gloves. 'He doesn't travel without them.'

Ivy smiled. 'Of course. Did he tell you about the rehearsal

last night? He had the show committee eating out of his hand. The children following direction for the first time ever. And he revised the script into something coherent in the space of an evening. It was quite something to watch.'

'Trip has a way with people,' Brooke said. 'And he doesn't do half measures.' She gave Ivy a curious look. 'He was out later than I thought he would be.'

'We took the scenic route back to my car,' said Ivy.

'Hm,' said Brooke. 'Wasn't it a bit dark for a stroll?'

'Um. The moon came out,' said Ivy, and for some reason she felt her cheeks getting pink.

'Well.' Brooke regarded her in silence for a moment, then said, 'I'm looking forward to seeing Seal Island. Another Fox Bay secret?'

Ivy yawned into her coffee. 'I mean. It's an island, there are seals.'

'Apparently it's a dead ringer for Saltwater Isle in *Ocean Deep* though,' said Brooke, pulling out her phone and clicking on a link. 'Look.' She held out the phone. 'In this interview, Kathleen Lee says it's *exactly* how she imagined it when she wrote the book. She said, and I quote, "*Fox Bay could have been conjured up out of my own imagination. It's exactly where I imagined the captain returning when he comes home and finds love again*".'

'So you *are* a Kathleen Lee fan then?' said Ivy curiously. She was sure she remembered Brooke saying the opposite.

Brooke shrugged and Ivy thought that she was also flushing. 'Yeah, I mean her books are okay. I quite like them.'

'I'm sorry. They're *okay*? You *quite like them*?' Trip appeared, holding his backpack and tugging on his beanie. 'Come on, Brooke, be honest now.' A look of mischief crossed his face. He turned to Ivy. 'Ivy, I think it's time for me to tell you my sister's deepest, darkest secret,' he said. 'She loves— Oof!'

He broke off as Brooke elbowed him hard in the ribs. 'Shut *up*,' she hissed. 'And come on, will you? We'll be late.'

She stalked down the street.

'What?' whispered Ivy as they hurried after her. 'What's your sister's deepest, darkest secret?'

'Brooke loves rom coms,' said Trip, his long legs keeping pace easily. 'She's the biggest Kathleen Lee fan. She's read all of them. She goes on Reddit forums talking about them. And everything else. Jilly Cooper, Emily Henry, Tessa Bailey, Danielle Steele. Brooke is never without at least one of those on her bedside table.'

'Really?' whispered Ivy, panting as she struggled to keep up with Brooke's rapid stride. 'But that seems so unlikely. Rom coms are all about love and optimism and Brooke is . . .' *Hard as nails*, she wanted to finish, but she bit her tongue. 'She seems more of a realist.'

'Oh, Brooke loves a love story,' Trip said. 'Romantic movies too. She's always curled up watching something, so long as it has a happy ending . . . Name a Hallmark movie and she'll have watched it. In fact, she usually clears this time of year just for that. The whole of December. She said otherwise she doesn't have time to finish them all before Christmas Day, what with all the subsidiary channels.'

Ivy couldn't help laughing, breathless from the pace the siblings were setting. 'Brooke *is* just like the heroine at the start of every Hallmark movie, before she meets the smalltown man who melts her heart. I had no idea she was such a fan.'

'That's why she's here,' said Trip. 'To see if—' He broke off.

'What?' said Ivy, frowning. 'To see if what?'

'To see if Fox Bay is how she imagined it when she was reading *Ocean Deep*,' he said, rather woodenly, looking straight ahead. There was something unconvincing in his tone that made Ivy study him closely. 'Look,' he said, pointing, 'there's Old Bill.'

Old Bill was sitting on the edge of his faded blue boat, whittling some indeterminate piece of wood.

'Ah, you're here for the island trip,' he said, standing up as they approached. 'Kate! Customers are here.'

Kate, a lean, tanned woman who Ivy knew used to run the surf school with Jacob, stuck her head out of the boathouse. 'Hey, Ivy,' she said. 'Nice to see you back. How's art school?'

'It's okay,' said Ivy evasively. One day she would have to come up with a better answer. 'Are you doing boat tours with Bill now?'

'The surf shop is mostly shut up in the winter,' she explained. She emerged holding a cup of tea and zipping up her jacket. 'Apart from a few die-hard enthusiasts. Old Bill gave me this gig.'

'What she's not telling you is I'm not allowed to do long trips now. I've got to be careful, the doctor says,' grumbled Old Bill. 'Eyes aren't what they were, neither's my balance. I promised

Simi I'd be careful and she's watching me like a hawk. Although I *would* be fine . . .' He shrugged. 'Anyway, Kate's been helping me out till it's lighter.'

'Sorry it's so early,' Kate said, taking a final swig of her tea and setting the tin cup down on the harbour wall. 'The tours start at eight and we're still booked out after the Kathleen Lee stuff last summer.' She pulled on a bright orange bobble hat. 'Shall we go?'

'Sure,' said Brooke, hopping neatly into the boat. Trip followed and both siblings settled themselves with ease. Ivy, who scrambled in far less gracefully, boat rocking, wondered if they were used to sailing. Whereas she, who had grown up by the actual sea, had barely set foot in a boat.

'Cast off,' bellowed Old Bill, seemingly oblivious to the early hour and the sleeping residents of Fox Bay. 'May you have fair winds and following seas!'

Soon they were heading across the water under a sky that was slowly turning gold. After about twenty minutes' sailing, Seal Island rose ahead of them and, as they neared the rocks, seals began to appear, first a slick head or two, then dozens of them, lounging like sunbathers on the rocks, slipping into the sea with curious glances as the boat approached.

Kate slowed the boat and the seals bobbed in the water, watching. Brooke, seated near the bow, laughed with delight at one particularly bold pup that barked indignantly at them. Trip pointed, wide-eyed, as another darted beneath the boat like a shadow. The siblings looked more alike when they were relaxed,

Ivy thought – Brooke in particular was transformed in this moment, her whole face alight with excitement.

Ivy wished, suddenly, that she could draw this and found herself reaching into her coat pocket – but she hadn't brought her sketchbook.

'Here.'

She looked up to see Trip holding out a leather sketchbook and pencil.

'You're looking for your sketchbook, right? Because I saw this in the stationery shop and got it for you. I meant to give it to you at the bookshop,' he said. 'In case you did want to have a go at drawing Fox Bay.'

'Oh.' Ivy felt herself going pink. 'That's really . . . thoughtful of you. Thanks.'

Trip turned back to look out at the sea.

Her cheeks still hot, Ivy opened the sketchbook. Her pencil moved almost instinctively, capturing Brooke's windswept profile and excited gaze, her pointing finger, Trip's eyes crinkled in laughter, the glistening water and the shimmer of movement beneath it.

She flipped the page and drew their feet in the bottom of the boat, her battered, paint-spattered DM boots, Kate's trainers, Trip's brown leather Chelsea boots and Brooke's expensive-looking hiking shoes. When she turned the sketchbook page again, this time she focused on Trip and Brooke, heads close together as they looked out at the seals clustered on the rocks, talking quietly.

She hadn't drawn like this in weeks, with the same ease and fluidity. Maybe longer. She leaned closer as she drew, trying to capture the siblings – and caught snatches of their conversation.

'Another place Gran would have loved,' Brooke was saying quietly.

'Yeah,' Trip said, voice barely audible above the gentle lapping sound of the water. 'She really would. She wanted to see seals one last time, didn't she? I had that trip planned to La Jolla, but . . .'

Ivy paused, pencil mid-line, struck by the expression on his face as she caught him in profile. The unexpected sadness. She couldn't resist drawing it. The frown between Trip's eyes, the way his mouth was set in a tight line, the way his hair fell over his forehead. She glanced away and slipped the sketchbook back in her coat, feeling like she had just seen and captured something she shouldn't have. The boat bobbed quietly for a moment.

'I need to get back,' Kate called over at last. 'My first tour's about to start.' She cricked her neck. 'Ugh, I've managed to pull a muscle,' she said. 'Today's going to be fun.'

'I can get us back,' said Trip. 'If you want a break.'

'Really?' said Kate gratefully. 'I wouldn't mind. If you're up to it.'

'Sure thing,' he said. 'I've been around boats since I was little.'

'You sail?' said Ivy, rolling her eyes. 'Sailing, theatre camp. Did you really have the perfect All-American childhood?'

'Um,' said Trip, avoiding her eye as he swapped places with Kate. 'Sort of.'

They began to sail back, Trip handling the boat with ease.

'You know what you're doing,' said Kate, impressed. 'Can you take over the rest of the tours today?'

Brooke snorted. 'Don't ask him, because he will.'

Trip shrugged. 'I wouldn't mind.'

'Trip needs to learn to say no,' Brooke said. 'I'm trying to train him.'

'There's one more sight to see on the way,' said Kate. She grinned. 'Only you can't actually *see* it, I'm afraid.' She squinted and pointed just behind Seal Island. 'Over there should be Mystery Island.'

'What's Mystery Island?' asked Trip.

'Old Bill claims there's a secret island near Seal Island, that only emerges during a full moon. Says that smugglers used to hide rum there, pirates would hide from the law – all sorts of tall tales. I've never found anything myself, but then again I've never looked that hard. I like the mystery aspect.'

'Mystery Island,' Trip said, his ready smile starting. 'I like that too.'

'Very Famous Five,' Ivy said. 'But it doesn't exist. Old Bill made it up, obviously.'

Trip grinned. 'Be cool if it did though, wouldn't it?'

All the way back, Ivy found herself watching Trip's hands on the oars and ropes, the flex of his muscles under his T-shirt as she listened to the hush of the sea between them.

Chapter Thirteen

With Trip at the helm, Erin, Mei and Callum on backstage crew and the committee put firmly in their places, the show kicked into gear. And, with less than two weeks to go and the script finally nailed down, rehearsals started in earnest.

As preparations ramped up, Ivy was so busy she barely had time to breathe. Her waking hours blurred into a carousel of bookshop shifts, ambitious papier-mâché projects, and emergency glue runs. She dashed between the shop and the town hall, hauling bags of shredded newspaper, swathes of material and whatever cardboard she could lay her hands on. She found that she was enjoying it more than she expected. With a proper brief to follow, it was a satisfying challenge conjuring scenery out of old boxes and egg cartons. After months of feeling insecure and anxious about her work, the chance to let her imagination run wild, via the recycling bin and the school's rapidly depleting art supplies, was unexpectedly freeing.

Soon she had transformed a pile of cardboard into a storm-tossed fishing boat, complete with splintering boards and faded paint. A stack of cereal boxes became a miniature pastel-painted harbour, with hand-drawn signs for the shops, and puns for the eagle-eyed audience members to spot. She built a stone circle out of chicken wire and papier-mâché and cliffs from cardboard, a backdrop of crashing waves from material and a silhouetted Jamaica Inn, sign swinging ominously.

And then, of course, there were the fish for Tom Bawcock's boat. There were to be hundreds of them, three-hundred-and-fifty to be exact, all to spill across the stage in a sparkling shoal. She had to enlist most of Year 4 for that. She could imagine how cool it would look, the audience gasping in amazement.

Her fingers were constantly covered in glue and paint. But for the first time in months, Ivy wasn't dreading each day, steeling herself for blank glances and eye rolls. She had to admit doing the props was kind of . . . fun.

The kids of Fox Bay rose to the challenge Trip set them. Ivy saw them studying their lines at bus stops and in the playground, reading their highlighted script with serious faces, lips moving silently as they committed their parts to memory. One boy called Miles, who was playing Merlin, even claimed to be growing a beard.

'That's some serious method acting,' Trip told him.

Ivy didn't see Trip much. Occasionally she caught glimpses of him at the town hall – mid-rehearsal, gently guiding the kids back to their marks, discussing technical issues with Callum or earnestly explaining the dramatic subtext of a scene to a group of seven-year-olds dressed as sardines. Always cheerful and upbeat, and managing, somehow, to get the best out of everyone.

Brooke hadn't been wrong when she had said that Trip could pull this off, Ivy thought.

His enthusiasm caught on. Posters for the show, designed by Ivy, printed by Kate and extravagantly coloured-in by Bethie and Liv, started to be splashed all over the town. Lou had promised to provide catering as her contribution to the library fund. Simi had promised wine for an after-party. The Seafoam Serenaders agreed to do the music and had even located an authentic folk band to help after the last one went on strike. The theatre critic for the *Fox Bay Sentinel*, an elderly man called Magnus who had refused to see the last three shows on the grounds that they were rumoured to have been simply too awful, had agreed to be in the audience on the big night. There was a buzz in the town and it was all down to Trip.

Ivy told herself she was *glad* she was seeing a bit less of him this week. His relentless good mood would surely have started to wear thin. Besides, she still had an art project to pin down. As well as working on the show, she was desperately throwing ideas around in her head, googling concepts and themes, even ransacking the eclectic art book section at Wildest Dreams in between serving customers. Words swirled in her brain. *Impermanence. Ephemerality.* Ideas would strike, only for her to realise a little later how stupid they were.

She couldn't help returning to Trip's question the night they had walked through Fox Bay in the winter darkness. '*Why don't you ever draw Fox Bay?*' More and more she found herself picking up her sketchbook to capture something in front of her: a child dressed as an octopus; Simi on a ladder stringing fairy lights above the door at the Mariner's, her and Lou exchanging a brief kiss during a busy shift; Mei, headpiece on, barking orders; Callum, eyes closed as he conducted the Fox Bay youth choir in the carol section; Erin snorting with laughter at one of the children calling St Piran 'St Piranha'.

And when things were quiet at Wildest Dreams she'd draw things she remembered: children, lost in a book, heads bent together over the pages; Aunt Josie doing her mantras before the shop opened; the cups of tea and melting candles. All of the cluttered cosy charm that she associated with Wildest Dreams and the quirky characters of Fox Bay would pour out on to the page. At least she was enjoying herself, she thought, although it didn't add up to a project of any sort.

'Morning, Ivy,' said Fin, dropping on to a stool across from her on Thursday morning as he set down Josie's sourdough. His eyes drifted to the open sketchbook on the counter. 'Is this part of your big project Josie was telling me about?'

Ivy groaned. 'This? No, I wish. It's just scrappy sketches. Silly stuff. It's not worth—'

But Fin had already pulled the sketchbook gently towards him, flipping through the pages. Ivy watched him. Fin was an artist and had been selling rugged seascapes of the area around Fox Bay for years, some for serious money. He might not be her tutor, but Ivy suddenly found herself anxiously wondering what he thought of her work.

She watched as the images flicked before her. A kid in a

seagull costume mid-squawk. Brooke frowning over her emails, coffee gripped in her hand. Trip laughing. The beach, the boats, the Stargazy Pie. Ivy's notes were scrawled in the margins – snatches of overheard dialogue, music that was playing.

Fin kept turning pages, slower now, eyes keen as he assessed the pictures. Ivy found herself holding her breath. Eventually, he closed the book, resting a hand on it.

'Ivy,' he said, looking up at her, 'these are *really* good.'

She flushed. 'It's just stuff I didn't want to forget.'

'Exactly,' he said. 'There's real heart in these. Real warmth. And a wicked sense of humour. That sketch of Bill in the pub – you can hear the tall tales he's spouting just looking at it.'

Ivy laughed, surprised and a little embarrassed. 'Fin. They're only silly. They don't add up to anything proper.'

'I disagree. There's a lot to be said for capturing ordinary life like this. The small stuff. Like a story without words.'

Ivy looked down at the book. For the first time this year, she felt a spark of confidence returning, a small flame licking into life.

'Maybe I'll keep going then,' she said shyly.

Fin nodded. 'You should. Not every masterpiece has to be brooding and abstract, you know. There are plenty of small ones. Sometimes the magic's in showing life as it is. You can't force something that isn't there, Ivy. I've always been drawn to painting the sea and I can't imagine anything bigger or more endlessly interesting than that. If I tried to do something else . . . it would ring hollow. Maybe you like drawing people doing everyday things. For now, anyway.' He winked. 'Even artists are allowed to change their minds, you know.'

Ivy nodded, storing the words away to think about later. 'Thanks, Fin.'

He stood. 'Don't thank me. Just keep drawing. The world's weird and funny and beautiful and you've got an eye for all of that.'

And with that, he was gone, leaving Ivy alone with her sketchbook and the warm loaf of bread. The unexpected praise settled on her. She felt cheerful and encouraged. Whether or not there was a project in this, it nevertheless felt *right*.

She flipped to a fresh page of the sketchbook and began to draw.

Later that morning, Brooke marched down the stairs while Ivy was pricing up a handful of remaindered paperbacks. 'What,' she said, dropping a photocopied flier down on the counter, 'is this? Because I don't recall you adding it to my list of must-see Fox Bay highlights, Ivy. Have you been holding out on me?'

Ivy turned the flier round. *See Fox Bay Come Alive With Winter Magic!* the flier screamed in comic sans font. Two snowmen danced with pointing disco fingers on either side.

'Oh, that's just the Fox Bay Winter Wonderland opening,' Ivy explained. 'It's tonight, I guess.'

'Winter Wonderland?' Brooke questioned.

'Yeah. It stays open through to January but they do a cheesy opening ceremony. Do you have that back home? Everyone counts down and then they turn on the fairy lights. Sometimes they drag out a local celebrity – and I use the word *celebrity* very loosely. But sometimes it's funny.' Ivy smiled, remembering. 'One year they got this talking dog from a few towns over to do it. Only he couldn't really talk, obviously, given that he's a dog, so he barked the countdown.' Ivy found her smile widening at the memory. She had actually loved the Winter Wonderland when she was younger. It had felt magical.

'There's more,' said Brooke, tapping the flier with a manicured nail. 'Stalls, artisanal crafts and carol singers. It sounds like a Hallmark film.' There was real excitement in her voice and she took out her phone and began to type. 'I'm texting Trip. This is so far up his street I can't even tell you. He'll *love* this. You'll take us along, won't you, Ivy?'

Ivy hesitated. They finally had a night off from rehearsals, and she had been hoping for a peaceful evening of moody music and tortured creative brainstorming. The days were slipping by and all she had were her handful of scrappy, saltwater-stained sketches, even if Fin's pep talk had made her feel better about them. But she had always loved the lights. Maybe this would improve her mood? And Brooke looked genuinely thrilled. Trip would love it. It might be fun to go along . . .

Just then, her phone buzzed so she pulled it out. It was her WhatsApp group with Mei, Erin, Callum and now, of course, Trip.

Mei: is everyone going to the lights tonight? Shall we get there early to get a good spot? Hot chocolates, cider?

Erin: Absolutely! I heard Fin is going to dress up as Jack Frost.

Callum: There's live music from six. One of the bands sounds cool, here's the link.

Mei: Can't wait! I feel like the holidays have well and truly kicked in when the lights go on!

Trip had thumbs-upped every message. Obviously.
    And then another text came through, from her mum:

Hey love! Just a reminder about the lights later. I imagine you'll come straight from work so we'll see you there? Waffles and hot chocolate like the old days! Oh and Miss Wheeldon will be there. She can't wait to hear all about art school. Love you.

Suddenly, panic swept over Ivy like cold water. Miss Wheeldon, her adoring Sixth Form art teacher, who had predicted great things for Ivy and raved over her final piece. No – she couldn't do it. She couldn't spend the evening with her hyper-enthusiastic-sort-of-school-friends and her over-excited mum and sister, all of them radiating jolliness while she felt like the ghost of a festive dishcloth. She couldn't tell her old art teacher, who had always had such high hopes for Ivy, that she was about to fail.

'Sorry, Brooke,' she said. 'I can't make it tonight. You and Trip should totally go, though. If anywhere is excessively welcoming, it's Fox Bay.'

To her surprise, Brooke paused her typing and looked up, a glint in her eye. 'Come on, Ivy,' she said. 'Ditch the snark for five minutes. What *are* you going to do this evening? Sit around feeling sorry for yourself?'

Ivy flinched, startled at the confrontational note in Brooke's voice. 'I don't *feel sorry* for myself,' she said defensively. She gathered herself. 'Why is it any of your business what I do tonight anyway?'

Brooke shrugged, going back to her phone. 'You're right,' she said. 'I forgot I was talking to Fox Bay's biggest rebel. Of course, you wouldn't go to something as cheesy and tacky as a Winter Wonderland. What would Patti Smith say?'

Ivy stared at her, then looked down at her vintage *Horses* tee, temporarily too indignant to speak. Brooke typed away, unconcerned.

'Look, we can't all be ridiculously cheerful like your brother,' Ivy said at last. 'Life isn't that easy for everyone, you know. Some people don't lead a charmed existence just because they have a great smile.' *And amazing hair*, she thought.

Brooke glanced up at her again, an odd expression crossing her face. 'Is that what you think about Trip?' she asked curiously. 'Like he has everything easy all the time? A charmed existence?'

'Look at the evidence,' said Ivy. 'He's barely been here a fortnight and the whole town has fallen at his feet. He's charmed the show committee and all the kids. Swapped recipe tips with Fin and taught Old Bill yoga. *Everyone* loves him. And when he's done here he'll fly off to Florence or Mexico City or Osaka or wherever he's decided to go to next and everyone will love him there too. He's clearly one of those people.'

Brooke nodded slowly. 'I'd say Trip gets back what he gives out,' she said. Then she stretched. 'I'm going for a walk. Sorry about what I said.' She nodded at Ivy's shirt. 'I like Patti Smith. And I forget you're just a kid.'

Ivy stared after her as the door banged shut, fuming, mouth wide open. *Just a kid?* Well, of all the patronising, stupid, unfeeling . . .

She looked down at the flier. *Should* she go along tonight and prove to Brooke she could be as full of Fox Bay festive cheer as the next person? No. She wasn't in the right place for it. Another evening with Mei, Erin and Callum, pretending not to care that everyone else seemed to be thriving, while she was horribly stuck.

She was sitting this one out.

Instead, as soon as work was over, she holed up in the school art room, surrounded by paint pots, vast quantities of cardboard and the beginnings of a moody, slightly lopsided backdrop of

Tintagel Castle, with the beach below. Liv's big Arthurian death scene needed atmosphere, and Ivy had decided foggy cliffs and dramatic skies were the way to go. She jammed her headphones on and let angry, crunchy guitars fill her ears as she scowled at the scenery and painted in big, angry brushstrokes.

How, Ivy thought, had it come to this? The most promising art student in her year, who had always received top marks and glowing feedback from every teacher, painting the backdrop for a kid's show in a deserted primary school on a Thursday night while the rest of the town partied under sparkling lights?

When Ivy had last been in this room, her future had felt full of promise and excitement. She had expected big things for herself. And now she was back, sitting on a bench that seemed far too small, knees hunched up, trying to work out why Arthur's horse looked more like a cow.

What are you going to do this evening? Sit around feeling sorry for yourself?

Ivy caught herself. Was Brooke right? Was she wallowing in self-pity?

Ivy was just layering in some delicate purple borders to the brooding storm clouds while PJ Harvey blared in her ears, when she felt a tap on her shoulder.

Ivy jumped hard and her brush skidded across the canvas, leaving a bright purple streak where there should have been misty grey. She yanked off her headphones, ready to yell, then stopped. Trip was standing there, looking mortified.

'I'm sorry,' he said, holding up both hands. 'I didn't mean to scare you. I was here putting away the costumes and I thought everyone was gone. I was just locking up.' He pulled a face, looking down at her painting. 'Sorry about that too. It's really good.'

Ivy looked down at the ruined clouds, now slashed through with vivid purple. She gave an unwilling smile. 'It *was*, maybe. Now Tintagel looks decidedly glam rock.'

Trip tilted his head. 'Very magical, actually. Mystical purple. King Arthur meets *Stranger Things*?' He waited as Ivy wiped her brush. 'Brooke mentioned you're not going to the lights?'

'I'm clearly very busy,' she said, gesturing to the paint-splattered table. 'And to be honest I can't face a festive crowd. Not because I feel sorry for myself,' she added hastily. 'I'm just not feeling it. You go ahead. Don't worry, I'll make sure everything is locked up.'

Trip didn't say anything for a second. Then he said, 'You know, most people would rather face a festive crowd than spend the evening haunting their former elementary school like an art ghost.'

Ivy gave a reluctant laugh. 'I told you, I'm just not in the mood,' she said, rinsing her brush in a jar of cloudy water.

'Okay,' said Trip, 'if you're sure. Only, I'm walking down there now. You wouldn't have to stay long,' he added. 'You could just . . . walk down with me. Show me the good stalls. Mock the singing if it makes you feel better. Tell me how cheesy the whole thing is. That kind of thing.' He gestured around. 'It seems a bit lonely here.'

Ivy's mum's words that first week home came back to her. *You seem lonely.*

Ivy looked down at the mess she'd made of the backdrop. It would still be there tomorrow. And, really, what *was* she doing holed up in her old art room, listening to angry music and whingeing about how she hadn't fulfilled her potential? Even Patti Smith would tell her she was overreacting.

'Fine,' she sighed, pulling off her paint-smeared hoodie and reaching for her coat. 'But if there's a dog counting down this year, I'm off.'

Chapter Fourteen

The Fox Bay Winter Wonderland had always been the most lavish of the town's many traditions, but this year, with the influx of tourists, it seemed like the event committee had really outdone itself. The whole square was strung with fairy lights, the air thick with the scent of cinnamon from the mulled wine and frying dough.

The fair was also full of Ivy's own personal ghosts. Everywhere she looked she saw people she knew from childhood, bundled up in scarves and woolly jumpers; there were plenty of strangers too, watching in wide-eyed wonder at the perfect, real-life postcard unfolding before them.

The choir was clustered beneath the bandstand, warbling their way through a slightly off-key version of *Winter Wonderland*. A local author, who Ivy vaguely recognised as Serena Woods, who wrote racy romance novels, was signing books next to the mulled wine stall. *She must be the year's designated celebrity*, Ivy thought.

Ivy could see Josie holding forth to Simi with lots of hand gestures, while Fin did a roaring trade in sausage rolls and hand-printed cards featuring The Mariner's Arms with a wreath above its door. Mr Hargreaves was talking animatedly to a group of tourists, handing out fliers for the show. Bethie and Liv twirled by the tree in their bobble hats, while Ivy's mother darted here and there – handing out change, picking up a brush to help with the face painting, chatting to old friends. Ivy watched her mother affectionately. How had the ultimate joiner, who believed passionately in community spirit, who never let a local cause go unchampioned, managed to produce such a loner as herself?

'This is incredible,' Trip said, as he took it all in. 'It's like a Hallmark movie exploded. In the best way.'

'You haven't even tried my hot spiced cider yet,' Lou said, holding out a tray of little white cups, steaming in the cold air. She looked a little tired, Ivy thought. She hoped all the tourists weren't too much for her.

Trip took a cautious sip and then nodded appreciatively. 'Dangerously good,' he told Lou, who beamed. 'Hey, look Ivy – it's the guys.'

Ivy followed his gaze to where Mei, Erin and Callum were standing under a lamp post sipping hot chocolate and eating marshmallows, chatting and laughing. Ivy followed Trip over, wondering when her sort-of-schoolfriends had become 'the guys'.

'Hey,' she said.

'Ivy!' cried Erin, enveloping her in a hug. She looked adorable, with fluffy earmuffs over her perfectly tousled hair. 'Good to see you. We weren't sure you were coming. You didn't reply to any messages.'

'I thought I might have to work,' said Ivy. 'But Trip persuaded me out.'

'Did he now?' said Erin, eyeing Trip speculatively.

'She can't spend all night in the school art room,' said Trip. 'Shall we look around?'

They wandered between stalls, Ivy pointing out the best fudge and home-made cake – all the old favourites she remembered, as well as some new entrepreneurs. It was busier than normal, but it was still full of the usual Fox Bay quirks. Some of these stalls had been here since she was little – the one with the misshapen knitted jumpers, the one that sold Norwegian-style felt gnomes, the one that – for some inexplicable reason – sold portraits of pop singers painted on rocks.

Ivy bought a rock with Taylor Swift's face on it for Liv and continued on. Everywhere she walked, someone came over to say hello. Fin asked her to help him wrap a seascape he had sold, Simi asked how the coursework was going, Tamsin offered her a free tarot reading and Old Bill called her over to decide the gingerbread-house competition vote. Kids she had known as babies were running around, giddy with the party atmosphere.

In a quiet moment, as the others browsed, Ivy felt her fingers groping for her little sketchbook. She pulled it out and, in the lamplight, began dashing off small vignettes – Bethie with her face smeared with chocolate, the serious faces of the judges at the gingerbread-house contest. A dog looking longingly at a kebab rotating temptingly out of reach. Someone jostled her and spilled hot chocolate on one page, apologising profusely.

Dabbing it off, Ivy couldn't help smiling. The impressionists had left sand on their paintings after all; surely a hot chocolate stain conveyed the sticky, imperfect charm of the night.

As the evening wore on, Ivy found herself laughing more than she expected, relaxing in the comfort of knowing nearly everyone; the familiar glow of Fox Bay now gaudily dressed in tinsel. And Trip, as ever, was an excellently appreciative audience.

'It's just so *nice*,' he kept repeating, looking around, dazed and happy. 'I love it.'

'You love *everything*,' Ivy told him, but she couldn't help smiling back.

'Hey, guys,' came a familiar voice and they turned to see Brooke, wearing a jumper with the words 'Yule Be Back' shakily embroidered on it. 'I just got this. What do you think?' She twirled. 'Shall I wear it to work?'

'Absolutely,' Trip said, slinging an arm round his sister's shoulders. 'Isn't this amazing? It's just like a Winter Wonderland should be.'

'I knew you'd love it,' she told him. She looked cheerful and relaxed, and Ivy remembered that Brooke loved Hallmark movies. 'Glad you made it after all, Ivy,' she added. 'Embracing tradition. I had you down as a Scrooge.'

'Actually, I used to love Fox Bay's weird events,' Ivy retorted. It was true. The thrill of marching in the Easter Bonnet Parade with her handmade creation on her head, the excitement of the summer pie-eating competition, the Valentine's postbox in Wildest Dreams. 'It just seems a bit silly now.'

Both siblings gave a gasp and turned to her, eyes wide.

'*Tradition* seems silly?' said Trip, staring at her.

'Well, yeah . . . It's all just a bit . . . over-the-top and – and unnecessary,' Ivy finished lamely. That line sounded good in her head but faced with Trip and Brooke's astonished expressions she began to wonder if she *was* Scrooge.

'I love holidays,' declared Brooke. 'Always have.'

'Our gran always made a big thing of them,' Trip said wistfully. 'Our parents would be busy working, so we'd go to hers. For Christmas dinner, we didn't have anything boring like turkey. She'd invite all her friends and they'd all bring a dish. Thai, Persian, Mexican . . . we had all the cuisines. And at Easter, she'd leave a trail of chocolate eggs from our door all the way through to the backyard where she'd hidden our treats. We had to work for them, she said.' He sighed. 'It was great.'

'That sounds nice,' admitted Ivy. 'But you know, you were kids. We're older now.'

'So?' said Trip, looking bewildered.

'So . . .' Ivy trailed off. Suddenly she wasn't sure exactly what her point was.

Brooke shook her head at her sadly. 'Ivy, as you may have guessed, I'm a realist,' she said. 'I don't like kittens or babies or bubble bath or anything remotely whimsical—'

'Unless it's within the pages of a Kathleen Lee novel,' teased Trip, and Brooke glared at him.

'But come on, Ivy,' Brooke went on, 'this time of year is great. This . . .' she extended her arms to take in the fair, '*this* is great.'

Ivy looked around the fair, the chattering, bustling crowd of people she had known her whole life, all wearing bobble hats and eating mince pies. It *was* kind of great, she thought. Maybe she had been too close to it to see it properly. And now, through the excited gaze of these newcomers, she was seeing it for what it was: one of Fox Bay's entirely unnecessary and yet brilliant traditions.

A microphone squawked and the crowd began to gather round the darkened tree. Ivy could just make out the usual lopsided tinsel star on the top, now almost bald.

'Time for the countdown, everyone!' Simi called into the mic. 'Everyone, please welcome Serena Woods!' There was a smattering of applause as people assembled. 'Serena, can I ask you to do the honours?'

Preening, amber beads jangling, Serena Woods took to the little stage and made one of her speeches about how much she loved this sweet town and how delightful it was to be back and that she had copies of her latest book, *Desert Heat*, for sale at her stall. Then she called, 'Fox Bay, are you ready to welcome the holiday season? Then let's get this tree lit!'

There was a cheer and Selena cleared her throat dramatically. 'Ten . . .'

Like everyone else, Trip and Ivy turned towards the wonky tree, shoulder to shoulder in the crowd. Around them, people cheered and raised their phones to capture the moment, cups of hot spiced cider sloshing alarmingly. Ivy and Trip were close, enough that Ivy caught the warmth of him, along with the faint clean scent of his shampoo.

'Eight!'

Ivy watched Trip, watching the tree. His grin was wide, and his face had that same awed expression she had seen a thousand times since he had arrived in Fox Bay, as though each of these mundane moments was something incredibly special. The light caught his cheekbones and his eyes were warm. He really *was* handsome, Ivy thought, startled by the revelation. It had crept up on her. He was so doggedly cheerful, so entirely un-brooding and unlike a tragic artist in every way, that she had somehow missed the full force of it. But now, she understood what everyone had been making such a fuss about.

'Seven!'

She tore her gaze away from Trip's cheekbones and tried to focus on the lights.

'Six!'

Tried not to notice how the crisp night air had flushed his cheeks, or how his chestnut hair was curling slightly beneath his beanie.

'Five!'

Or how his eyes were especially caramel-brown in the light.

'Four!'

When Ivy darted another surreptitious glance, she found that Trip was looking right back at her. 'Hey,' he said in a low voice.

'Hey,' she whispered.

'You've got something on your cheek,' he said quietly, reaching out and gently brushing the side of her face with his thumb. 'I think it's icing sugar from all that gingerbread.'

'Three!'

As Trip's thumb brushed her cheek, Ivy froze. His touch was light, but her cheek burned. She wasn't used to being looked at like that, so serious and intent.

'Two!'

'Any second now,' said Trip. But he wasn't looking at the tree. He was still looking at her. He had taken his hand away, but her cheek tingled from his touch.

'One!'

The square exploded into light. The crowd whooped and cheered, music burst from crackly speakers, but Ivy barely heard any of it. In that moment, it was as if the entire square blurred into nothing. She was only aware of the lights and the steady thud of her heart in her ears. Trip was gazing at her, with those warm brown eyes, and everything else had fallen away.

'Well,' she said at last. Her voice came out as a croak and she cleared her throat. Her heart was knocking against her ribs. 'That was the famous Fox Bay Winter Wonderland light show. All ten seconds of it. Was it all you imagined?'

'It really was,' he said.

Neither of them moved and neither looked away.

And then, 'There you are! I lost you in the crowd. Cute, wasn't it?'

The spell was broken. Ivy looked away quickly, her cheeks hot. It was Brooke. She was clearly well into her second cup of cider and, along with her jumper, she was now also wearing a reindeer-antler hairband that was slightly askew. She looked happy and relaxed as she approached, but then her expression changed. Her eyes darted quickly from Ivy to Trip and back again.

'Really cute,' said Trip easily.

'Properly Hallmark,' Brooke went on, her gaze still flickering between the two of them. 'Everything I hoped for and more. I was a bit worried the tree might fall over but Simi told me it's always at an extreme angle like that.'

'It's rustic,' said Trip. He sounded entirely casual – as though that loaded moment between him and Ivy hadn't happened. Maybe, Ivy thought confusedly, it *hadn't*, except in her own fevered imagination. Maybe she had hallucinated a romantic moment with her employer's over-enthusiastic guest. Trip was nice to *everyone* – she wasn't special. But had she imagined the serious expression in his dark eyes, his hand on her cheek?

'Well, I think the show's over,' said Brooke briskly. She tugged off the antlers. 'Should we be getting back, do you think?'

Ivy noticed that the crowd had indeed thinned and the stallholders were packing up. Families were beginning to head home, although Bethie and Liv were still doggedly selling show tickets to strangers.

Ivy's mum saw her, waved and called, 'Come on, love! I need your help persuading this one into bed.'

'Coming!' Ivy said.

'At this rate, they're going to sell out the whole town hall,' she added to Trip and Brooke.

'True. In fact, I think we should consider extra seating,' said

Mr Hargreaves, hurrying past, bobble hat bouncing jauntily. 'The sales have been through the roof. Perhaps we could also offer a video recording, Trip, for a fee – what do you think? Bring in some extra funds?'

'Sure thing, Mr H,' Trip called after him. 'I'll get Cal to look into it.'

'I'd better go with Mum,' Ivy said. 'Night, guys. See you in the morning.'

Ivy caught Trip's eye and smiled. 'Bye,' she said and Brooke gave her a little wave.

Ivy hurried off after Liv and her mother; Liv was still enthusiastically waving fliers at anyone they passed and her mum was busily chatting about plans for the next event in Fox Bay's social calendar – a winter beach barbecue with live music. Ivy listened to their chatter, smiling at their excitement – but all she could think about was Trip and that moment by the tree.

She could feel the touch of his hand on her cheek all the way home.

Chapter Fifteen

The next morning, Ivy found herself waking to a grey dawn. Fox Bay felt fresh, rinsed clean by a night of sea mist and frost. She stretched, wriggling in the bed, and the memory of Trip's fingers brushing her cheek came flooding back. She pushed it away and went to get ready but, when she was in the shower, his gaze under the fairy lights flashed into her mind and she blushed from head to toe.

It was nothing, she told herself as she massaged shampoo into her hair. Nothing. So why was she grinning like an idiot?

'You look very cheerful, love,' her mum said in the kitchen, wrapping sandwiches for Liv's lunch. 'Did you have an artistic breakthrough in the night?'

'Oh that,' said Ivy, pouring a glass of juice, feeling herself going pink once again. 'No, sadly inspiration didn't strike.'

Her mum squinted at her. 'Well, *something* has changed. You're positively glowing.'

Ivy flushed deeper. 'Maybe the Winter Wonderland magic is getting to me after all.'

'Hmm.' Her mum thrust one of the foil-wrapped bundles at

her. 'I hope so. You always loved it as a kid. Now, remember to have lunch. I'm worried you're being run ragged down there between the shop and the show.'

Ivy found herself smiling again as she gave the car its customary warm-up, repeatedly turning the ignition and praying the engine co-operated. She switched on the radio and when a cheesy ballad came on, she didn't turn it off in disgust. She even found herself humming cheerfully along. All she could see, as the darkened houses flashed by, was Trip, looking down at her as the lights flared into life, his expression serious and questioning.

She shivered happily. Suddenly she couldn't wait to see him, irrepressible good humour, endless chatter and all.

Ivy parked down one of the cobbled side streets. She headed to Fin's bakery and carefully selected the fluffiest, butteriest-looking croissant for Trip and then chose some more pastries for Brooke, Josie and herself. She was in such a good mood she even bought Pushkin a cat biscuit.

'You seem happy, love,' said Fin, handing her the paper bag. 'Going well at the shop, is it?'

'Yeah,' said Ivy. 'It is actually.'

Whistling, she headed up the street and pushed open the door to Wildest Dreams, suddenly breaking off mid-tune. Trip and Brooke were standing by the counter, wearing coats and hats, with suitcases at their feet.

Josie was already behind the counter, pencil tucked behind her ear. 'Morning, darling!' she called. 'Glad you got here in time to say goodbye. These two are making their escape from Fox Bay.'

'Oh,' Ivy said, feeling like she had suddenly been soaked in cold water. Her gaze darted to the cases. *Goodbye?* 'You're . . . leaving? Did the Winter Wonderland put you off?' She gave a nervous laugh, but she felt uneasy.

Trip shook his head, smiling as he tugged on his gloves. 'It's not really goodbye – we're just off to London for a few days. Someone called Ted is driving us to the station.'

'And he's late,' added Brooke, eyeing her Apple Watch crossly. 'Honestly, I said 8.30 a.m.'

'London?' said Ivy. She felt a rush of relief that he wasn't leaving for good.

'Didn't Trip tell you?' Brooke said, smoothing down her navy coat. 'We're catching the nine o'clock train. Or we should be, if this guy ever shows up. Does everything in this town run half an hour late?'

'No, I—' Ivy paused. 'You didn't mention London.' She hated how crestfallen she sounded.

Trip looked, Ivy thought, slightly evasive. 'Brooke said I needed a proper city fix.'

'You can't come to the UK and not go to London,' Brooke said firmly. 'I've booked us a great boutique hotel in Covent Garden.'

'But what about the show?' Ivy asked, trying not to sound forlorn.

'Mr H says it'll be fine for a few days,' Trip said. 'I chatted to him last night. I've left all my notes and Callum has the sound cues down, Erin is up to speed on the script, Mei was born to be stage manager . . . she's like a different person with that headset on.' He shivered. 'A slightly intense one, but she's working wonders.'

'Yeah, I think the Fox Bay extravaganza can cope without you for a few days,' said Brooke.

Josie tutted. 'Still, you're going to miss all *sorts* of fun things,' she said. 'There's going to be the annual bonfire on the beach and dancing. It has an almost *pagan* energy.'

'That's a shame,' said Trip, sounding genuinely regretful. 'I love a bonfire, especially a pagan one.' He glanced at Ivy. 'When is it? Maybe we'll try and come back in time.'

For a moment, Ivy imagined being on the beach with Trip, branches crackling as the flames flickered into the dark night, woodsmoke scenting the chill air. His arm round her, pulling her close—

'It's on Monday night,' she said quickly. 'The bonfire. If you wanted to come back for it, I mean.'

'I'm not sure we'll make it,' said Brooke. 'We're going to be pretty booked up till at least then.'

'Booked up?' said Josie, frowning. 'With what?'

'Oh, you know. Shows, restaurants, shopping,' said Brooke vaguely. 'Can't bring my little brother to the big city and not give him the full tourist experience, can I?' She tapped her foot. 'Where *is* this Ted person?'

Ivy considered Trip. It was odd that he would leave the show for sightseeing in London when he was so into it. But she supposed Brooke knew him best.

'Ted usually waits in the lane,' Josie said. 'Make sure he takes it easy on the narrow roads and don't let him go too fast. His eyesight is not what it was – his cataract op is coming up.'

'Good to know,' said Brooke, hoisting her case. 'Come on, Trip.'

'Right,' said Ivy, gathering herself. She realised her expression must be hurt and she pasted on a cheerful smile. 'I hope the journey is okay. Oh, I forgot,' she held out the paper bag, 'I bought you breakfast.'

'Sweet of you,' said Brooke, taking the bag. 'Thanks.'

Ivy hesitated. Something felt off, she was sure of it. Brooke was smiling, but it didn't quite reach her eyes. There was a tension in her posture. Wary, almost. And Trip *definitely* seemed oddly evasive – not his usual chatty self. But why? What had changed?

'See you then,' said Trip. 'Keep an eye on the show for me. Don't let Mr H make any unscripted changes or snap decisions. Tell him absolutely no fires. Sketch what I'm missing maybe? And if you see a single snowflake, you have to alert me *immediately*.'

'Will do. Have fun,' Ivy said, trying not to wonder why she already missed him when he hadn't even left yet.

After they said goodbye and the door swung shut behind them, Ivy went to the window and watched them, Trip chatting all the way up the street. She went back to the counter and switched on the computer, thinking that the shop suddenly seemed very quiet.

Josie gave her a pointed look over the top of a box of returns.

'What?' Ivy said, pulling the day's orders up on the screen.

Josie raised an eyebrow. 'Oh, please. I know a lovestruck expression when I see it.' She sighed happily. 'It's as I predicted.

You and Trip are *drawn* to each other.' She sounded pleased with herself. 'I predicted that his positive energy and your own more . . . muted aura would collide and fireworks would ensue. I knew it.'

'You know nothing,' Ivy said briskly, keeping her eyes on the spreadsheet. 'Trip and I are just friends. Wait, scrap that. Acquaintances. Acquaintances who see each other every day. Is there a word for that? Anyway, that's what we are.'

'All right, darling,' Josie said as she started shelving books, 'if you say so. But all of my senses are tingling. I am never wrong about affairs of the heart.'

'Fin was besotted with you for five years before you noticed,' Ivy pointed out. 'He had to order your entire back stock of Russian novels in an attempt to save you from penury before you paid attention to him.'

Josie waved her hand. 'The mysteries of our *own* hearts are impenetrable,' she declared grandly. 'But *your* heart, my dear, is as clear as glass.'

Ivy's phone buzzed on the counter and she grabbed it. Her heart leapt when she saw Trip's name on the screen.

This guy Ted drives like a maniac. See you in a few days, I'll bring you something crassly commercial and unnecessary from Camden Market.

Ivy bit back a smile. Her heart began to flutter in her chest, just as it had when the fairy lights had come on and she had found herself lost in Trip's serious, intent gaze.

Josie smirked. 'Just acquaintances, hmm?'

'Stop,' said Ivy, turning back to the spreadsheet. She couldn't stop the smile from breaking out as she began to work through the orders.

But all the same, she couldn't quite forget Brooke's evasiveness and couldn't help wondering what had taken the pair to London at such short notice.

Later that afternoon, the bell above the shop door jingled and Erin strode in, grinning broadly.

'Well, well, well,' she sang, brushing the drizzle off her coat. 'If it isn't Ivy Pearson, Fox Bay's most secretive resident. Anything you would like to tell me? About you, the Wonderland lights and a certain very hot American tourist? Hmm?'

'They're just acquaintances,' said Josie, around a mouthful of sourdough. 'Apparently.' When Ivy shot her a glare, she held up her hands. 'I'll be in the back, stocktaking. You talk to your friend, darling.' Josie slipped out of sight, chuckling under her breath.

'I'm not being secretive,' Ivy said, 'and I have nothing to tell. What are you talking about?'

Erin leaned on the counter, her bouncy hair tumbling over her shoulders. 'Oh, *please*. I am – and so is all of Fox Bay, to be honest – talking about you and Trip and the positively *electric* chemistry we saw last night.'

'I don't know what you mean,' said Ivy, flushing. 'There was no chemistry, electric or other—'

'Electric,' Erin said firmly. 'We saw you during the countdown. The way you were looking at each other was intense. Like something out of a film. Mei was annoyed about it for five minutes because she kind of liked him, but she says on reflection you're clearly meant to be and you can't fight chemistry like that. So she's cool with it, in case you were wondering.'

'Cool with *what*?' Ivy said, feeling the heat in her cheeks flooding down to her neck. One of the (many) problems she had with Fox Bay was the fact that nothing escaped its residents and *everyone* talked. There were no secrets. 'And no, I wasn't wondering. Because literally nothing happened. We stood under a tree watching the lights.'

'Watching each other more like,' said Erin knowingly.

Josie snorted from the back room. 'You should see them in the shop together,' she called.

'We're friends,' wailed Ivy. 'Acquaintances, I mean. And anyway, he's gone to *London*.'

'I heard. Ted told me he dropped him and Brooke at the station this morning.'

'Of course he did,' muttered Ivy. 'Does anything in this town stay private for five minutes?'

Erin frowned thoughtfully. 'That Brooke girl is mysterious, like an MI6 agent. I spent half an hour last night at the fair trying to find out what she does for a living and I still don't know. Honestly, maybe she's secretly working for a global shadow organisation.' She smoothed her hair. 'Usually, I can get to the bottom of someone pretty quickly, but she's a closed book.'

Ivy didn't have a retort for that. If Erin, with her keen instinct for gossip, suspected something was up with Brooke, she was probably right. And Brooke *was* mysterious. And, just when Ivy had thought they were becoming friendly, she had whisked Trip away at the speed of light.

Her phone buzzed, and she automatically glanced at the screen. Another text from Trip lit it up:

We're here! And I think we've found the best cinnamon bun in London. Not as good as Fin's though.

'Mmm,' said Erin, craning her neck. 'A text from Trip by any chance?'

'He's just telling me they got to London okay,' Ivy said, putting her phone in her pocket, away from Erin's beady eyes.

Erin let out a happy sigh and clasped her hands. 'Midwinter romance. The best. Our angsty little artist and an all-American tourist. This writes itself.'

'She's right, Ivy. I know destiny when I see it,' said Josie, watching fondly from the door of the stock room. 'And destiny is right in front of your face in expensive knitwear.'

Ivy rolled her eyes. 'You're both being ridiculous,' she said. 'I don't believe in destiny *or* romance. Now if you don't mind, I need to get some of these orders sent out.'

But all that day, every time her phone buzzed with another message, she felt a warm glow inside.

* * *

Trip texted off and on all the next day. He was having an amazing time – eating Greek food in Primrose Hill, seeing the Impressionists at the National Gallery, cocktails in Soho, watching Shakespeare at the Globe.

You are like the world's most committed tourist.

My sister is determined I get the full experience. She thinks we might stay an extra day or two. But I really want to make it back for this pagan bonfire.

Ivy closed her eyes and allowed herself to imagine it again – her and Trip on the beach, drinking Lou's hot spiced cider, giggling about the show, looking at pictures of his time in London. And then, maybe their eyes would meet again. Maybe his hand would brush her cheek. Only this time—'
   Ivy forced herself to get back to shelving. Honestly, she was as bad as Josie and Erin and all the other Fox Bay gossips, desperate for a whiff of romance. Imagining things that weren't there. She wouldn't get ahead of herself. She would just . . . see what happened.
   On Sunday, though, Ivy couldn't help but notice that Trip's texts were coming in fewer and further between. Ivy was sure something had changed. The texts, which yesterday were full of his observations and sweet jokes, started to feel clipped. His replies were shorter and there were longer gaps between them. Ivy told herself not to read anything into it. He was probably busy sightseeing or eating his way through all of Borough Market.

Still, around early afternoon, she couldn't resist checking and double-checking her phone, noticing that her text about Old Bill being spotted wearing a nicotine patch had gone unanswered.

Trip didn't owe her anything, she told herself.

All the same, she wished he would text back.

Later, when she texted him a photo of a cardboard castle turret she'd finished for the set, he reacted with a heart emoji. No comment.

Ivy stared at the screen a little too long. Then locked her phone and shoved it in her pocket.

She wasn't *bothered*. Not really.

Except . . . she kind of was.

Josie glanced at her from where she was wrapping up a stack of hardbacks in brown paper and string, which she was adorning with lines of Russian poetry using, Ivy noted, an actual quill. 'Any word from our American in London?'

Was Josie actually psychic like she insisted she was, or just a good guesser? It was hard to tell. 'Nothing. He's probably busy,' Ivy said lightly. 'They're doing all the tourist stuff. It sounded like Brooke had a pretty packed itinerary.'

'I'm sure you're right,' said Josie. 'Besides, he'll be back soon. It'll be nice to have him around the place again.'

Ivy smiled. As she turned away to start shelving, though, all she could think was how Trip's silence, now that she had got used to his chatter, his warm texts, his jokes and teasing, seemed weirdly loud.

Chapter Sixteen

On Monday, Ivy woke in the early hours of the morning with her stomach in knots. It was the day of the bonfire. The bonfire that Trip had said he might come back for. But why should that make her feel so sick and hopeful and nervous and excited, all at once? She glanced at her phone, but he hadn't texted.

And when she thought about it, what on earth was she doing, getting attached to Josie's irritatingly peppy guest? At the end of the holiday, Trip would head off to some other cool European city or one of the many colleges where he had an offer. She would never see him again. There was no *point* in getting attached. This – whatever it was – could go absolutely nowhere. She'd heard of a *summer* fling, but never a *mid-December* fling.

Ivy lay staring into the darkness of her room as the minutes creaked by, but sleep eluded her. She should be focusing on her art project, she thought, instead of obsessing over Trip. Eventually, she threw off the covers, showered, dressed and arrived at the shop far too early, the morning air still grey and damp, the kind of chill that clung to her clothes and made her feel miserable all the way through. It pretty much suited her mood.

She found Josie already there, wearing what looked like Fin's pyjamas with a thick fisherman's jumper thrown over the top, barefoot and humming, lighting tea candles round the front counter like it was a shrine. The scent of pine filled the air, along with the undertow of coffee and cinnamon buns from the bakery.

'Good morning, darling,' said Josie, glancing up with her ready smile that crinkled her eyes. 'I had a feeling you'd be in early today. Couldn't sleep either?'

'No,' admitted Ivy, dumping her tote on the floor. 'I'm not sure why.'

'Hm.' Josie rested her hand on a bundle of twine. 'Well, since you're here, I'd love your help. I thought we might make some winter crowns for everyone to wear at the bonfire later out of all this foliage. And I have cookies in the oven for customers. We're going to really lean into winter this year, darling.'

She nodded to the corner and Ivy saw a stash of pine branches and sprays of red berries.

'*That's* what that smell is,' Ivy said, smiling in spite of herself.

'That's right,' said Josie, pouring her a cup of coffee. 'Winter has come to Wildest Dreams and about time too. Now. Garland time. I don't think we should be constrained by anything as narrow and unimaginative as a *colour theme*, should we? You're an artist after all. We should just do something wonderfully rustic and pagan.'

Ivy snorted. 'Some artist,' she said. 'Painting props for a kids' show is the pinnacle of my creative achievement at the moment.'

'Please. If you have an artistic soul it can't be denied, whatever the outlet. Go on, darling, let your instincts take hold. Run wild. Trust yourself.'

Ivy obediently took a bundle of dried flowers and pine and began to weave, working in strands of ivy and gold stars, trying to let her instinct take hold. She and Josie worked together, occasionally humming along to the songs playing quietly on the radio.

Then, as Ivy started on a second crown, making it smaller with Liv in mind, Josie spoke softly. 'Funny, isn't it? How love shows up in ways you don't expect.'

Ivy glanced over, caught off guard. 'What do you mean?'

Josie eyed her own crown critically and then reached for some glitter. 'I thought I'd already had my great love, once. Years ago. Your mum would remember him – Peter. He was a teacher here in Fox Bay. We were going to see the world together. Quote Russian poetry to each other in Paris and Rome. And then he *died*. Can you get more tragically romantic than that?' She paused, eyes on the flickering candlelight. 'Afterwards, I didn't think I'd ever feel anything close to that again. I was content to find my romance in the great Russian novels, in long ago poets. Believe me, I wasn't even *looking*.'

Ivy stayed quiet.

'And then, last summer, love found *me*,' Josie continued. 'Someone who had been right under my nose all this time. Not at all what I thought a great romance would be. No drama, no grand declarations – well, maybe one,' she said, going pink. 'But he's so ordinary, I never expected it.'

'So Fin is the *second* great love of your life?' Ivy asked.

'I suppose he must be,' Josie said thoughtfully. 'I just didn't think the second great love of my life would wear fleeces and cargo trousers with zips.'

Ivy fiddled with a sprig of holly, unsure what to say. 'I thought I'd fall in love at college,' she said at last. 'I thought he'd be an artist like me. Moody and intense and serious . . . I even met someone I thought was perfect. But he turned out not to be, I guess.'

'Well, you and I are a little alike, dear,' said Josie. 'We're always going to hanker after a grand idea, a great, sweeping love affair. Artists like us . . .'

Ivy refrained from asking what kind of art Josie actually did.

'But you're happy with Fin, right?' she asked. 'Even though it's not super romantic?'

'Oh, I never said it wasn't romantic, darling! Fin is the most romantic man I have ever met. But his idea of romance is making my tea just how I like it or putting a hot water bottle in the bed before I get in because he knows I get cold feet at night.' Josie slipped the end of a branch and added a crown to the growing pile. 'I wonder if . . . maybe you don't always get the kind of love you think you want. But sometimes you get the love you need.'

Ivy smiled. Occasionally, Josie, for all her strangeness and flights of fancy, could be surprisingly wise and down-to-earth. 'The love you need. I like that.'

She thought of Trip, showing up full of good humour when

she had been at her lowest. Of him jumping in to save the show and the way Liv's face had shone with relief. Of him dragging her out of the darkened art room to experience Winter Wonderland. Unlike Raff, with his moods and reveries, Trip had kept showing up, endlessly cheerful, exactly when she needed him.

But if so, a little voice nagged, then why hadn't he texted?

'I don't know about me,' Ivy said, 'but you and Fin seem really happy, with your hot water bottles and tea.'

'We *are* happy, darling,' said Josie, starry-eyed in the warm light. 'And I'm so glad I found him *now*, not ten years ago. Back then I might have thought a love like this was dull, instead of seeing it for what it is. Utterly romantic.'

Ivy stepped back, considering the little stack of slightly wonky flower crowns. 'These will look brilliant in the firelight later,' she said.

'They will.' Josie picked a berry-laden crown off the pile and balanced it on top of her head. 'We might need a few more though, darling – can't have anyone feeling left out.'

Ivy looked at Josie, detangling a grey curl from a spiky branch and grabbed for her tote bag. 'Hold still a minute, will you?' she asked, taking out her sketchbook.

'Don't draw me for goodness' sake. I'm a mess,' protested Josie.

'You look great,' Ivy told her, pencil flying over the page. She swiftly captured Josie, cheeks as flushed as a child's, the wild tangle of foliage and hair, the striped pyjama bottoms and her bare feet, the glitter covering her hands. She tried to imbue the sketch with all that she could feel in the room – the warm glow from the candles, the strands of ivy and dried flowers, the sleepy, cosy, stillness of this dawn moment.

'There,' she said, picking up a crown that she'd attached tiny silver bells to, and dropping it on Ivy's head. 'A perfect fit. Now, let's do one for Fin.'

Once the pile of crowns starting wobbling precariously, Ivy brushed the glitter off the counter and they stood admiring their work.

'I think that's perfect now, darling,' Josie said. 'Just the right side of gloriously excessive.'

'I'm not sure,' Ivy said doubtfully. 'We could put on a few more of these berries?'

Josie shook her head vehemently. 'Part of great art is knowing when to stop,' she said firmly. 'And besides, I think we're due our breakfast now, don't you?'

Ivy helped herself to one of the buns and sat cross-legged on the worn armchair while Josie perched on the stool behind the till, eating yogurt out of a jar. For a little while, they didn't say much, just the flicker of candles and the quiet clink of spoon on glass between them.

'I suppose *I* could text *him*,' Ivy said at last. 'Trip, I mean.'

Josie smiled at her. 'I knew who you meant, darling,' she said. 'And why not?'

Ivy reached for her phone. She would just send a quick

message. Tell Trip she was looking forward to seeing him soon. It was nearly seven now, a perfectly socially acceptable time to text. She would sound breezy and casual.

She clicked on his Instagram first. If Trip was awake, she thought he might have posted something excitable – *final bacon sarnie in London*. But there was nothing – nothing, in fact, all week, since he had put up a picture of him and Brooke giving a thumbs up by the lighthouse, a photo that Ivy had taken. But then Ivy noticed he'd been tagged in a photo yesterday. She idly clicked on the post and nearly choked on the remains of her bun.

Blue sky behind the London Eye. Trip, smiling, arm slung round a startlingly beautiful girl with perfect white teeth, wide brown eyes and glossy black hair. Ivy clicked on the post and was taken to an Instagram page. Her name was Madison White. *Actor, activist and cat-lover*, read her bio. She and Trip, with their matching wide smiles and gorgeous, happy faces, looked undeniably, unbearably perfect together.

Ivy stared at the screen a moment too long before jabbing the lock button and shoving her phone quickly into her pocket.

'Did you text him?' asked Josie, looking up from her yogurt. 'Because you and Trip really did have—'

'Do *not* say we have chemistry,' Ivy snapped. 'We have nothing.'

'Oh,' said Josie, looking taken aback. 'Well, in that case—'

'And no, I didn't text him,' Ivy went on. 'Because honestly, I've realised it's been a bit of a relief having him gone. All that endless optimism and the good deeds . . . like, has he ever had a bad day in his life?'

'Well, I'm sure—'

'The answer is no, he hasn't. Because everything's easy for him. He swans around the world on some sort of never-ending gap year. Deciding which of the many colleges he might grace with his presence. With his perfect hair and his perfect teeth, rushing around Fox Bay like some sort of boy scout. No, actually, he's like a golden retriever, always under my feet. Well, he wouldn't be so cheerful if his life wasn't so charmed.'

Josie blinked. 'Darling, this all sounds a little—'

But Ivy barrelled on, all her hurt and confusion at Trip's radio silence and then the picture on Instagram pouring out as one long diatribe. 'And don't even get me started on his name. Trip. *Trip*. Who names their kid that? It's not a name. It's a hazard. It's what happens when you don't look where you're going and end up hurting yourself.'

'Ivy—'

'No, seriously. You can't trust anyone who sounds like an accident. I hope he and his fake sunshine stay far away in London—'

'*Ivy*—' Josie's tone was sharp.

'What?'

She followed Josie's gaze towards the doorway and froze.

Trip stood there in the open door, weekend bag slung over his shoulder, expression unreadable except for the slight tightening round his mouth and an unmistakable flicker of hurt in his eyes.

'Morning, guys,' he said politely.

There was a horrible extended silence.

'What are you doing here?' Ivy managed at last in a strangled voice. 'You're meant to be back this afternoon at the very earliest.'

'We thought we'd get a late train yesterday instead,' he said. 'But it broke down last night outside of Truro. We ended up staying the night in a Premier Inn and getting a taxi back first thing. Brooke's gone for coffee and I thought I'd come along here and see if anyone was up.' He hesitated. 'Anyway, I think I'll go up and shower. It was a long night.' He headed for the door to the stairs. 'See you guys.'

Then he walked out without another word.

Silence crashed over the room. Ivy sank her head into her hands, cheeks burning. 'Oh God,' she whispered. 'How much do you think he heard?'

'Er,' said Josie. 'Maybe not much.'

There was another long silence and then Ivy lifted her head. 'Do you think he hates me now?' she asked weakly.

'Of course not, darling,' Josie said stoutly. 'I don't think Trip is the hating type. And besides, you can always apologise, can't you?'

Ivy groaned. She had, yet again, made a huge mess of things.

After a long, miserable day in the shop, Ivy would have much preferred to avoid the Fox Bay pre-winter solstice bonfire in favour of going home to stare at the ceiling, fuming over Trip and Madison. But Josie had insisted on dragging her down to the beach, marching Ivy between her and Fin like a prisoner in a sparkly flower crown. 'I will simply not have you brooding, darling,' she had said firmly. 'My prescription for heartache is a cold winter night on the beach, a blazing fire and some good music to get the blood going.'

Fin had patted her arm. 'Josie might be right about this one,' he had said gently. 'Sometimes holing up and fretting doesn't do any good.'

Ivy had been too crushed to protest. She had been coming to this bonfire since she was five, when the tradition had started. It was just as she remembered it, the fire roaring in the centre of the sands, blooming bright and golden and sending up sparks that disappeared into the velvet sky. Lanterns bobbed on strings between lamp posts, casting a soft glow. It was as ramshackle and enchanting as Ivy remembered it.

The Seafoam Serenaders were already in full swing by the time they arrived, their fiddles whirling through sea shanties and jigs with cheerful abandon. Kids darted past with sparklers, scrawling neon shapes in the air, and Lou handed her a paper cup of mulled apple juice before she could protest. The scent of woodsmoke and winter spices hung thick in the air.

Everyone was there: her mum and Liv, Bethie and her mum Lydia, Simi and Lou, Old Bill and Kate, Mr Hargreaves. Even Ynez the postie was dancing near the chip van as Josie started distributing flower crowns to the crowd. And there too, of course, was Trip, nodding enthusiastically at Callum as he seemed to be explaining something. She turned away before he could catch her looking.

Erin appeared at her side with a cider. 'Ivy, we're all over here. Come and hang.'

Ivy gave her a weak smile. 'Maybe in a sec.'

Erin rolled her eyes. 'You don't need to be tortured the *whole* time, you know.' Her voice was slightly slurred. 'It's a party. You could loosen up, hang with us, dance . . .'

'I'm okay here for now.'

They stood in silence for a moment, watching the flames twist and crackle, before Erin nudged her gently.

'You know,' she said, 'I'm studying psychology at Bristol. And I aced my end-of-term exams.'

'Right, I know,' said Ivy, confused, and then remembered her own average marks. 'Good for you.'

'And if you'll allow me to psychoanalyse *you*, Ivy, I'd say that I think sometimes you're scared.'

Ivy stared. 'Scared? Me?'

'Sure. At school for instance. You barely spoke to us. Or to *anyone* except Raye and the art teachers. You always acted like everyone else was beneath your notice. We'd try – we'd ask you for coffee or study sessions or to go to the cinema – but you'd always make up some excuse and scuttle off. I remember asking you to my twelfth birthday. You told me, if I remember correctly, that you were *allergic to bowling*.'

'I think it's the varnish they use,' said Ivy weakly. 'It gives me a headache.'

'We couldn't work out if you were shy or grumpy or just hated us or what. But I figured it out the other day at Winter Wonderland. You're *scared*.'

Ivy glanced at the cup in Erin's hand. 'How much of that cider have you had?'

'You're scared of all of it,' said Erin, waving her cup expansively, sloshing some cider on to the sand. 'Life. People. Romance. The future. You keep this little buffer of sarcasm and cynicism around you like bubble wrap, and I have to say, it's very effective. Because no one dares get close.'

Ivy opened her mouth to protest, but Erin cut her off by holding up a mittened hand.

'I'm not judging you. I get it. It's easier to assume everything's going to disappoint you than risk opening up, being wrong and getting hurt. But, I don't know . . . it must be kind of lonely, right? Shutting people out.'

Ivy stared into her own cup, momentarily lost for words. There it was again. That word people kept using about her. *Lonely*. She took a sip of her drink. The juice had gone cold.

'I don't shut people out,' she said at last, in a small voice.

'You shut *us* out,' Erin said. 'At school, I mean. Me and Mei and Callum.'

'I . . .' Ivy's voice trailed off. 'All those times you asked me to do stuff, I thought you were just doing the right thing. I didn't think you really *wanted* me there,' she finished lamely.

'Why wouldn't we?' Erin said softly. 'You're cool. We like you.'

Ivy thought back over the last few years of school. All that time saying no. Her and Raye hiding out in the art room, making fun of the cool kids with the great hair and their denim shorts, their bowling parties and cinema trips. She had been so sure they were only tolerating her, when actually . . .

'You mean you properly wanted to be friends?' she asked. 'All this time?'

Erin slapped her forehead dramatically. 'Yes, Ivy. We properly wanted to be friends. All this time.' She sighed and downed her cider. 'Listen, I'm going to dance now, because sometimes people like to do that at parties. But think about it, Ivy. If you keep shutting people out, insisting they're acquaintances rather than friends, you'll end up with a pretty small world. And you know who *else* you've shut out, right?' She nodded meaningfully to the cluster of kids by the fire, where Trip was standing, head thrown back, laughing at something the others had said. Erin squeezed Ivy's arm. 'Come over and join us any time. And the pagan-crown look suits you, by the way.'

Erin headed over to the fire, slipping an arm round Mei's waist. As the music swelled and more people joined the dancing, Ivy felt herself drifting at the edge of it all – full of confused thoughts, too tired and sad to figure them out. She told her mum she had a headache and left before the final song, boots crunching over the frosty path as she made her way back through the dark.

From the beach, she thought she heard someone call her name, but she didn't turn back. She just needed to be home.

Chapter Seventeen

For the next couple of days, Ivy buried herself in work and the show. She put in long shifts at the shop, then headed to the school art room where she busied herself setting up displays and crafting props like her life depended on it. She finished a papier-mâché boat, finessed her hand-painted Arthurian castle and gave herself a migraine gluing feathers to angel wings for the carol section. Anything to stay busy. Anything to stay out of Trip's way. The hurt look in his eyes as he stood in the doorway of Wildest Dreams kept replaying itself in Ivy's head as she lay in bed at night. But so did the image of his arm round Madison.

Her desire to avoid him seemed to be mutual. Aside from two polite 'good mornings' and a 'good luck at rehearsal', she and Trip barely spoke. Not properly. She hardly even *saw* him, just a glimpse here and there – deep in conversation with Callum about the sound cues, a distant laugh in the rehearsal hall, chatting to the piano tuner, bussed in from Truro to try and persuade the piano into something approximating the right key. As the days passed, Ivy was no longer sure who was avoiding who. She learned to listen for footsteps on the old staircase, so she could vanish behind a stack of hardbacks or slip out to the stockroom the second she sensed his presence.

And yet, she couldn't really escape Trip because, everywhere she went, someone was talking about him. It was like the residents of Fox Bay were his biggest fan club.

'After seeing him sail, I'd trust him with my own boat,' Old Bill told her seriously, clapping a hand to the faded wood as Ivy went for a brisk walk along the beach one morning to clear her head. 'And look at this.' He held out his arm, sleeve rolled up, to display a nicotine patch. 'I've gone four days without my pipe,' he said proudly. 'The hypnosis podcast Trip sent me really works.'

'Can you tell Trip we need numbers for the food for the after-party?' Lou said, thrusting a piece of paper into Ivy's hand as she stopped by the Mariner's Arms to collect some old cardboard boxes to use as props. 'He can choose anything on here and I'll do him a special on the pizza.'

'He's such a sweet boy,' her own mum said outside the Co-op, fondly looking after Trip as he disappeared round the corner, whistling loudly. 'You should see him with the kids at rehearsals, Ivy. Livvie adores him and you know she's a tough nut to crack.'

Outside the corner grocer, Ivy nearly collided with Melissa, the town librarian, who was balancing two canvas bags full of what looked like books and packets of biscuits.

'Oh! Ivy. It's you,' Melissa said, slightly breathless. She had a bobble hat pulled down against the fierce wind over her crew cut. 'I was just thinking about you.'

'You were?'

'Well, not *just* you,' Melissa said, hoisting the bag higher. 'The whole lot of you. Mr Hargreaves, all of you wonderful young people, the children putting on the show. I can't thank you enough. Things have been pretty tight at the library. I can't do it all by myself, you know – it would mean the world to hire an assistant. But there's some good news – Trip helped me put in an extra funding grant application for additional staff. He made a very impassioned case about literacy funding. He said the show will only get us so far.'

'Oh,' said Ivy. 'Well, he's right about that.'

Melissa beamed. 'He's a good person. I work with books. I'm *excellent* at reading people.'

Ivy smiled and nodded, but her insides twisted every time someone said how kind or funny or sweet or helpful Trip was. She wasn't proud of what she'd said about him the other day and even less proud that she had accidentally said it all to his face. She hadn't even meant it, not really. She had just been lashing out because she'd felt foolish and exposed and humiliated. Like she had put herself out there for a change, allowed herself to believe in some good luck, and it had backfired.

All the same, she thought, he'd had no reason to look so hurt. *He* had been the one to stop texting *her*. Left *her* hanging.

And then he'd been all over Instagram, grinning like he was in *People* magazine, with that shiny-haired, beautiful girl. Madison. So how dare he look like a wounded puppy?

So why did she still feel so guilty?

On Thursday, with only two days to go until the show, Ivy had ducked out of the art room to decompress after gluing countless newspaper barnacles on to the boat hull, a thankless, sticky job. She was just taking some gulps of biting afternoon air when Brooke appeared, perfectly composed as always, wearing an expensive-looking puffer coat with a beige cashmere turtleneck underneath, and carrying a travel mug in one hand.

'Hey,' she said briskly. 'I was coming to find you. Trip said you'd be up here. Got a sec?'

Ivy tensed, feeling unaccountably nervous. 'Kind of in the middle of—'

'Because I'd still love to see that cove,' Brooke said. 'The one from the *Ocean Deep* launch party that was all over Insta? I've got an hour to kill and I can't find it on Google Maps.'

'You won't find it on Google Maps,' said Ivy. 'It's hidden. Although it's kind of an open secret to everyone around here.'

'Cool. Another Fox Bay secret.' Brooke bounced on her feet in a way that reminded Ivy of Trip. 'Shall we go then?'

Ivy stared at her. 'Wait. You mean, now?'

'Sure. That is if I can tear you away from the play prep.' She glanced at Ivy's paint-stained hands. 'I'd really appreciate it.'

Her expression was neutral, but again Ivy couldn't quite read what was underneath. Still, curiosity won. 'Fine,' she said. 'I need a break anyway. My car's just down here.'

Brooke took a seat in the battered Fiat, gingerly moving the crisp packets and rolls of canvas aside so she could sit down. She buckled herself in, then sneezed several times in rapid succession.

'Would you mind if I open the window for some air?' she asked politely as Ivy pulled out. She began to pick fluff off her coat. 'Only I think I'm allergic to . . . something in here.'

'It's quite old,' said Ivy apologetically. 'We think the previous owner was a smoker because the seats have always smelled a bit weird. Um—' she went on, as Brooke's window stubbornly refused to budge despite her efforts. 'You have to sort of hit it with your elbow . . .'

'You know what, it doesn't matter,' said Brooke. She opened her shoulder bag and drew out a clear plastic pouch full of various pills and vitamins. 'I'll just take an antihistamine.'

The drive to the cove was quiet, the kind of silence that wasn't entirely comfortable. Ivy kept her eyes on the road while Brooke watched the sea as they curved round the bay, her legs crossed, perfectly still.

The car lurched down the lane and up on to the verge in the unofficial parking space that Ivy knew so well. When she was little and the main beach was busy, her mum would say they could visit the secret cove and take a picnic and swim. The cove was usually deserted, with only the occasional visitor. Even after

Wildest Dreams had thrown a seriously aesthetic book launch for *Ocean Deep* here, and it had become semi-famous with booktokers and travel instagrammers, its whereabouts seemed to have remained secret. As far as Ivy knew, no tourists had discovered it.

'I haven't been here for ages,' said Ivy, turning off the ignition and still struggling to make conversation. 'I hope it's worth seeing.'

'I'm sure it is,' said Brooke, shoving the door open with difficulty and stepping outside, her hiking shoes sinking into the sand. 'Down here?'

The cove was tucked into the coastline, hidden by cliffs on either side, the path so narrow and overgrown that walking down here almost felt like trespassing. Brooke and Ivy half walked, half skidded their way down until they emerged into the little clearing. The sea here was always quieter than anywhere else along the coast, curtailed by a crescent of white sand. The wind was hushed by the shelter of the cliffs and an old boat sat half-buried at one end of the beach, blue paint worn and faded, its name illegible. Over the years, local children had turned it into a pirate ship to play on or a fairy castle. Last summer, it had apparently become a makeshift bookshop for the *Ocean Deep* launch party, strung with fairy lights and bunting.

Ivy found herself drawing a long breath as the memories came flooding back to her. Memories of scampering over this sand as a child, bucket and spade in hand. Her college deadline, her insecurities, the hurt look in Trip's eyes – it all melted away. Ivy closed her eyes and took herself back to a time when all she'd had to worry about was whether she would be allowed an ice cream before dinner.

When she opened them again, she saw that Brooke had whipped out her phone and was taking a series of rapid photos in the grey afternoon light. She scrolled through before nodding, satisfied. 'Incredible,' she said, almost to herself. 'This is *perfect*.'

Ivy, meanwhile, was turning in a slow circle around the cove. She had known this quiet beach her whole life, yet, as with her trip to the lighthouse the other morning, she felt like she was seeing it afresh. The new and familiar combining. She thought of Trip's words. *'Sometimes a break from a place isn't a bad thing. You come back, you see it differently.'*

'It's so peaceful,' remarked Brooke. 'Even the birds are quiet. I could use a place like this from time to time.' She glanced at Ivy and drew a deep breath. 'Listen, Ivy,' she said decisively. 'I've got to admit to an ulterior motive in getting you to drive me here today. I wanted to talk to you. About Trip.'

Oh God, Ivy thought, panicking. Had Trip told his sister all the mean things she'd said? Was Brooke going to tell her off? 'You really don't have to—'

'No, I think I do,' said Brooke, lifting her chin. 'I wanted to clear something up. You seem to think he's had this charmed life, right? Idyllic, all-American childhood. Sailing lessons. Theatre camp. Trips to New York. A choice of any college, travelling round the world . . .'

'Well, when you put it like that, it does sound pretty great,' said Ivy, smiling nervously.

Brooke didn't smile back. She walked towards the edge of the water, hugging herself against the soft breeze. Then, without looking back, she said, 'Trip's life hasn't been all sunshine, you know. Our parents were never around. We get along fine, but they were always too busy working or socialising to spend that much time with us. Poor little rich kids, right? So we spent all our time with our gran in Santa Cruz. Gran was *amazing*. Like, the definitive hippie, super cheerful and chilled and up for anything – she was like Trip and our mom in that way. A real "yes" person.' Brooke smiled fondly. 'Josie reminds me of her too, in fact. She had an incredible old house and her neighbours along the beach all shared a sailboat and she had loads of bohemian friends who would have us to stay. Art shows, trips to NYC. She was all about *silver linings* and *glass-half-full*. She always thought things would work out for the best. I never once saw her sad. If she was, she never let us see it.'

'She sounds great,' said Ivy. 'I can see where Trip gets his optimism from.'

'Yeah, Trip . . . he was this sunny little boy who always saw the best in people. Never really talked about our parents.' Brooke sighed. 'So, I had to be the realist. When our grandma got sick a few years back, I was the one who had to break it to Trip that she wasn't going to get better. And then this spring, when she died . . . We knew it was coming, but still. It hit us both hard – and as usual Trip wouldn't talk about it. Our parents offered to pay someone to clear out her house but Trip and I didn't want that. So we spent months going through everything.'

She gave a shaky laugh. 'Which, when you're dealing with the estate of an eighty-four-year-old hippie activist with hoarding tendencies, is intense. We were pretty exhausted. It's part of the reason we decided to do this trip. We both needed a break.'

Ivy let out a breath. She'd had no idea that behind Trip's cheerful façade lay this recent sadness. 'I'm sorry,' she said quietly. 'That must have been really hard. I just assumed—'

Brooke turned to face her. Her expression was open and for a moment she looked like her brother.

'I'm not blaming you, Ivy. I know how it seems. And Trip would never share a sob story. I wish he *would*, I think it would do him a lot of good – but he's perennially allergic to anything sad. I'm only trying to give you the whole picture, because . . . well, because I think he really likes you.'

Ivy felt a mix of emotions. Guilt, that she had so quickly dismissed Trip as a spoiled rich kid with no idea what the real world was like. Embarrassment, that she'd subjected him to an unfair character assassination just because she felt insecure. And sympathy, that he had spent the year grieving.

'Trip's all in, you know,' Brooke said slowly. 'That's what he's always been like, even as a kid. He doesn't stop to think too hard – he goes with his gut. When he commits to something, he *commits*. You've seen him at the rehearsals. Full steam ahead. It wouldn't occur to him to be careful. That he might get hurt.'

They stood side by side for a moment, the wind tugging at their coats and the sea lapping against the pebbles. The cove, with the grey skies and lowering clouds, was suddenly very quiet and the silence felt loaded. Ivy was the one to break it. 'You think I'm going to hurt Trip?' she said at last.

'I think he's too nice for his own good,' Brooke said. She pushed a strand of her hair behind her ear. 'Luckily, he also seems to have an instinct for decent people. I'm not blind. I can tell there's something going on between you two. I knew right away that Trip was smitten. But I want him to focus on his future. You don't seem in a super-happy place and you also live across the world from Trip. I don't want him distracted or upset more than he has been already.'

The words hung in the air. Ivy's chest felt tight. Brooke thought she would upset Trip.

'I'm not trying to be a villain here,' Brooke said. 'But I need to look out for my little brother, you know?'

'I get it,' said Ivy tightly. 'Besides, you've got it wrong. Trip likes someone else. This girl Madison.'

Brooke frowned, looking confused. '*Madison?* Oh.' She gave a faint smile. 'Trust me, Ivy – that's not what you think.'

Before Ivy could ask her what she meant, Brooke was heading back up the beach, striding against the wind. 'Shall we get back?' she called as she went. 'Fin promised me scones for tea.'

Chapter Eighteen

Ivy sat on the bench outside the Driftwood Café the next morning, the cold from the wood seeping into her jeans and through to her thermal leggings. After all the activity and chaos of the past few weeks, the show was tomorrow. And she couldn't stop replaying the conversation between her and Brooke in the cove. It had left her feeling hollow and frustrated, like she had been unfair to Trip and now had no way of making it right.

She sighed and pulled out her phone. Raye answered on the second ring. 'If you're calling to ask me again if I'm coming to the show, I've already told you I will do my absolute—'

Ivy huffed a breath, somewhere between a laugh and a groan. 'I think I've blown it.'

A pause. Then, sounding mystified, Raye said, 'Blown what?'

'Blown *it*. With Trip.'

There was a beat of complete silence. Then Raye said, '*Wait*. Trip. The super cheerful guy who is driving you crazy? I'm sorry, you *like* him?'

Ivy rolled her eyes towards the grey sky. 'Yes. Yes, I really do.' Saying those words aloud was partly a relief and partly terrifying.

'But you said how annoying he was.'

'Yeah.'

'You sent me that text saying he was like a golden retriever, in a bad way.'

'Yes!'

'And now you *like* him? When did this happen?'

'I don't *know*, Raye!' Ivy groaned. 'I just – he makes things feel better. Happier. He makes me feel like the world isn't all doom and gloom.'

'Well, you could certainly use someone like that in your life,' Raye said, considering.

'But then I said something mean about him because I was in a bad mood—'

'You, in a bad mood?' broke in Raye. 'I don't believe it.'

'—and he overheard me. And now he's pulled back and maybe he thinks I don't like him because of all the horrible things I said, and I *do*. I'm a complete idiot. Anything good, I always mess it up.'

There was a rustle of movement on Raye's end of the line, probably as she flopped on to a pile of cushions or a coat she never hung up. 'Okay. First of all, you're *not* an idiot. You're just you. And you and feelings, Ivy . . . well, sometimes you don't mix. It's no wonder you didn't realise you liked this guy. For someone so clever, you're pretty bad at seeing the blindingly obvious.'

Ivy made a small noise of protest but didn't disagree.

Raye continued. 'Second of all, you haven't blown anything. You're still doing the show together, right?'

'Yeah,' said Ivy, fiddling miserably with her boot lace.

'Well, why don't you bite the bullet and say sorry? Tell Trip how you feel, take a chance for once and put yourself out there? And then you can make up before the show. Which, by the way, I am going to try to make. Cleo has her ballet recital in London tomorrow, but we're hoping to leave straight after.'

'Really?' said Ivy hopefully. Suddenly she wanted to see Raye – who seemed to have transformed from manic pixie dream girl to wise woman of the world in the space of a few months – more than anything.

'I wanted to see the show anyway – you know, I have never missed a single one, not since Mr H got the drama bug in Year Two. But now I have an added incentive. I need to see how this *romance plays out.*'

Ivy pressed the phone tighter to her ear, the lump in her throat surprising her. 'I want to tell Trip I'm sorry,' she whispered. 'And I want to show him how I feel. But . . . I'm scared.'

There was quiet on the other end of the line for a moment. Then Raye added, more softly now, 'Oh, Ivy. You can let people in, you know? Let some cracks in the façade show. You might find that people will surprise you. They're not *guaranteed* to let you down.' She laughed. 'Or so I'm discovering, anyway.'

Ivy closed her eyes. 'Okay.'

'Okay,' Raye echoed. 'Now I've got to go and finish packing. But try and be brave. You've got it in you, Ivy Pearson, I know you do.'

The atmosphere in the hall when Ivy arrived for the prep session that afternoon could best be described as the sort of controlled chaos Jackson Pollock might have been aiming for. There was order in there somewhere, Ivy thought, she just wasn't sure where.

Josie had shut the shop early so they could both help. Children tore up and down the corridor outside the main hall, trailing ribbon and shrieking. The pixies had lost their tights. Sweyn Forkbeard had lost his helmet. One of Ivy's carefully constructed barrels of whisky for the *Jamaica Inn* scene had been crushed after a Year 5 boy insisted he could barrel dance on it. King Doniert's Stone, which Ivy had spent weeks stippling so it mimicked actual rock, had somehow gone missing and was eventually found in the toilet. The photo montage of the St Ives artists' movement had permanently snagged on a slide of Barbara Hepworth.

There was, however, something warm and thrilling about the chaos. Ivy couldn't resist taking a late-afternoon break, perched on a stepladder with her sketchbook, capturing vignettes until her tea went cold: Josie pinning costumes, Mr Hargreaves sitting on the stage breathing into a paper bag, Callum humming the notes for his self-penned ballad, *The Mermaid of Lamorna*, the children doggedly performing their lines, The Mariner's Arms' dog breaking in and savaging a cushion, sending feathers flying.

Ivy was in the middle of drawing Merlin's concentrated little face as he mouthed his lines when she realised that someone had paused just behind her. She glanced up, her hand flying out instinctively to cover the page.

'Sorry,' Trip said, 'I couldn't help noticing. They're really good.'

'They're just scrappy little sketches,' Ivy said, flushing.

'Well, I like them,' he said. There was a pause. *Be brave, Ivy*, she thought. This was the perfect moment to apologise and tell him how she really felt. Even if it was glossy Madison he liked, she could at least be honest with him.

'Trip,' Ivy said, trying to keep her voice from shaking. 'Can I—'

Just then Mei ran over. 'Trip, can you look at the sound cues for the Jamaica Inn sequence?' she said. 'I think Cal's been a bit ambitious on the storm front. He wants thunder, lightning waves *and* gunshots – no one will be able to hear the kids.'

'Sure,' said Trip, allowing himself to be tugged away with an apologetic smile. 'Speak later, Ivy.'

Ivy sighed and watched him go. It had been a mistake to try and talk to him before the show. Trip was, of course, the one holding all the chaos together. Calling out suggestions, ushering children off and on the stage, taking the dog back to the pub, encouraging the performers, reminding them of their cues. Calling Fin to repair a leaky pipe, Ted to move chairs, Lou to set out trays of glasses for the interval and collecting the programmes Kate had printed for them at the surf shop. His good humour never faltered, even when Mr Trenwith announced dramatically that one of the twins had gone AWOL.

By the time early evening hit, they had managed one full dress rehearsal, complete with thunder and lightning and the fog machine on full blast. There were hiccups – Sweyn walked off the stage the wrong way, smack into one of the lobsters – but, all in all, it was a success. The rogue twin even returned with a bag of Haribo in time to finish his epilogue.

Then, when darkness had fallen and the children had been collected by their parents, chattering off into the evening, when the chairs were set in neat rows and the props carefully labelled and collated backstage, when Ivy had glued and patched everything together and begun to hope that they would, in fact, open tomorrow . . . disaster struck.

'Um,' said Fin, appearing in the doorway of the hall, a worried look on his face. 'Ivy, I was just fixing the pipe in that back room and . . . was this important?'

With a sinking heart, Ivy followed him into the back room and groaned. One of the key set pieces of the Historical Cornwall section involved the Legend of Tom Bawcock and his loyal cat, Mouser; the tale of a man who had braved a terrifying storm to bring back fish and feed his starving townsfolk. The reveal would be a huge net of origami fish, which were to be released on to her recreation of the famous harbour to – Ivy had hoped – great applause. Ivy had spent hours painstakingly folding the paper fish, in silver, gold, pink, grey and brown, along with most of Year 4. She had stored them carefully under the backroom table – right under the vigorously leaking pipe, it turned out. They were now, Ivy realised, a soggy, waterlogged mess.

'Oh no,' whispered Ivy, pulling out a handful of wet paper and squelching it in her fist.

Fin grimaced. 'Unsalvageable, I take it?'

'Unless the starving townsfolk of Mousehole are going to feast on a pile of mush, I'm going to need to do this again,' Ivy said.

'Ivy, we'll all help,' said Josie, squeezing into the room behind Fin. 'I can round up Simi and the others and we can have a marathon folding session together—'

'It's okay,' Ivy said. Yet another thing she'd managed to mess up — she couldn't even look after a stupid box of paper fish. 'I'll sort it. Liv and Bethie will be bouncing around at home having a pre-show sleepover. I could use some peace and quiet. I'll do it back at the shop, if that's okay, Josie?'

'Just call if you need reinforcements,' Josie told her. Fin squeezed her arm, handed her a box of biscuits, and made her promise not to work too late.

Ivy went first to the art room at the school, where she packed up fresh paper, folding instructions and a Thermos of tea and then escaped, laden with her supplies, to the closed bookshop. She couldn't help breathing a sigh of relief when she went inside — after the chaos of today, the place was still and, as always, faintly cinnamon-scented.

Ivy spread out her supplies on the counter, cracked open her tea, and began work. The fairy lights cast a soft glow across the shelves, and for the first time that day, she felt herself relax, sinking into the paper-folding rhythm. She didn't have enough of the original colours and decided that these fish would have to be of the more exotic sort than those usually found in a Cornish sea — lime green, purple and fuchsia pink.

She'd barely folded six fish, though, when the bell over the door jangled. She looked up, startled.

Trip stood there, wind-tousled and flushed from the cold, holding two steaming paper parcels with 'Cod Almighty' emblazoned on them.

'Hey. I thought you could use some fish,' he said. 'And chips. But mostly fish.' He winced. 'Sorry, that's a bad joke. I brought fish because you're folding fish and . . .'

Ivy let out a laugh. 'Got it. That's a *terrible* joke. But, thank you,' she added shyly. 'I'm actually starving.'

'Me too.' He held out one of the bags. 'Take a break?'

They sat in a fort made of beanbags and cushions in the kids' section, legs crossed, paper crinkling between them. They ate in comfortable silence and Ivy couldn't help wondering whether she had imagined the awkwardness of the past few days. It felt as easy as always between them – or almost. The warm light of the shop made everything look cosy – the stacks of books, the painted backdrops stacked against the walls that Ivy would take to the town hall in the morning, Josie's array of crystals and the glinting bottles left over from last summer, when everything had changed for Fox Bay.

'How are you feeling about tomorrow?' Ivy asked at last. 'Your big UK directorial debut.'

'I'm nervous for all the kids,' Trip said. 'They're so excited. I really hope they nail it. But *I'm* excited too. When I started this, I thought it would be fun . . .'

'You thought putting on a show in a draughty town hall with a collection of Cornwall's biggest divas – and I'm not talking about the kids – would be *fun*?'

'Yeah, I did. But I hadn't realised *how much* fun.' Trip turned to her, eyes crinkling. 'Is that lame?'

'No,' Ivy said, flushing under his gaze. She turned back to her food, rooting around for a big chip. 'I don't think that's lame.' She meant it, she realised. Trip's enthusiasm for the Fox Bay show, his friendliness and kindness to everyone, his willingness to throw himself into the least likely projects – even his concern for Old Bill's health – were all what made him so special.

They fell silent again, the distant sound of the waves barely audible through the shop walls. Ivy recalled Raye's advice. *Be brave.* Which meant addressing the elephant in the room.

'Listen,' said Ivy, clearing her throat. 'About the other day . . . what I said when you got back from London. I'm sorry. You weren't meant to hear all that and I didn't even mean it. But I still shouldn't have said it.'

'It's okay,' Trip said, staring at his chips, 'you don't need to apologise. I know I can get carried away. And talk a lot and be annoying. Brooke's always telling me to chill out. It's fine.'

'No, it's not. I was being mean, and childish, and—' Ivy took a deep breath. *Be brave, be brave, be brave.* 'Well, honestly, I was kind of jealous.'

Trip looked up sharply. 'Jealous?'

Ivy gave a half-laugh. She was embarrassed but determined

to plough on now she had started. 'Yeah, I mean one minute we were texting loads and making jokes and then . . . suddenly it stopped. I knew you were busy but . . . well, then I saw a picture on Instagram.' She risked a quick glance at him and saw he was looking utterly confused. 'It was of you and a girl,' she went on. 'An incredibly pretty girl. Her hair was all . . .' Ivy flapped her hand, 'all shiny.'

There was another beat, in which Trip looked even more bewildered. Then his expression cleared. His eyes widened in realisation. His mouth opened slightly, then closed again.

'Oh,' he said at last. 'Right. *That* incredibly pretty girl.'

Ivy hurried on. 'I know you don't owe me any explanation—'

'The thing is . . .' Trip rubbed the back of his neck, 'the thing is, Ivy, I wasn't telling you the whole truth about why Brooke and I went to London.'

'You weren't?' said Ivy, startled. That wasn't what she had been expecting Trip to say at all.

'Yeah. We didn't go there for sightseeing, you see. I mean, we saw some stuff, but we went for another reason – something I can't tell you about yet.'

'You . . . can't tell me why you went to London?' asked Ivy, now feeling increasingly bewildered herself.

'No. I promised I wouldn't.' He looked sheepish. 'But I *can* tell you that I wasn't avoiding you.'

'Wait,' said Ivy. 'You're telling me that you and Brooke were doing something *top secret* in London?' Maybe Brooke really *was* a spy, she thought. 'With that incredibly pretty girl? Come on, Trip. You can just say if you have a girlfriend, rather than make up some—'

'I don't have a girlfriend!' said Trip. 'Me and that girl—'

'That incredibly pretty girl,' Ivy reminded him.

'Right, me and that incredibly pretty girl only hung out for an hour or so and it definitely wasn't whatever you were thinking it was.' There was a flush on Trip's cheekbones. Quietly, he added, 'If I could've spent that whole weekend talking to *anyone*, Ivy, it would've been you.'

A beat passed.

Then Ivy's shoulders relaxed a little. 'Really?'

Their eyes met. 'Really,' Trip said.

Ivy found herself grinning, a huge grin that hurt her cheeks. Trip would rather have been talking to her than that girl, and suddenly that was all she needed to hear. And okay, the secrecy around the trip to London was pretty weird – but he seemed genuine and besides, he *had* brought her fish and chips . . .

'Okay,' she said, feeling like a weight had been lifted off her chest. 'I guess I'll find out what you were doing in London one day, right?'

'Yeah,' he said, nodding vigorously. 'Definitely. One day really soon. And you'll like it. I think.' He shook his head. 'I'm not great at keeping secrets,' he admitted ruefully.

'That is not a surprise.' Ivy dunked a chip in her ketchup and glanced around at the stacks of origami paper, the piles of cardboard. 'I forgot how much fun this can be,' she said suddenly.

'This?'

'Yeah. This last-minute, putting-on-a-show stuff. All the rushing and the mess and the weird creative decisions that don't make any sense until suddenly they *do*. It reminds me of my A-level art show. It reminds me why I loved it so much. Especially when stuff doesn't go to plan. You end up with something even more spectacular.' She giggled. 'Like acid-green fish.'

Trip smiled. 'Don't tell me the Fox Bay show has inspired you artistically?'

Ivy didn't answer for a moment, then nodded slowly. 'Maybe.' She thought of her sketchbook of hasty drawings and wondered.

For a moment, the two of them just sat there, legs touching slightly, fingers salty, surrounded by greasy paper and cold chips. Trip leaned his head back against a beanbag. 'Oh, man. Tomorrow's going to be completely ridiculous, isn't it?'

'Completely,' Ivy said. She groaned and wiped her hands on a napkin. 'Speaking of which, I had better get back to these fish. It's going to take all night.' She flexed her fingers. 'Time to get folding.'

'I can help, if you want,' he said.

She glanced at him. 'Was origami one of your Boy Scouts' badges?'

'I have literally no idea how to fold an origami fish. But I learn fast.' He stood and held out his hand. 'Come on.'

And so, perched at the counter on stools, they folded to the sound of a George Michael marathon on the radio. Slowly, awkwardly at first, then with growing rhythm. Coloured paper piled between them, Trip's hands working steadily. Ivy kept sneaking glances at his face, soft in the low light, intent on his work.

The hours passed. They made jokes about tomorrow's show and took bets on which of the twins would forget their lines first and whether the lightning blast that heralded King Arthur's entrance would ever land on cue and if they should put a warning at the start in case of nervous dogs.

At last, as the hands on Josie's ancient clock turned two in the morning (which actually meant it was twenty past), Ivy reverently laid down her last fish.

'Done,' she whispered, cradling one exhausted hand in the other. 'Three-hundred-and-fifty paper fish.'

Trip laughed and pushed back his hair. 'Phew. I'm going to see these fish in my dreams later.' He clambered off his stool. 'I'm going to pack them up. In a *waterproof* box.'

When the fish were safely sealed up and by the front door ready to go in the morning, Ivy and Trip looked at each other.

'Can I walk you to your car?' he asked.

'I left it back at the town hall,' Ivy realised.

'We could walk along the beach at this time, right?'

'At two-thirty in the morning? Sure, why not?'

Fox Bay was asleep, so they talked in hushed whispers until they reached the beach. The tide was out, and the sand stretched pale-grey under the sky. The moon cast silver light on the ripples of the sea. They could see harbour lights twinkling alongside the stars.

Trip and Ivy walked side by side, shoes in hand, toes curling into the cold sand. Her coat flapped lightly in the sea breeze.

'Ivy,' he said, 'what you said the other day. Do you really think I'm like a – a golden retriever?'

Ivy groaned, pressing her mittened hands to her face. 'Oh my *God. No.* Trip, I really am so sorry—'

'It's okay.' Trip bit his lip. 'Like I said, I'm too enthusiastic. It's a problem. I need to learn to be a bit cooler.'

'It's *not* a problem,' said Ivy, through a lump in her throat. 'It's a *good* thing to be enthusiastic and cheerful and nice to everyone you meet, even when they don't deserve it like Mr Trenwith.' *And me*, she thought. 'You don't want to be a massive pessimist like – well, like me. I can't even make it through a term of art school without having a crisis and thinking about quitting.'

'I don't think you're a pessimist,' he said. 'Not really. A pessimist wouldn't have believed they could make three-hundred-and-fifty rainbow-coloured fish for a kids' show in the space of a few hours.' He drew a deep breath. 'Look, what you were saying – that I'm on this endless holiday, doing whatever I want, swanning all over Europe – the thing is . . .'

'I know, Brooke told me,' said Ivy, jumping in. 'About losing your gran and why she was so special to you. I'm really sorry about that too. I should have asked you more questions, instead of jumping to the conclusion you were just some spoiled rich kid. To be honest, it says a lot more about me than you. I was mega resentful.'

They walked on in silence for a moment, the sea breeze whipping their hair about. 'When Gran died—' Trip said, then broke off. 'It still feels weird to say that, you know? Like she's about to show up any second and tell me off for thinking she's gone. Tell me not to be silly. It feels *impossible* that someone that loud and cheerful and stubborn isn't here.'

'She sounds awesome,' Ivy said tentatively.

'She is – was – my favourite person. Always laughing. Loads of friends who adored her. She saw the beauty in everyday things – a fresh peach, a fat peony, a good meal. I don't think I ever heard her say, "not now" or "maybe later". There were no rules or bedtimes or homework when we stayed with her, not if there was something more fun to be doing. She used to say, "You can have a lifetime of adventures, just by saying yes."' He laughed. 'Which I loved, of course. Brooke . . . I don't know. I think it stressed her out a bit. She had to be the sensible one.'

Ivy didn't say anything, just walked alongside, listening.

'Gran came to Cornwall once,' Trip continued, 'when she was a kid. She spent Christmas here and it snowed on the beach. She said it was magic – *impossible magic*. She never forgot it. She was talking about it when she was in the hospice. And I know it sounds silly, but I wanted to come here and see it too. Snow on the beach.' He rubbed the back of his neck. 'So, when Brooke suggested we finish up our trip in Fox Bay, it seemed . . . fate. I guess this year has been me trying to do what Gran did. Say yes. Find magic.' He grinned wryly. 'Even if it's directing the Fox Bay show. Like I said, silly.'

'That's not silly,' Ivy said. 'Saying yes, finding magic. It's . . . kind of amazing.'

Trip shrugged. 'You said it never snows in Fox Bay, though. So it sounds like it was a waste of time anyway.'

'But it wasn't a complete waste of time, was it?' Ivy asked in a small voice. When he didn't reply, she hurried on. 'I mean, you did the show. Taught Old Bill yoga and helped him to stop smoking. Helped Melissa get a grant for the library.'

Trip laughed. 'How could I forget Old Bill's yoga? You're right. It *wasn't* a waste of time.' He glanced at her and his expression grew serious. 'Not at all.'

'Well, that's good to know,' said Ivy.

'She'd have liked you, I think,' Trip said. 'Gran, I mean. You'd have gotten along.'

'Really?' said Ivy. 'Because you make her sound like human sunshine. And I'm . . . what? Human cloud cover? Mild drizzle? A bit overcast?'

'She was good at reading people. Saw through all their defences to what they're really like. Kind, funny, clever.' He flushed. 'For instance.'

'You don't think she'd tell you to run a mile from the moody artist with a chip on her shoulder?' Ivy asked, thinking of Brooke's words at the cove. *I need to look out for my little brother, okay?*

'I think,' said Trip quietly, 'you're exactly the kind of person she'd tell me to keep close.'

There was a silence in which Ivy could hear her heart thudding.

'I meant what I said earlier, by the way,' said Trip. 'Your drawings are really good. And what you've done with the set is unreal. So don't give up on the art just yet, will you?'

'Okay,' said Ivy. She stopped and stuck out her hand. 'If you don't give up on that snow.'

He laughed and shook it. 'Deal.'

This time, he didn't keep her hand in his, but the silence felt different now – easier and lighter. They turned down a street and reached Ivy's car. She hesitated, not quite wanting the night to end, but Trip was already jamming his hands into his pockets and turning to go. 'See you tomorrow,' he said. 'Ready for action. Don't forget the fish.'

'See you tomorrow,' Ivy said. 'Goodnight, Trip.'

When she reached the flat, she tiptoed into her bedroom, where she could hear the quiet, even breathing of two exhausted eight-year-olds, squished into Liv's single bed. She leaned against the door for a second, thinking about her and Trip and their conversation in the dark. She understood Trip better now, she thought – the boy who wanted to say yes to everything. Who wanted to see snow on the beach, find impossible magic. Who saw her, not as moody and difficult, but as a good person having a tough time. Who believed in her.

So don't give up on the art just yet, will you?

An idea had formed in her head on the drive home, and now she felt sure it was the right thing to do. Ivy went to her desk and, quietly so as not to disturb the girls, she opened her laptop. She sat down, took a deep breath, started a fresh email, and began to write. It took her another hour to draft what she wanted to send and review the attachments. Then, when her eyes were swimming with tiredness, she stood and stretched. She'd check that over in the morning.

She brushed her teeth, tugged off her jeans and rolled into bed. She was beyond exhausted. Still, even as sleep reached out for her, she couldn't help thinking of Trip's expression as they had walked along the moonlit beach – eager, a little shy as he had talked about his grandma. That serious look on his face. *Snow on the beach. Impossible magic.*

Ivy knew she had to be realistic about this. Brooke had made it very clear – there was no future for her and Trip. He would leave soon, go to college in the States, and Ivy would stay here in Cornwall. They were polar opposites. All the same, Ivy thought of his grandmother and their shared dream. If only she could do something for Trip before he left to make that dream real.

Ivy drifted off, wondering if there might be some way . . .

Chapter Nineteen

As Ivy woke on Saturday morning, the day of the show, she was struck by a bolt of inspiration. She sat up so fast the covers tangled round her legs. There it was, unfolding before her: a way to make Trip's dream come true. In a manner of speaking, at least.

To make it happen, though, she had some work to do. She jumped in the shower and threw on the first outfit she could find. Then she forced herself to sit at the desk and read through the email she had drafted last night. Was she really going to do this? *Yes*, she decided. She was. She was going to be brave.

Taking a deep breath, she pressed *send*.

She rushed to the front door, snatching a piece of toast from Liv's plate on her way past the kitchen.

'I'll see you at the show, love!' her mum called, and Ivy mumbled a reply through a mouthful of toast. There was no time to waste – she had a plan for today, and it started at the shop.

After parking up, Ivy let herself into the shop, grabbed the box of paper fish and headed into the back room to look for her satchel of paints. She turned to go, then paused.

She could hear something. Voices. Something about the tone made her edge to the bottom of the stairs and listen.

'You can't keep putting this off, Trip.' It was Brooke. Underneath her even tones, Ivy definitely caught a note of worry. 'The buyer's ready. We might not get another opportunity like this. The house is just sitting there, gradually falling apart, I might add. One day that money could help you do something great.'

'But why rush it?' came Trip's voice. His voice sounded so strained and quiet, Ivy almost didn't recognise it as his. 'I don't see why we need to make a decision *now*. That place meant so much to Gran. To us—'

'Do you think I don't know that?' Brooke snapped, her patience clearly fraying. 'We had an amazing childhood there. But now we need to move on.'

'I'm just – not ready.' There was a crack in Trip's voice that caught at Ivy's heart. 'It's only been a few months. Can't we wait till next year?'

There was a pause, then Brooke spoke again, her voice gentle now. 'No. What would be the point? We've put this off for long enough. I need you to be serious, Trip. We have to do this. You have to let it go or else I don't think you'll ever make a decision about the future. Gran wouldn't want you to put your life on hold. There's so much you could be doing. Go to college. Have adventures. *That's* what she would have wanted and you know it.'

A heavy silence followed.

'It's time, Trip,' Brooke added softly. 'It's time to let her go.'

Ivy belatedly realised she was eavesdropping on a highly personal conversation, holding her breath so as not to miss a single word. She took a step back, accidentally knocking a mug off a shelf as she did so. *A Tale of Two Kitties*. It clattered loudly to the floor and she ducked into the kitchen.

She heard the sudden creak of the stairs, a door shutting and then nothing. When Ivy emerged a few minutes later, clutching the pieces of broken mug, there was silence.

Having swept up and thrown away the broken mug, Ivy headed out of the shop into the street, colliding with Josie in the door.

'Ivy, goodness – where's the fire?' said Josie, laughing.

'I need the morning off,' Ivy said, without preamble. 'Please, Josie, it's something I have to do for Trip.' She bit her lip. 'Maybe it's silly, but all the same I want to—'

'Enough,' said Josie, holding up her hand. 'I can see in your eyes it's important. Take all the time you need, darling. I'll see you when I see you.'

'Thanks,' said Ivy, whisking out of the door. 'I'll be at the town hall. But don't tell Trip!'

Even though the show was hours away, the hall was already in a frenzy. Ivy grabbed a handful of kids to help guard the door of one of the back rooms, then set herself up to work, with chairs piled against the door for security, until she was happy with her surprise. Now she just had to get it out and hidden safely without Trip seeing.

Ivy smuggled her secret project into the prop room and made

sure everything was ready. She emerged, delighted that she'd managed to keep it hidden – only to discover that Trip wasn't even there to hide it from.

In fact, Ivy couldn't see him anywhere.

She was immediately put to work by Mei, headpiece secured and in her element. There were children to shepherd, mermaid tails to arrange, lines to run, anxious adults to soothe. Mr Hargreaves was a blur of tweed and fluffy white hair. Erin was a honey-blonde tornado of activity, flashing her bright smile left and right while being devastatingly efficient. Callum was running through his sound and lighting cues with Mei. It felt like the whole of Fox Bay had decided to muck in and everyone knew what part they had to play. Simi bustled past with boxes and crates, Josie added extra chairs to the rows, Fin carried in box after box of tablecloths, paper cups and napkins for the after-party.

The only person who *wasn't* rushing around organising and sorting was Trip. He was still nowhere to be seen.

Ivy texted him, trying to sound breezy and unconcerned. She texted again, half an hour later. Then, ditching the breeziness, she called him. The messages went unanswered and the calls went to voicemail. Every time Ivy asked about him, she was met with a shrug.

'I'm sure he was just here,' Mei said, waving vaguely. She was up a ladder, grappling with the topmost corner of the massive map of Cornwall Ivy had painted. 'But it's okay, he'll turn up. And we have strict instructions.'

'Yeah, he must be out back,' Erin said, stabbing a straw into a carton of juice and handing it to a Year 4 who was encased in a giant cardboard Stargazy Pie. 'He's *always* here.'

But Trip wasn't in the back. He wasn't in the little kitchen or the corridor. Ivy checked the music room. The stage. *Under* the stage. The tech table. Nothing.

As the time ticked on, Ivy began to worry.

'It's just not like him,' Ivy said, pacing up and down in front of Josie, who was doing some last-minute costume alterations for the tiny smugglers. 'He's put everything into this show and now it's crunch time. So where is he?'

'Maybe he's talking to Lou about the catering,' said Josie, through a mouthful of pins. 'I wouldn't worry, darling. Trip has a very reliable aura.'

'Yeah,' said Ivy, 'you're right. He must be doing something like that.' *Still, it is weird*, she thought.

Without his cheery-but-firm leadership, things were starting to go wrong. Tempers were fraying, cues were being missed, kids were flagging, and so was Mr Hargreaves. An argument broke out over who had the most recent script. Eventually, with barely more than two hours to go until the audience arrived and still no sign of Trip, Ivy couldn't handle it any more. Putting the final touches to the standing stones could wait. She threw down her brush and headed out into the streets of Fox Bay, down to Lou's pizza van on the beach. Lou was stoking her pizza oven and Ivy could feel the heat from a distance.

'Have you seen Trip?' she called, shading her eyes against the dazzling winter afternoon sun. 'Only we're curtain up in two hours and I can't find him.'

'Haven't seen him all day,' Lou called back. She looked tired but happy, resting a hand on the small of her back. 'But I know exactly how many pizzas and the toppings and all that.' She gave Ivy her warm smile. 'Don't fret, love. He'll turn up – he won't miss the big day, not after all this work.'

Ivy nodded, but her stomach had an uneasy feeling. She pulled out her phone and tried calling him. No answer. Texted. Nothing.

All of a sudden, she knew she wasn't overreacting. Trip was . . . well, he was Trip. *All in*, like Brooke had said. He had shown up for every rehearsal, every blocking and sound session, supervising the front of house, the costumes, the script. She had seen him rally, encourage and bolster these kids, not to mention the show committee. He had even appeared last night, parcels of fish and chips in his arms, to help her re-make the three-hundred-and-fifty paper fish. There was *no way* he would just disappear on the day of the show itself. Not without a good reason anyway.

Then Ivy thought of the conversation she had overheard that morning between him and Brooke. She thought of the pleading note in Trip's voice and Brooke's gentle words: *It's time to let her go.*

Ivy was sure then. Something *was* wrong with Trip – and she had to find him.

Chapter Twenty

Ivy burst into the bookshop to find Brooke, looking irritatingly calm, typing on her laptop and eating a scone, with the radio on in the background.

'Trip's gone,' Ivy announced breathlessly.

'What do you mean, gone?' said Brooke, setting down her scone and wiping her fingers on a napkin. 'He was right here, this morning. You artists are very dramatic.'

Ivy drew a deep breath. 'I mean *gone*. Vanished, disappeared like a puff of smoke. He is not at the town hall. And before you ask – yes, I already checked the bakery, the pier and The Mariner's Arms. The play is starting in two hours and he's the only one people listen to. I can see the cracks already. The twins are arguing with Merlin about his entrance. Mr H is panicking about the running order. No one seems to agree on the latest script. We need Trip. He would never vanish today of all days. So where *is* he?'

Brooke shut her laptop and stood, frowning slightly. 'Maybe he's gone out to get the cast and crew coffee or something. Some big, cheesy pre-show gesture?'

'Nope. I've tried the Driftwood Café. I've asked everybody I can think of and no one has seen him.' Ivy sighed and flopped down into the nearest armchair. 'I've been calling and texting and nothing. Straight to voicemail. It's like he's turned his phone off.'

Brooke grabbed her own phone and pressed *dial*, then held it to her ear. After a few seconds, she lowered it. 'He's not picking up,' she said slowly.

'Told you,' said Ivy, relieved that Brooke might be finally taking it seriously.

There was a pause, filled only by the faint hum of the radio. Then: 'You don't think something actually happened to him, do you?' Brooke asked, her voice quieter now. 'Like I say, I saw him earlier and he was totally fine.'

'Totally fine?' Ivy narrowed her eyes. 'Was he? Really? You didn't have, say, a pretty emotional conversation this morning about *selling your grandmother's house*?'

Brooke flushed. 'You were listening?'

'I didn't mean to eavesdrop,' said Ivy, 'I was out back getting something and then I realised you guys were talking. Trip sounded pretty upset.'

'Yeah, he was. But it was a conversation we had to have. Trip needs to face reality.' She chewed her nail. 'You think he took off because of that?'

'I don't know. But it's weird otherwise, isn't it? The day of the show. He would *never* disappear like this without a reason.'

They exchanged a look. 'You're right,' Brooke said at last. 'We need to go look for him.' She grabbed her coat. 'Come on.'

They headed back out on to the streets and searched, more methodically this time under Brooke's strict guidance. They re-checked the town hall, the bakery and even the library. Most shops were closed up as people prepared for the show. It felt like everyone in Fox Bay was in the town hall – except Trip.

'Let's head down to the beach,' said Brooke at last. 'Maybe he's meditating or doing yoga and is totally oblivious.'

The walk along the harbour was quiet. On the beach, both of them scanned the coastline. But there was no sign of a familiar figure, bouncing along petting dogs and chatting to anyone he could find.

Brooke stopped. 'Okay, so he's *not* at the beach, the pub, the bakery, the town hall or the library. Fox Bay is like a ghost town today so we're running out of options. Where else?'

Ivy bit her lip. 'He's thinking about your grandma a lot. Was there anything special they liked to do together?'

Brooke smiled faintly. 'It's hard to narrow that down to be honest. Grandma would say yes to literally anything Trip wanted to do. She used to pick him up after school and just drive. No map, no plan. She'd always say that the best days started with a detour—'

'Ivy! Brooke!'

Old Bill, his flannel shirt flapping in the breeze like a flag, waved them over. He was breathless from walking fast.

'I heard you were looking for Trip and figured it might be worth my saying,' he puffed. 'My boat's gone.'

Brooke blinked. 'Gone? As in . . . it's been stolen? Don't tell me Fox Bay has actual *crime*.'

'Borrowed,' Bill corrected, wheezing as he got his breath back. 'Sometimes things get borrowed. And I'm pretty sure whoever borrowed my boat was Trip.'

Ivy's eyes widened. 'Trip? Why do you think that?'

'Well, I told him he could take it out whenever he wanted, you see,' said Bill. 'And I saw him walking along the harbour earlier. Seemed quiet. Not his usual self.'

Brooke groaned. 'He borrowed a *boat*? Why on earth . . .?'

Ivy's gaze drifted out over the water, towards the curve of the bay where the small, green, tree-covered islands rose from the sea.

'Where do you think he went?' she asked. 'Did he go back to Seal Island for some reason?'

'Nothing much out there apart from that,' said Bill. 'Aside from Mystery Island, of course.'

Ivy said slowly, 'Mystery Island.' She turned to Brooke. 'Trip and your grandma loved adventures, right? Well, what could be more adventurous than an excursion to Mystery Island?'

'But it doesn't exist, right?' Brooke said, looking confused. 'It's just another one of Bill's stories.'

Bill chuckled behind them. 'Oh, it exists all right.' He squinted at the late-afternoon sun. 'But if you want to get to Mystery Island, you'd better start now.'

'How come?' Ivy said.

'It only appears at low tide.'

Brooke spluttered indignantly, pulling up her iPhone notes. 'But – but you told Kate it's a ghost isle that only appears at the full moon, for other ghostly smugglers to hide their whisky, if they chant the name of Davy Jones! And now you're saying you can get there in the middle of the day? By regular boat?'

Bill looked sheepish. 'Well. I may have embroidered the truth a little. It's not even really an island, to be honest.' He shrugged. 'Just a promontory round the southwest side of Seal Island. It's rarely above water, which is why it's hidden – but it would be about now.'

'Did you happen to tell Trip any of this?' Ivy pressed.

'Hm.' Bill considered. 'May have given him a little hint. He was always asking a lot of questions.'

Ivy looked back at the water. Trip was hurting, she was sure of it. He was alone. And he couldn't miss the show he'd worked so hard on.

'Brooke, are you up for a sail?'

Brooke exhaled. 'Fine. If you really think Trip's out there – and let's face it, taking an impromptu trip to a hidden island sounds *exactly* like the sort of thing he'd do – then yeah. Let's go get him.'

Ivy turned to Bill. 'Can we borrow your back-up boat?'

Bill grinned. 'Thought you'd never ask.'

They dragged the spare boat, a marginally more modern vessel than Bill's old one, out to sea, Ivy's teeth chattering as they waded into the icy water. Brooke hopped in elegantly, then held out a manicured hand to Ivy, hauling her into the boat.

'You're rowing, by the way,' Ivy said. 'One of us works out and it's not me.'

Brooke smirked. 'Rowing is all about teamwork, Ivy. And besides, this was your idea.'

A few minutes later, with both of them pulling on the oars, the little boat was speeding – or rather, lurching – out to sea. The sea was peaceful, but Brooke's rowing technique was decidedly aggressive, while Ivy was struggling with the heavy oars.

'Can you put a bit more effort in, Ivy?' said Brooke. 'Come on. Focus. Work smarter, not harder.'

'How do we *steer* this thing?' Ivy hissed, water splashing up her arm and soaking her jacket. 'How are we going to aim for a hidden island that only appears at certain times of the day if we can't co-ordinate?'

'If you would just slow down and concentrate,' Brooke said, maddeningly, 'then we'll find this place just fine.'

But doubts were flooding in thick and fast now. *What if Trip wants to be alone?* Ivy thought anxiously. *What if he doesn't want us to find him? What if he's angry with me?*

When Seal Island finally came into view, quiet and green, they stopped rowing, catching their breath.

'I swear,' Brooke muttered, scanning the shore, 'if he's over there chatting to the seals, perfectly fine, I'm going to make him swim back.'

But Ivy caught the note of worry in her voice again.

'According to Bill, Mystery Island is just round there,' Ivy said, brushing thick waves of hair out of her eyes. 'Ready for the final push?'

Brooke nodded. 'Come on. And let's synchronise this time, for God's sake.'

Chapter Twenty-one

Brooke and Ivy walked across the sands of Mystery Island in the pale gold light of the afternoon sun. The tide slapped lazily against the rocks and curlews wheeled above in long, slow arcs.

They had managed, with much bickering, to ease the boat into the shallow, *almost* hidden, bay. Sure enough, the island seemed to have risen from the water as if by magic. *So not all of Old Bill's tales were* entirely *made up*, Ivy thought. And there, seated on a rock, near Old Bill's little boat, was Trip.

His back was to them and his legs dangled over the side. As they drew closer, Ivy saw that he wasn't humming or smiling. For once, he was still, looking out over the water.

Ivy and Brooke exchanged a glance. 'Come on,' said Ivy.

They picked their way carefully over the rocks. 'Hey,' called Trip, glancing over his shoulder. He looked surprised. 'You came all the way out here?'

'Yes, because you went *missing*,' said Ivy severely.

'I wasn't missing,' he said, looking confused. 'I just needed to get away for a bit. I didn't mean to worry you.'

'Well, you did,' Brooke said, her usually steady voice faltering. 'You can't just take off like that, okay?'

'I'm sorry,' he said quietly, looking at his lap.

There was silence. Ivy nudged Brooke. 'You go,' she whispered. 'Talk to him.' She hung back, pretending to examine the shells that had washed up on the shore, but she was unable to resist listening in.

Brooke approached and climbed up on to the rock beside Trip, sitting close to him. 'I'm sorry. I was just worried about you, buddy,' she said quietly. 'You're my little brother. What's up?'

'I was thinking . . . I wish Grandma had seen this place,' Trip said, eyes on the horizon. 'She'd have loved it. The quiet. The ridiculous seals. Magical.'

There was a long silence.

'I'm sorry,' Brooke said at last. 'About Grandma's house. About this past year. I rushed through the funeral and clearing her house and the sale like a checklist of things I had to do. And then I hurried you off to Europe. I didn't let you have time. I thought I was doing the right thing but I was so busy trying to organise everything I didn't let either of us *feel* anything.'

Trip turned to look at her. 'You were just doing your best,' he said. 'It's not your—'

'Can you let me finish?' Brooke said, exasperated. 'Don't do the thing where you jump in and make everything okay. I'm trying to apologise here.'

'Fine,' said Trip, grinning. 'In that case, continue.'

'I thought if I could only . . . keep moving, do the next practical thing, we could skip the worst of the pain. But that wasn't fair. You lost her too. And I should've let you grieve.' She rubbed her forehead. 'This whole year, I tried to think about what Grandma would have wanted for you. I set up adventure after adventure, because that was your thing, wasn't it? You and her, having adventures. And then I thought you'd be done with adventures and you could go to college and get back on track.' She gave a shaky laugh. 'I was trying to be so *logical*. So, I'm sorry.'

Trip nodded. 'Fine, apology accepted. But now I get to make one too, okay?' He reached out and squeezed his sister's hand. 'I'm sorry for not helping more. For letting you do everything.'

Brooke shrugged, blinking fast. 'I *am* the big sister,' she said, her voice wobbling. 'That's my thing.'

She let her head rest briefly on his shoulder, just for a second.

'Um,' said Ivy. 'I'm really happy you guys have worked things out . . . but . . . the play is in an hour.' She squinted at her phone. 'Wait, less than an hour. And Trip, I think they need you.'

Trip glanced up and shrugged. 'Do they?' he said flatly. 'I don't know, Ivy. Maybe you're right and getting so involved was a bit stupid. It's just a school play – I'm sure they'll all cope fine without me.'

'No!' cried Ivy. 'I wasn't right at all. Things are totally falling apart without you. I'm worried there might be some sort of mutiny at this rate. Seriously, Trip we *need* your optimism and over-investment and annoying sunniness.' She noticed Brooke fighting back a smile and powered on. 'And we need you *now*. The twins were holding Merlin hostage at sword-point when I left.'

Trip hesitated, a smile of his own tugging at the corner of his mouth.

'The twins are holding Merlin at *sword-point*?' he said at last.

'It was a cardboard sword,' Ivy confessed. 'But still. We need you, Trip. The play needs you.'

'Okay, okay,' he said, jumping to his feet and brushing down his jeans. 'Say no more.'

Ivy gave a laugh of relief. 'Thank goodness. I feel like this island might be submerged soon, anyway. Shall we get back in the boat? I don't want to end up as the subject of one of Old Bill's tales.'

Brooke laughed too and slid off the rock. 'Yeah, I'd rather not be the ghost of the American tourist who vanished on Mystery Island, thanks.'

Trip came closer to Ivy and touched her arm. 'I'm sorry, Ivy,' he said. He looked pale and tired and his hair was rumpled, but he seemed calm. 'I shouldn't have taken off like that. I just needed some alone time.' He smiled wryly. 'And that is not something I ever thought I'd say.'

'Solitary brooding behaviour does seem out of character for you.' Ivy swallowed. 'I wanted to make sure you were okay,' she added in a small voice.

'Well, thanks,' Trip said. Their eyes met, and Ivy noticed the different lights in them. Caramel, gold, flecks of bronze. 'Thanks for coming to find me.'

Brooke rolled her eyes. 'Come on, you two. Let's go put on a show.'

Chapter Twenty-two

'Has anyone seen Arthur's crown?' Liv shrieked, standing on a chair in full tinfoil chainmail. 'I literally just had it. It was on the prop table two seconds ago!'

'It's on the lighting board,' called Bethie-as-Mordred from the wings, rustling in her own armour. 'You put it there when you were dancing to Dua Lipa earlier. Hurry! We can't duel if you haven't got your crown.'

'Right.' Liv hopped off the chair and began pushing her way through the crowd. 'Out the way, people. King coming through.'

Ivy ducked as a tiny Lancelot with ginger plaits ran past her, holding a wooden shield. She lugged the stone into place and carefully ensured the sword was wedged tightly enough to be convincing when Liv pulled it free, but not so tightly that it never emerged at all. The smell of hairspray filled the air and, somewhere near the dressing rooms, the guising band were loudly tuning up. Amidst the discordant chorus of fiddles, concertinas, tin whistles, euphoniums and flutes, Ivy could discern the squeaky opening of *Joy To the World*.

'Is it meant to sound like that?' Ivy asked no one in particular.

'They'll get there,' said Callum, bustling through with a sheaf of sheet music. 'They just need to warm up a bit.'

To her right, Trip was talking to a Year 4 with stage fright, getting him to breathe in and out.

'You're going to be great,' he said soothingly, his hands on the boy's shoulders. 'Just remember, you've got this. Remember to breathe. Remember to project.'

'Thank goodness you're back, dear boy,' Mr Hargreaves said, hurrying past with a handful of reserved tickets. 'I have to admit, I was starting to *worry* earlier. I wasn't sure what we'd have done without you.'

Trip glanced over his shoulder and gave his usual sunny smile. 'No need to worry, Mr H,' he said. He caught Ivy's eye. 'I wouldn't have missed this for the world.'

With Trip's return, the atmosphere had swiftly been downgraded from borderline hysterical to a controlled chaos. Beautiful, glue-encrusted, poster-paint-spattered, cobbled-together-with-masking-tape chaos. And Ivy loved it. It reminded her of all the art shows she had put on over the years. Dusty clothes, hair shoved up into a messy bun, paint under her nails, on her hands and knees adding last-minute detail; fixing, gluing, sewing. She had forgotten how much fun this was.

'You look . . . *happy*,' said Erin, hurrying past with a basket full of toy pistols. She paused to rest it on her hip and study Ivy. 'It's very off-brand.'

'I know,' said Ivy, getting to her feet and dusting off her knees. 'I've been trying to open myself up a bit.' She paused, smiling shyly at Erin. 'A – a friend told me things could get a bit lonely otherwise.'

Erin smiled back. 'That's what friends are for,' she said. 'To deliver the occasional home truth. You don't get your artist card revoked for loosening up a bit, Ivy.' She nodded across the room, to where Trip was now adjusting the waistcoats, wigs and flowing shirts of the Fleetwood Mac tribute band. He looked completely in his element – focused, cheek smudged with paint, sleeves rolled up. 'Glad you found him,' she said, with a wink, and carried on.

Ivy and Trip's eyes met. It kept happening – as she hauled scenery into place, fixed paper crowns and hemmed robes. And each time he gave her his excited grin.

Then Trip glanced at the clock and hopped on to an upturned crate, cupping his hands over his mouth. 'All right, people!' he called. 'Places, please! This is not a drill! We are starting in TEN!'

The children began to scurry to their places, led by various members of the show committee. They had rehearsed this yesterday and Ivy, shepherding a cluster of mermen, couldn't help but think it was going relatively smoothly. Until—

'WHERE IS MERLIN?' screamed Mr Hargreaves. 'Why does he keep disappearing like this? Why does—'

'I'm RIGHT HERE,' announced eight-year-old Merlin, emerging from a broom cupboard wearing a long silver robe and what looked suspiciously like a towel tied round his neck for a beard. He was rubbing his eyes. 'I was meditating. Josie said it would help with stage fright.'

'You were sleeping,' said Mr Hargreaves crossly. 'I distinctly heard snoring. Now, go and join Morgana.'

Ivy did a last-minute check on her backdrops. The pretty streets of 1970s Redruth. The barn for the folk dancing. The windswept Bodmin moor, where Jamaica Inn stood, sign blowing, dark secrets hidden within. The earthen mound for the wrestling display. Tintagel Castle, where King Arthur was born. Dozmary Pool, where the lady in the lake would emerge with Excalibur. The mighty stone with Caliburn buried inside. Finally, the castle with a little beach below, where Arthur would meet his fate.

At that last one, she stepped back and looked at the finishing touches she'd added that morning. It was subtle, but she hoped it was enough. A little surprise for Trip.

Okay, so maybe she was being ridiculous because Trip was about to leave Fox Bay and she would never know what might have been between them. But then she recalled her tutor's words: *find what you care about*. At least, in some way, Ivy had done that – even if it was painted on cardboard.

She ducked behind a curtain and looked out at the hall. The audience had begun eagerly filtering in before the official start time, coats bundled over arms, cheeks pink from the cold. They took their seats on folding chairs – some borrowed from the library, others from the Driftwood Café. The front row had already been claimed by the early birds.

Ivy dropped the curtain and wove her way through the people backstage until she found Trip, eyes on the actors lining up. 'How are you feeling?' she asked.

Trip bit his lip, looking around at the nervous children, clutching their wooden swords and pistols, their folk instruments and guitars. 'I hope they'll be okay,' he said.

'They'll be great,' Ivy told him, and she meant it. 'They're ready, thanks to you. This is your moment of glory. Enjoy it.'

He smiled. 'Thanks. You go and watch from the wings and I'll see you on the other side.'

Ivy watched the audience take their seats. Ynez the postie had somehow snagged a seat in the centre of the front row. 'Had to sprint,' Ivy could hear her telling people. She nodded proudly towards the stage. 'Grandson's an exciseman.'

Ivy's mum had also wangled a front-row seat and was talking animatedly to Fin, who was holding a large Tupperware container of gingerbread, and Josie, who was showing her pictures of the campsite she and Fin had booked in Italy next summer. Simi was holding Lou's hand as Kate clambered over their knees. Tamsin was clutching a tiger's eye crystal for good luck and Mr Trenwith took up an entire four seats with his camera equipment, bickering with his wife over lighting settings. There were toddlers wriggling on laps, visiting students pretending they weren't excited, and at least three dogs who had snuck in with their owners and were now curled up under chairs.

Brooke, stylish even in a puffer coat with windblown hair, slipped in and walked past the stage to her seat. Ivy stuck her head out from behind the curtain and waved to her.

'It's going to be great,' Brooke called. Her gaze landed on Trip, who could just be seen making a last-minute adjustment to the smoke machine, then she looked back to Ivy. 'Glad we got him here?'

'Yeah,' said Ivy. 'I really am.'

Mr Hargreaves beamed and gave them an excitable thumbs up, practically bouncing up and down in his chair. The room was buzzing with that particular warmth that Ivy associated with Fox Bay events. She could hear whispers all around. 'Looks all right this year, doesn't it?' 'Bethie's getting to kill Arthur at the end.' 'Do you think they'll make it to the end this time?'

Ivy couldn't help but smile. This loyal audience kept on doggedly showing up, year after year, no matter how disastrous Mr Hargreaves's last show had been.

There came a sudden burst of energy near the side doors and she heard someone shrieking '*IVY!*' and a blur of purple hair and leopard print hurtled into view.

'Raye!' cried Ivy, waving frantically. 'You made it!'

Raye hurtled down the hall towards the stage, her coat flapping behind her like a cape, dragging a tall, elegant girl in leggings in her wake. Ivy scrambled down and hurried over. 'We literally drove straight here from Cleo's ballet recital,' she said, talking fast. 'She got a standing ovation and did a solo. So, you know, this has a lot to live up to. Oh.' Raye went slightly pink and pointed to the girl standing next to her. 'Ivy, this is Cleo, Cleo this is Ivy. You literally *have* to like each other, I can't handle it any other way.'

Cleo, breathless and amused-looking, held out her hand. She looked effortlessly cool, with cropped hair and red lipstick. But,

Ivy thought, eyeing her as they shook hands, her expression was fond as she looked at Raye.

'Hi,' Cleo said, with a Scottish accent. 'You must be the famous Ivy. I've heard a lot about you.'

'I've heard a lot about *you*. And I can't believe you came all this way,' said Ivy. 'That's far.'

'Well, I thought it sounded so romantic here,' said Cleo. 'If a bit weird, to be honest.'

'Yup,' said Raye cheerfully. 'I told Cleo that Fox Bay is the cultural beating heart of the southwest. And that Mr H's shows are guaranteed to be *memorable* at least.'

'There's nothing like a bit of winter weirdness,' Cleo said, smiling at Raye. 'Or a bit of winter romance either.'

Romance and weirdness. That was Fox Bay all over, Ivy thought. She hugged Raye again before she could stop herself. 'God, it's good to see you,' she whispered into her friend's shoulder.

'You too,' Raye whispered back. 'And by the way, you sound, like, a thousand per cent happier than you did on the phone. I was getting a bit worried about you. Something or someone must have turned things around.' She pulled back. 'Speaking of which,' she said, 'did you manage to talk to Trip?'

'I . . .' Just then the lights flickered. 'I'll tell you later. I think it's starting,' Ivy said. She frowned, glancing at her watch. 'They're a whole two minutes early. Mr H will be freaking out.'

Someone clanged a triangle offstage and Ivy heard a muffled yelp. 'I told you, not yet,' someone hissed. *Mei*, she thought.

'Sit down,' hissed Ivy, climbing back on to the stage and darting back to the wings. She watched as Cleo and Raye melted into one of the rows.

'Everything okay?' Trip whispered, as he hurried past doing final checks.

'Really good,' she told him. 'My best friend Raye made it. Er, are we ready for this?'

'More than,' he assured her.

'But the triangle came in early . . .'

'From this point on,' Trip said firmly, 'we just need to go with it.'

The murmur of the crowd quieted to a hush as the velvet curtain began to part, slowly, creakily at first – and then flew open with a loud *bang*.

'Oops,' Ivy heard Merlin whisper. 'I think I pulled too hard.'

A banner was jerkily lowered: *A (Somewhat) True History of Cornwall.*

A serious-looking child in a tea-towel robe emerged from the shadows, a spotlight fixing on him as he solemnly declared, 'We begin with Saint Piran, patron saint of Cornwall – that's me. And also, we'll explain how surfing made it from Peru to Perranporth.'

Three more children, all in wetsuits, came out and began to speak, their voices carrying loud and clear in the hall. The audience chuckled benevolently.

'And now,' the boy said, when the brief history was finished and the canvas behind him shifted to Redruth, 'for a Fleetwood Mac medley, in honour of Mick Fleetwood's Cornish roots.'

'Team Stevie though,' whispered Ivy to Trip as he sent the band on in their flowing sleeves. He laughed, as the opening chords of *Go Your Own Way* struck up.

The evening wore on, to regular bursts of genuine laughter and unforced applause from the audience. There was a brief explanation of tin mining, folk dancing and a dramatic reading of *Jamaica Inn* (including a terrifyingly realistic depiction of the alcoholic inn owner by an utterly angelic seven-year-old called Daisy). There was a shadowy cove made of cardboard boxes and toilet rolls and tiny smugglers wearing eye patches, swigging from bottles marked SECRET WHISKY. The fog machine was in overdrive, with Mei going for maximum drama as instructed.

'Great cove,' Trip told Ivy.

'Thanks,' she said. 'I made it myself.'

Then, after the blood-curdling theatrics there was a call and response section, in which Year 4 taught the audience certain key phrases in Kernewek to much hilarity.

After the wrestling, with the requisite audience participation – Joan from the sweetshop proving especially sprightly – it was time for Tom Bawcock's dramatic attempt to brave the seas outside Mousehole, returning with his net full of fish, which were released to gasps from the audience on to the stage in a great, shivering shoal. The boy playing Tom bowed while children dressed as Stargazy Pies danced in celebration. Pushkin, reluctantly playing Tom's cat, Mouser, looked out coldly at the audience, held in the boy's firm grasp. As soon as the boy set him down, Pushkin bounded into the front row and leapt on to Josie's lap, where he glowered.

Ivy realised that Trip had joined her again and was watching, his eyes keenly following the actors. 'Think it was worth it then?' Ivy whispered. 'Staying up all night making all those paper fish.'

Trip's voice was a breath against her ear, making her shiver as he answered. 'I think so, yeah.'

And then, Ivy knew, it was the grand finale. The series of scenes from King Arthur's life, from his birth at Tintagel to his death at the hands of Mordred on a Cornish beach. Ivy prayed that the round table would hold, that the aged, gold-painted papier-mâché goblets would look the part. She glanced at Trip.

'I think you should watch this one from the audience,' she said quietly. 'Come on.'

He smiled down at her. 'Okay. I think my work here is done anyway.'

Silently, they made their way down the side stairs and to the back of the hall.

The lights shifted. A hush fell. As the scene began, the backdrop fell seamlessly into place to a chorus of gratifying murmurs of amazement from the audience. Ivy let out a sigh of relief. It was all going to plan – or at least pretty much, she thought, as Liv let out a huge sneeze that dislodged her crown.

As the actors guided the audience through the key moments from the legendary king's life, complete with clanking armour, sloshing wine (Ribena) and dramatic declarations, Ivy found herself beaming with professional pride. The kids were acting their hearts out, the music and sound cues were on point, the smoke machine was in full flow and, though she said so herself, the sets looked pretty damn good.

As the final backdrop fell into place with a gentle *swoosh* and Bethie and Liv took up their fighting stance, faces hidden by their visors, Ivy leaned forward slightly. The beach backdrop she'd painted hung, hidden slightly in shadow, as Erin coaxed the lights to shift from sunrise to daylight, painting the hall in shades of amber.

Liv, as a valiant but slightly exasperated Arthur, declared, 'Do your worst, traitor!'

'Then I shall end you, Arthur,' cried Bethie-as-Mordred. 'Your time as king is at an end.' They battled for a few moments in fierce silence, huffing and puffing behind their visors – then Mordred dealt the final blow.

There was a tragic silence before Merlin cleared his throat. 'Um. Happy holidays, everyone,' he said simply. 'This has been fun. And now,' he waved his hand, 'it's time for us to say goodbye or, as we would say in Cornish . . .' He held a hand to his ear and, as one, the audience chanted back:

'Duw genes!'

That's when the lights came up on the backdrop that Ivy had spent the morning retouching, painting it in the rich yellows and oranges of a Cornish coastal sunset. Her gaze flew to Trip, wondering if he would notice the additions that she had added – the white snow falling from the purple streaked sky, past the castle and on to the beach below, where it clustered in great flurries. She'd told herself that it wouldn't matter if Trip noticed or not. But really, she wanted him to see and understand.

Trip leaned forward slightly, eyes scanning the backdrop, frowning. 'Ivy,' he whispered. 'Did you . . .'

'Wait,' she said. 'Just wait.'

All around them, people were applauding as the kids bowed. Ivy took it all in – the poster paint, the wooden swords and folk dancers and squeaky instruments and kids who had acted their hearts out, their faces shining in the stage lights, basking in the praise, the cheers and whoops crashing over them.

And then, with all the cast gathered on stage, it began to snow.

Not real snow, of course. Handfuls of tiny pieces of white paper, painstakingly torn by Year 5s and stored in a bin labelled SECRET! (DO NOT THROW AWAY!!) fluttered down like a paper blizzard, thrown by Erin and Callum up in the rafters. It caught the light from the fairy-lit battlements, dusted the cardboard castle in glimmering white, landed on Liv's shoulders and crowned Bethie once more. The fans Ivy had placed in the corners blew it merrily around the hall.

The audience gasped, then applauded wildly. The little kids shrieked and leapt off their parents' laps, running about in front of the stage, trying to catch paper flakes on their tongues. Trip laughed under his breath and tilted his head back to watch it fall. The snow was catching in his hair, clinging to his cashmere jumper.

He turned to Ivy. 'I thought you said it never snows here?'

She blushed. 'I couldn't let you leave without getting your dream.'

'Snow on the beach,' he said. He took her hand in his and squeezed. 'Thanks. And what a show. You did it, Ivy.'

'*You* did it,' she told him. She gestured around at the hall. 'This was all down to you. This is one for the history books – the first Fox Bay show that wasn't an unmitigated disaster.'

Trip's smile was open, like a kid on Christmas morning. Ivy's chest ached, in the best way. Suddenly the town hall that smelled of sandwiches and socks, with Trip's hand in hers and shredded paper landing on her hair, felt like the most romantic place on earth.

Chapter Twenty-three

The applause and the bows went on *for ever*. The crowd, packed on to the creaky folding chairs, stamped and cheered like they were at Glastonbury instead of Fox Bay town hall. Liv took a fifth bow and then a sixth. Bethie gave a sword flourish that nearly took out a light and even the smallest of the smugglers got their turn in the spotlight.

Mr Hargreaves ran on to the stage and flapped his hands for silence. 'Congratulations, everyone!' he cried. 'Now, while the actors were all wonderful, I think we are missing some unsung heroes who deserve their own applause. Let's hear it for the backstage production team! Trip, Ivy, Erin, Mei, Callum – get up here!'

'Oh no,' said Ivy in horror. 'This is the whole point of being *backstage*. No one pays attention to you.' She looked around wildly for an escape, but—

'There's Ivy!' cried Liv, darting over to her, and before Ivy could flee, she found herself dragged physically by small sweaty hands on to the stage. But as she faced the rows of people with delighted faces, most of whom she had known all her life, Trip's hand stayed in hers, warm and sure. The applause swelled as they took their bows.

Ivy's face was burning, but Trip took it in his stride, waving and grinning like he genuinely loved every absurd second of this. He high-fived Merlin and the troupe of sardines. In the audience, Ivy could see Josie blowing effusive kisses, her mum whistling and Raye beaming.

As soon as she could, Ivy tugged Trip down off the stage. 'Phew,' she said. 'That was more intense than I—'

A slight figure barrelled into Ivy, nearly knocking the breath out of her.

'You magician,' Raye said into her ear, still squeezing. 'The snow? The backdrop? The swordfight? I loved it.'

'You hate theatre,' Ivy managed, grinning. 'You said you get second-hand embarrassment from all the pauses.'

'I liked *this* theatre,' Raye corrected. She looked past Ivy and raised an eyebrow. 'And *you* must be Trip,' she said, sticking out her hand. 'I've heard all about you. Incurable optimist? Director of the first coherent Fox Bay show in living memory? Sunshine to Ivy's storm cloud?'

Trip, unfazed, extended a hand. 'That's me. Hi. And you must be Raye, Ivy's Fox Bay partner-in-crime and fellow creative?'

'Guilty,' said Raye, graciously shaking his hand. She turned and beckoned to Cleo. 'Cleo, this is Ivy's friend, Trip. The director of the masterpiece you just witnessed.'

Cleo smiled warmly. 'Congratulations on the show. Completely unhinged, in the best way.'

'Now,' called Mr Hargreaves from up on the stage, 'the after-party! Everyone grab a chair and stack them up and then we'll bring out the food.'

The audience did as they were told. Parents were hugging their kids, teachers were congratulating each other, toddlers were running wild with bits of leftover paper snow stuck in their hair. The hall buzzed with victory. Out of all the strange and unwieldy plays that Mr Hargreaves had come up with and the inhabitants of Fox Bay had patiently sat through, this was the only one that had been an unqualified success and the audience could hardly believe their luck. Lou bustled in with trays of pizza and Simi poured glasses of wine.

With great care, Fin directed a team of eight people carrying in a long trestle table that bore an enormous, burnished Cornish pasty. They all gathered round and watched with bated breath as it was measured.

'Only thirteen-and-a-half feet,' said Kate, shaking her head regretfully. 'And the entry in the *Guinness Book of Records* is fifteen. Sorry, Fin. There's always next year.'

'Oh well,' said Fin, sighing. 'It's good to have dreams.'

'And I bet it tastes amazing,' said Josie loyally, slipping her hand into his.

'We have,' Mr Hargreaves bellowed from the stage, 'done the final count of the ticket takings and we've officially smashed our fundraising goal, people! In fact, it's nearly double what we needed. The library is saved!'

'Who needs public funding when you can exploit child labour

to raise the money,' muttered Ivy, but she couldn't help smiling at the look of joy on Melissa's face.

The party wore on and Ivy quickly lost Trip in the crowd of well-wishers. She was hearing all about dinner with Cleo's parents from Raye when a sudden, delighted squeal rose up from the corner. She looked over to see Lou, cheeks glowing, standing with one hand protectively over her belly, and Simi beside her, grinning like she'd won the lottery.

'You're pregnant?' cried Kate. 'That's so exciting. We all thought you were hiding a secret wedding.'

'Yeah, I can't believe you thought we'd get married without telling anyone,' Simi was saying. 'We've been having IVF. We didn't want to say anything till we had the twelve-week scan – you know what this place is like.'

'A summer baby!' cried Josie mistily. 'Oh, this will be *wonderful* for the psychic energy of Fox Bay.'

'Let it Snow' was playing and Ivy found herself beaming.

Raye darted into the crowd to introduce Cleo to her parents. Ivy glanced over to see that Mei, Erin and Callum were sitting on the edge of the stage, sharing a bag of crisps and giggling at something on Callum's phone. Ivy watched them, their heads bent close in the way of old friends. She hesitated a moment, then took a breath and walked over, nerves tugging at her stomach.

'Hey,' she said. 'Can I . . . interrupt?'

'Of course you can,' said Mei, looking up. 'What's up? Relieved that it's over?'

'I guess. But I'll miss it, in a way.' Ivy scratched the back of her neck, feeling intensely awkward. 'I just . . . I wanted to say sorry.'

'Sorry?' said Callum, frowning.

'Yeah. I know you guys always tried to be friends at school and I shut you out. I tried to tell myself I was a loner, but the truth is . . . I was being defensive.'

Callum raised an eyebrow. 'She admits it.'

Mei elbowed him. 'Shut up, Cal. It's fine, Ivy.'

Erin shook her head, smiling her megawatt smile. 'Yeah, it's totally fine. You don't have to apologise.'

'I do, though,' Ivy said. 'And I know I've been rude all holiday. To be honest, it was hard seeing you all settle in so fast at uni. You sounded like you were having the best time ever and I—' she took a deep breath, 'I've been *hating* it.'

'You have?' said Erin, frowning.

'Big time. I'm lonely, I have zero friends, I had one relationship that lasted a fortnight and I think I'm going to fail the year because my marks are so bad. It couldn't really have gone worse. You guys seemed really happy so I felt embarrassed admitting it's been a disaster. Especially when I made such a big thing out of leaving Fox Bay to go to art school.'

For a moment, the gang were silent.

Then Mei spoke, her voice gentle. 'Ivy, you've got it all wrong. Uni hasn't been easy for us, either.'

'Seriously,' Erin nodded. 'I felt totally out of place for the first month. I didn't know anyone. I missed home like mad. I spent Fresher's Week alone eating brie in my room. I cried to my dad nearly every night. I nearly dropped out.'

'Same,' said Callum. 'I mean, I like the course but . . . I still think about being here. Working at the shop, biking around the cliffs, playing football. Everyone knows me here. It's safe, you know?'

Mei sighed. 'And I've been juggling way too much. Classes, societies, the bar, trying to keep up with everything and everyone. Sometimes I feel like I'm barely holding it all together.'

Ivy looked at each of them, surprised. 'You're struggling too? Why didn't you say anything?'

'We thought *you* were having the best time,' Callum said. 'You seemed okay. Moody as usual, but okay.'

'I'm not actually that moody. That's just my resting artist face,' Ivy muttered.

They all laughed, the tension breaking.

'Ivy, we like you,' Erin said simply. 'Even if you were a hermit all through school.'

'Even if you called me a jock with no soul,' added Callum.

'Yeah,' Mei agreed. 'We really like having you in the mix.'

Ivy smiled, a little teary-eyed now. 'Thanks, guys. I'd love a second chance, if you'll have me. I just needed some time to figure things out.'

'Well,' Callum said, raising his paper cup, 'here's to figuring things out.'

They clinked cups in a clumsy toast.

And then Liv cannonballed into them with a shout of, 'We

did it!', and Ivy found herself collapsing into laughter. With her friends. Not acquaintances – but her actual friends.

'Ivy,' said Brooke, appearing at her shoulder. She looked purposeful but slightly nervous. 'Can I talk to you for a sec?'

'Sure,' said Ivy. 'As a matter of—'

But just then, her phone rang. When she saw the number, Ivy felt her heart thumping.

'Excuse me, Brooke,' she said, 'I have to take this.'

She hurried out into the corridor. 'Ivy Pearson speaking,' she said breathlessly into the phone, letting the door shut on the noise of the party.

'Hello, Ivy.' Her tutor Jess's amused voice came down the phone. 'I got your email. You've certainly had a productive few weeks. I wish all my students were this busy during the holidays.'

Ivy could scarcely breathe. 'You saw my sketches?' she asked.

'I found them delightful. Deftly drawn. Wonderful snatches of everyday life. And these photos of your set design, of this . . . is it a lobster with a rum bottle?'

Ivy flushed. 'I know it's silly. It was just to give a sense of . . .'

'I thought the sets were charming,' Jess said.

Ivy drew breath. 'I know my work last term at Truro wasn't exactly . . . great.'

'No,' Jess said honestly, 'it wasn't. To be honest, I was worried you were on the wrong course. And now I'm sure of it.'

'Oh,' said Ivy, faltering.

'That's right. I think you're a talented draughtsperson who found yourself on the multimedia and fine art course when you should have been honing your illustration skills. I've spoken to the tutor on the illustration course here at Truro and she would be delighted to have you. I want to stress that I will work with you on your final piece if that's what you want and do my very best to hone your work. But I think it might be a good idea, given the work you've produced this past few weeks, to reconsider the course. The illustration tutor thinks, and I agree, that it is really quite extraordinary.'

'Really?' whispered Ivy. 'You don't think I'm a failure?'

'Far from it. You've got a flair for illustration, and clearly, a strong eye for atmosphere and character. Now, tell me more about this show.'

'It just finished,' Ivy said, laughing shakily. 'We're having the after-party. But it was great. I painted backdrops, made costumes, even made a big . . . er, papier-mâché fish pie.'

Jess laughed. 'A *Stargazy Pie,* by any chance?'

Ivy nodded. 'That's the one.'

'Well, Ivy, it's a big decision, so I'll give you a few days to decide.' Jess's voice down the phone was warm and encouraging. 'But I *will* say this. You're clearly talented. You've got strong instincts, and it's obvious that, whatever happened last term in Truro, you've reconnected with what inspires you. That matters more than you realise.'

Ivy let out a breath. 'Thank you,' she whispered. 'So, you won't fail me?'

Jess laughed. 'Not after this project. I have a feeling you've only just got going.'

Ivy felt something bloom in her chest. Not just relief – that the tutors still thought she had talent – but excitement. At all the ideas to come, the projects to embark on, the dust-filled, held-together-with-masking-tape shows she could see through to their joyful end.

'Thank you,' she said. 'Really. I was worried you'd think it was silly. Just drawings of the people in my town.'

She could hear the smile in Jess's voice. 'The world needs artists who can find the extraordinary in the everyday. Speak soon, Ivy. Now go and enjoy yourself at that after-party.'

As she walked back into the hall, Ivy sensed a shift in the atmosphere. A buzz, bigger even than the one accompanying Lou and Simi's announcement. The excited chatter was almost at fever pitch, but she couldn't work out what it was about. She caught snatches.

'. . . *Filming starting next spring!*'

'*Do you think the stars will come into the café?*'

'*Or take surf lessons?*'

'Ivy, get over here,' said Erin, waving frantically from the stage. 'This is important.'

'What?' said Ivy, heading over and hopping up to sit beside her.

'Have you *heard*?' Erin looked even more animated than usual. 'Did you *know*?'

'Heard what?' asked Ivy, bewildered. 'Know what? What's going on?'

'Brooke!' Callum cried. 'She's a secret agent. Sort of.'

'Make that a secret top Hollywood exec,' said Erin. 'Slow down, Cal, and tell her from the start.'

'I follow Kathleen Lee on insta,' Callum said breathlessly, 'and look at this! Posted just now.'

He held out his phone. It was Kathleen Lee's account, showing a picture of something that Ivy recognised – white sands, peaceful water.

'Read the caption,' Callum said.

Ivy read it aloud. 'The moment I've been waiting for – and I know you all have too. Filming for *Ocean Deep* starts in the spring! But I bet you can't guess *where* we're filming . . .'

Ivy looked up. 'Hang on. But that's . . .'

'The hidden cove here at Fox Bay!' Erin replied. 'I cornered Brooke just now and she confirmed everything. Brooke's been here in Fox Bay on a *mission*! For *Hollywood*! All this time. Can you believe it?'

Ivy tried to gather herself and failed. This was all too much after the call she had just had. 'Wait, *what*? Brooke is a Hollywood exec?'

'She's big-time Hollywood,' Mei said, eyes wide with conspiratorial excitement. 'They're in production for an adaptation of *Ocean Deep* and she's been secretly scouting the town. Kathleen Lee described it as exactly how she imagined the town in the book, so Brooke came to Cornwall to check it out. Apparently she went to other places too, but Fox Bay won.'

'She said it was *perfect*.' Callum waved his phone at Ivy. 'Look. There's a *Variety* article up. *Shooting is set to begin next spring on the hotly anticipated new adaptation of Kathleen Lee's biggest book to date,* Ocean Deep.'

Ivy took the phone and began to read:

Fans of Kathleen Lee can rest easy. Not only has the location been announced but it's one that *Ocean Deep* fans will be *very* happy about: Fox Bay, in picturesque Cornwall, a name familiar to those in the know. Producer Brooke Wakefield, who chose the location after an intense search, says, *'I can see why Kathleen fell in love with Fox Bay and I did too. The landscape, the locals, the charm. I can think of no more perfect setting than this in which to bring Kathleen's book to life.'* Fox Bay won't know what's hit it when filming starts next spring – but one thing's for sure, with a cast tipped to include some of Hollywood's hottest up-and-coming stars, things in the sleepy little town won't be the same again!'

Ivy looked up, dazed, and handed the phone back to Callum. 'But why didn't Brooke tell us?' she said.

'Apparently, she had to keep it an absolute secret in case anything was leaked and ruined things. But she told us she went to London last week to pitch it,' Erin chimed in, 'and meet with some actor. And they've got the green light! Hollywood is coming to Fox Bay!' She smoothed her hair. 'I wonder if they need a runner.'

'Casting has not yet been confirmed,' said Mei, reading on, 'but up-and-coming actress Madison White, hot off TV's coolest teen drama, *Joyride*, is tipped to play the Captain's daughter Lily . . .'

Ivy pressed her fingers to her forehead, trying to process what she'd just heard.

Fox Bay. A film location. Brooke, here on a secret mission. *Hollywood.*

All at once, it clicked into place. The trip to London. The half-truths, the secrecy, Brooke's forensic approach to sightseeing. And Madison White, the gorgeous girl on Instagram. The whole visit had all been about pitching Fox Bay as a location and meeting with actors.

She felt a tap on her shoulder and turned.

'I'm guessing you've heard the news,' said Brooke, shifting awkwardly.

'Um, yeah. It's all anyone is talking about.'

'Sorry, Ivy,' Brooke said. 'I couldn't tell you. I wasn't sure we'd pull it off and I really didn't want anyone to be disappointed. The higher-ups weren't sure about us filming on location like this. It's a big risk . . .' She drew a deep breath. 'But Kathleen was insistent that this place was magic and she convinced me in the end. Or rather, Fox Bay did. It won me over – all thanks to you, Ivy, showing me all the local spots. I met with the execs last week in London and showed them photos and they agreed too. Especially when I texted them pictures of the cove. How could they not?' She gestured around the hall. 'It's literally the most charming place in the world.'

Ivy opened and shut her mouth again. Her gaze landed on Trip, chatting away to Melissa, hands flying enthusiastically. 'I thought you were dragging Trip off to London because you were worried I'd hurt him,' she said bluntly.

'Well, to be honest, I was,' said Brooke. 'But I might have changed my mind on that one. My brother's an adult; he can make his own choices. I've treated him like a little kid for too long, I think. And besides,' she gave a wry smile, 'I think he could do a lot worse. You were a good friend to him today, Ivy. Thank you. I'm sorry I was so wary. Talk about overprotective.'

Ivy blushed. 'It's okay,' she said. 'I can see how I might have come across as a bit . . .'

'Moody? Solitary? Standoffish?'

'Yeah, all of those.' Ivy laughed ruefully. 'And I'll probably *always* be a bit grumpy, to be honest. But your brother seems to have brought out what there is of my optimistic sociable side.'

Brooke's eyes crinkled as she looked at her brother. 'He tends to do that for people,' she said. 'I can't live Trip's life for him, Ivy, I'm starting to realise that. He'll make his own choices and on reflection I think he'll do a pretty good job of it.' She smiled. 'Now, if you'll excuse me, I need to go and talk to Simi and Lou. I want them to take on the catering for next spring – and take on some Hollywood house guests too, if they're not too busy with the baby.'

As Brooke walked away, Ivy found herself smiling stupidly into space. She could hear the shrieks of surprise and confusion as Brooke's news made its way around the room. Hollywood in Fox Bay. *How wildly unlikely*, she thought. How unexpected. And how absolutely right. Because Brooke was on to something – it probably *was* the most charming place in the world. Suddenly Ivy felt excited that the rest of the world would realise it too.

She felt Trip before she saw him, his hand brushing gently against the small of her back, his voice warm at her shoulder. One word murmured in her ear.

'Beach.'

Ivy turned to him. He held up two wedges of Fin's celebration pasty. 'I come bearing snacks.' His expression was hopeful. 'I thought maybe we could go for a walk.'

And Ivy, for once, didn't hesitate.

'Yes,' she said. 'Let's go.'

Chapter Twenty-four

They slipped out through the side door, unnoticed by most, though Ivy caught Brooke watching them go. She was in the middle of a circle of avid townsfolk, who were hanging on her every word, stunned that a Hollywood producer had been in their midst all this time.

Outside, the air was crisp and the sky was bright with stars, the last of the paper snow still clinging to Ivy's coat. The laughter and bustle from the hall faded behind them, along with the music and kids' shrieking.

Trip took her hand like it was the most natural thing in the world and she let him. It felt completely natural. Different from when she and Raff had held hands, when Ivy would have been frantically thinking of something clever and impressive to say. For now, Ivy was content with quiet – and to her surprise, Trip was too.

They walked through the lanes of Fox Bay, past silent houses and sleepy cats curled in windows. Through the streets that Ivy had spent years dreaming about leaving behind. Now, as Trip laced their fingers tighter, she realised she didn't want to be anywhere else.

'Let's sit on the pier, like proper locals,' Ivy said. 'Which you sort of are. Honorary, at least, after pulling off that show.'

She and Trip sat side by side on the pier, legs dangling over the edge, the celebration pasty on napkins between them.

Neither spoke for a while.

'Are you relieved the show went so well?' Ivy asked at last.

'*Super* relieved,' he said. 'I was worried one of the twins would mess up. You know what a liability they are. I think Mr Trenwith would have leapt on to the stage and made us start again.'

She laughed. 'You've definitely got a knack for this.'

'What's *this*?' he asked.

'I don't know. Theatre? Organising? Bringing people together? Getting them to eat out of your hand?'

He shook his head. 'I don't know if it adds up to much of a plan for the future,' he said ruefully. 'I can't exactly do a degree in "organising random village shows".'

'No, but it's a starting point, isn't it?' said Ivy.

There was another pause.

Then Ivy asked, 'So, do I get to know all the secrets now?'

Trip let out a small laugh. 'Yeah. I think it's time.'

'Good. Because Brooke just gave me the topline and I need to know *everything*.'

'Brooke's production company optioned the Kathleen Lee book last year – she's a romance fanatic, so she pounced on it. She and Kathleen instantly got along like a house on fire. The production company was talking about shooting it all in LA and Kathleen wanted something different, something more authentic . . . she kept telling Brooke about this little village where she'd had her book launch and in the end Brooke agreed to fly out and take a look. Brooke thought I could come along too and do some sightseeing. Grandma always made Cornwall sound so magical.'

'That's why Brooke wanted to see all the sights,' Ivy said.

'Yeah, she needed a local to show her around, see the places that she might be able to film. Put her case to the big guns.'

'And that's why she was asking all those weird questions,' said Ivy, remembering. 'How many rooms Simi has and stuff.'

'Well, if Fox Bay is really going to be the location, then it's a big deal,' said Trip. 'Brooke was telling me all about it. They need accommodation, catering . . .' He looked out across the quiet harbour. 'I don't know if I like the idea of this place being overrun.'

Ivy thought about it. She thought about Fin's giant Cornish pasty and Old Bill's tall tales and the lighthouse, standing tall and proud on the cliff, shrouded in mist. She thought about Lou and Simi, and The Mariner's Arms and Wildest Dreams, Fox Bay's strange, hippyish beating heart.

'I think Fox Bay can cope with a visit from Hollywood,' she said slowly. 'It's about the people, isn't it, as much as this pier and the harbour and the lighthouse, the secret cove and Seal Island. And those people aren't going anywhere.'

He grinned. 'Maybe you're right. Maybe Fox Bay is tough enough to handle it.'

'So that's why you went to London? For Brooke to have meetings?'

'Yeah. I hated not being honest with you, so that's why I went radio silent. But yeah, a lot of meetings, a lot of sightseeing . . . One of the actors who has just been cast was in London too.'

Ivy nodded. 'Right. The incredibly pretty girl.'

'We met with Madison over afternoon tea.' He nudged her. 'Her *boyfriend* was there too. He's British, hence why she was in London.'

'You could've told me,' Ivy said gently. 'About all of this.'

'I *wanted* to,' Trip said. 'So many times. Believe me, I do *not* like keeping secrets. But I didn't want to jinx it. What if it got out and everyone got excited and then it didn't happen? But I won't keep any more, I promise.'

After a beat, Ivy asked, 'And how are *you*? About your grandma's house?'

Trip exhaled, eyes on the dark water.

'I think I'm all right,' he said. 'Saying goodbye to Gran's house will be really hard. But Brooke's right. Gran wouldn't want us to hang on to it and stay rooted in the past. She'd want us to keep the memories – all those special times she gave us – and do something with the money. Letting go doesn't mean forgetting her, I get that now. Besides, she's kind of woven into everything I do. Even saying yes to this ridiculous show. It's *exactly* the sort of thing Grandma would do. She'd have loved it here.'

'And Brooke?' Ivy asked. 'Are you guys okay? She really cares about you.'

He nodded. 'It was good to talk. I think it's time I grew up a bit and stopped leaving all the practicalities to her. She needs to kick back and let go sometimes too, you know?'

Ivy grinned. 'I mean, I can't exactly imagine Brooke *kicking back and letting go*,' she admitted.

'You should see her in the middle of a Hallmark movie marathon,' Trip said. He glanced at Ivy. 'She was right about me. I need to think about the future. I need to accept that change isn't all bad. Pick a college.'

Pick a college. Ivy felt a pang. Of course, Trip was going back to the States. Whatever almost-something this thing between them had been, it would be over before it had begun. They sat in silence for a while, two small figures against the dark sky, legs dangling.

Then Trip leaned a little closer, just enough for his shoulder to brush against hers. 'What about you? Back to your course with a completely brilliant project?' She hesitated and he shook his head. 'Come on. Those drawings you've been doing? They're really good.'

'You know what?' said Ivy, feeling the conviction swell again in her chest, 'I think they *are* good. But I'm leaving the course.'

Trip's mouth fell open. 'You're not! But Ivy, it was just one bad term. If art has been your dream your whole life . . .'

'It's still my dream,' said Ivy hastily. 'I haven't given up on anything. But maybe I was so focused on studying fine art that

I didn't consider all the possibilities. Jess thinks illustration will be right up my street. But there's another course to think about too . . .' She drew out the pause, grinning. 'Set design.'

Trip burst out laughing. 'That fish pie *was* pretty special.'

Ivy giggled. 'I'm joking. I've had enough papier-mâché to last me a long time. They need to review my application and confirm. But Jess sounded positive. She said the illustration tutor really liked my sketches.'

'Those scrappy little drawings?' Trip teased.

'Those scrappy little drawings.' *No serious subtext or meaning*, Ivy thought, *but real and human*. And maybe capturing what was under your nose was just as important, like people kept telling her. Like Trip kept telling her.

'I forgot, I got you something,' Trip said, 'in London. Something crass and commercial, like I promised.'

He held out a small paper bag with WELCOME TO THE UK stamped across the front. Ivy took it cautiously and peered inside.

'Oh my God. It's so . . .'

'Hideous?'

Ivy drew the item out and held it on her palm. It was a plastic snow globe. Inside was a luridly painted castle, complete with tiny plastic seagulls, glitter and a beach below.

Ivy stared at it. It *was* objectively hideous. She loved it immediately.

'It's like the show,' she said. 'The castle and the beach.'

'Yeah. I was going to get you something serious from the

National Gallery or the Tate, but then I saw that and it just . . . I don't know. I thought it might remind you of the show.'

Ivy snorted. 'There is a serious amount of glitter going on.'

'I know. But when it settles, it looks like snow.'

She turned it over, watching the sparkles catch in the moonlight. Her throat felt tight. She would keep the snow globe and remember this winter, she thought, long after Trip had headed back to America.

'It's perfect,' she said quietly. 'Thank you.' She glanced at her phone. 'I should get back,' she said. 'Mum will be wondering where I am.'

Trip gave her the warm smile she would miss so much and held out his hand to her. 'Come on. It's not that late. There's time for one more walk on the beach.'

Chapter Twenty-five

The evening was still. In the town hall, Fox Bay would be celebrating and tucking into the biggest Cornish pasty ever made (or *nearly* the biggest). It felt very far away to Ivy as they strolled slowly across the sand.

'I can't believe we pulled it off,' Ivy said. 'The props held up to some pretty strenuous sword-play. No one cried. Except Mr Hargreaves, but he *always* cries.'

'I'm sorry about London and Madison,' Trip said suddenly. 'I didn't want to give you the wrong impression—'

'It's fine,' Ivy said. *In a few weeks he would be gone anyway*, she thought. 'I mean, I didn't really care.'

'Right,' Trip said, his caramel eyes meeting hers in the moonlight. 'Is that why you painted the set with snow? Because you didn't really care?'

Ivy shrugged, flushing. 'I wanted to do something nice for you, that's all,' she said. 'Let's not make a thing of it.'

'I'm *absolutely* making a thing of it,' Trip said. 'It was really special. It's one of the nicest things anyone has done for me.'

'I just felt inspired. You'd been talking about snow on the

beach and I knew how impossible that was. And then I thought that art is all about impossible things and it gave me the idea.'

Trip nodded thoughtfully. 'Got it. So, what you're saying is . . . I'm your *muse*.'

She groaned. 'Oh no. I've created a monster. This is where your ego gets out of control.'

Trip stopped and traced a shape in the sand with his foot. 'You know Brooke will be here all next year, filming,' he said tentatively. 'We could hang out.'

Ivy took a deep breath and stopped too. 'Trip, let's be real,' she said, hardening her heart against his earnest expression. 'I think you're great. If we were in the same place? Then yes, I would definitely want to hang out. But what you're talking about is long distance and . . . well, I don't think so. We've only known each other for a few weeks. For long distance, you need some serious passion and commitment.'

'And you don't think we could have that?' said Trip, frowning.

'I – that's not the point. There's optimism, which I can just about get on board with, and then there's delusion. If you're studying in the States and I'm over here . . .' Her voice cracked and she trailed off.

'Right,' Trip said, his brow clearing. 'I see what you mean. Only you see, the school I accepted a place at isn't *in* the States.'

'It's not?'

'No.' He rocked on his heels. 'I went for UCL. Accepted the offer last week. And before you freak out and tell me I'm making a huge mistake picking a college based on a grumpy artist I've only known a few weeks . . .'

'Um,' said Ivy, 'you might have taken the words out of my mouth.'

'Well, first of all, it's my life. And second of all, the reason I wanted to go to London with Brooke last week was to check it out properly because I was *already* thinking of studying there. We went to the campus, looked around the halls of residence. Brooke's behind this too. UCL is the only college that does the exact philosophy course I want. There are loads of reasons for me to study here in the UK that are nothing to do with you, Ivy Pearson.'

'Fine,' said Ivy, a smile starting. 'I won't take it personally then.'

'But also . . . this is always going to be what I'm like, you know? I'm always going to say *yes* to something big and impractical and slightly ridiculous.' Trip shrugged. 'It's what Grandma would want me to do.'

There was a pause. Ivy could feel her heart beating fast in her chest. *Something big and impractical and slightly ridiculous . . .* but also, why not? Maybe she could get used to saying yes after all.

'It would still be long distance,' Trip went on. 'But, you know, slightly less long distance.'

His expression was serious, focused on her with the same searching look as that night at the Winter Wonderland. One that made her feel seen.

Ivy tilted her head. 'If we're really going to give this ridiculous idea a try . . .'

'Yeah?'

'Then I should at least know what Trip is short for,' she said.

A smile tugged at his mouth. 'Is that your condition?'

'It is,' Ivy said firmly. 'No more secrets, remember? Come on. Tell me.'

Trip hesitated, then looked sheepish. 'Um. Okay. Fine. It's short for . . . Edward.'

She stared. '*Edward*? Trip is short for Edward? But . . . how?'

He scratched the back of his neck. 'Trip's just because I'm the *third* Edward. Like, triple-Edward? Grandad, Dad, me. Three Edwards. But Mom and Dad didn't love it so they nicknamed me Trip and it stuck.'

Ivy burst out laughing. 'You're actually *Edward the third*? Like . . . like a king?' She was still laughing as she took a step closer, shaking her head. 'Edward. The Third.'

'Don't make it weird,' he murmured. 'Literally no one calls me that. I've been Trip since I was born.'

'All right, Edward.' She stepped closer and added softly, 'Do you hate it? If you hate it I'll forget I ever heard it.'

He considered her, reaching out a hand and pushing a lock of her hair behind one ear. She could feel her cheek tingling once again from his touch. She wondered if she would ever get used to it. 'I don't hate it from you,' he said at last.

Trip leaned in then, and she took yet another step closer. He kissed her.

It wasn't the gentle kiss Ivy might have expected. It was fierce, like all their moonlit walks and paper-folding sessions and hours spent in the town hall, covered in dust and paint, had been building to this. His hand slipped to her waist, pulling her in. It felt so unbelievably right, Ivy thought dazedly. Like they already knew each other.

And then, just as they broke apart, still smiling . . .

A snowflake landed on Ivy's cheek.

She looked up. There was another. And another.

Trip tilted his face to the sky, his eyes wide. 'No way,' he whispered. 'Don't tell me you organised this too.'

Ivy reached out her hand as the soft flakes fell, melting almost as soon as they touched her fingers. 'Looks like you finally got your magic.'